Published by

Windtree Press, Corvallis, Oregon

https://windtreepress.com

The Power of S.A.D. / Maggie Lynch.

Print ISBN 978-1-962065-28-3

Ebook ISBN 978-1-962065-27-6

Audiobook ISBN 978-1-962065-44-3

The Power of S.A.D.

Mariposa Lane Book 1

Maggie Lynch

Windtree Press

CONTENTS

*To all the foster children
raised by my maternal grandparents
and my aunt and uncle.
Thank you for bringing your
stories, your culture, and sharing your
strength and determination to
succeed despite the odds.
You have taught me so much.
I would not be the person I am
without you.*

From *The Popol Vuh*

We speak, Kojch'awik,
We listen, Kojta'onik,
We ponder, Kojb'isonik,
We move. Kojsilab'ik.

CHAPTER ONE

THE FOG OF UNCERTAINTY

It was early morning on New Year's Day and, after a week, Mama still hadn't returned home.

For the past week, Akna didn't leave the house or let her sisters out except when none of the neighbors were there. When they asked after mama, her story was so worn it was becoming unbelievable. It was always a version of the same lie.

"Oh, Akna, I haven't seen your mother lately."

"She's asleep," Akna would reply. "She's working nights now."

Most of the time that satisfied the busybodies. But the one who lived next store, Mrs. Gonzales, always probed further.

"Really? Asleep? Then where is the car?"

Akna had several ready responses and tried to keep her lies straight.

"It's in the shop."

OR if it was the end of the week:

"She met a friend last night and they partied a little too much, so she got a taxi home. Maria will pick her up later today to go get her car."

OR her favorite, if she really wanted to stop the questions, was:

"It's not here? Oh no, someone must have stolen it. By Mrs.

Gonzales, I have to go call the police and report it stolen." Then she would run into the house as fast as she could.

The truth was, Akna had no idea where her mama went when she disappeared for several days or weeks. And she'd learned years ago not to ask about it. It hardly mattered anymore whether she was home or not. When she was home, she stayed in her bedroom with her sickness unable to get up to cook or do anything.

Akna didn't mind, most of the time. Her mom always put money in the grocery jar so Akna could always get food and cook for her sisters. At eleven years old, there wasn't much Akna could do to help besides cover for mom. She couldn't drive. She couldn't get a job. The truth was she couldn't do anything without mom's permission…in writing.

She had the whole permission slip forgery down. Over the past two years, she always made a copy at the library whenever mama wrote or signed one. She would white out whatever the permission was for, then carefully copy her mom's handwriting for the new need. Then she would carefully write over each letter and word on the copy so it all looked new. In fact, she could sign her mama's name better than her mom could—especially when she was really sick and couldn't be roused from bed.

This time was the worst though. Not because of her being gone, but because it was the holidays. She'd never been gone before at Christmas.

Mama had left without notice the morning of Christmas Eve. She didn't even bother to leave a note. Akna had to be the one to take care of the Christmas Day rituals. She'd unboxed the two-foot tree and placed it on the end table after her sisters went to bed. She'd also found the stockings Nana had made several years ago and placed an orange in each one. If Mama had bought any presents, Akna hadn't found them in the usual hiding places. When her sisters asked about them, she explained that Santa had to decide who needed presents more than anyone else because there were many children with very little. It seemed to satisfy them.

Akna wasn't worried about how long Mama had been away. Not

yet. One more week and she would begin to worry. Before that happened, she needed to make plans about how they would live if Mama didn't come home soon.

EARLY NEW YEAR'S DAY, AKNA ROLLED OVER AND STARED AT THE bedside clock. 6:00 AM. Perfect! She'd awakened at the time she wanted. Her sisters should sleep for at least another hour. They'd never notice she was gone.

Akna slowly removed the arm that cradled her two sisters in their shared bed. She crawled from beneath the bedcovers, slipping off the end of the bed in silence. Carefully, she tucked the top sheet and Nana's crocheted afghan back beneath the mattress. Hai and Nakia breathed deeply, sound asleep. Gathering her folded clothes from the dresser, she tiptoed into the bathroom to change.

She slipped on her shoes near the front door and then put her arms through Mama's oversized coat. It came below her knees and the sleeves were too long for her arms, but it was the warmest coat in the house.

Twisting the door knob, she inched open the door, cringing when the bottom scraped against the torn threshold. She opened it only enough to get through. She'd be back in thirty minutes, an hour at most. Her sisters would never know she'd been gone at all.

She shimmied through the crack and stepped outside. The sudden cold forced out the breath she was holding.

"Where are you going?" Hai's voice whispered. Her foot stopping the door from closing. "Are you sneaking away like Mama?"

Akna dropped her head. "I'm not sneaking away," she whispered through the cracked door. "I just need—"

"I've heard you leave before," Hai interrupted. "You always sneak out when we're asleep. I keep wondering if this is the time you won't come back."

Akna sighed and came back inside, closing the door softly. She enveloped Hai in Mama's big coat. "I'm sorry. I didn't mean to frighten you. I'd never leave you and Nakia to fend for yourself. Never!"

She'd thought she'd been quiet every time. She never wanted to worry her sisters. It was her job to keep them safe. It was her job to make sure they didn't know how bad their situation was when Mama was gone for a long time.

"Where do you go?" Hai asked. "Do you go look for Mama? Do you ask her to come home?"

Akna unzipped the coat, then flopped on the sofa and patted the spot next to her. Evidently, she'd underestimated Hai. She'd treated her like Nakia, who was in kindergarten. But Hai was in the third grade. She was a lot smarter and noticed things more.

"I don't know where Mama goes. I don't know why she leaves us. I only know she always comes back and then we pretend she never left."

Hai nodded and worried her bottom lip with her teeth. She took a deep breath and then asked, "If you aren't looking for Mama, then where do you go?"

"I go to talk to Tata."

Hai wrinkled her brow and then waved her hands in Akna's face. "Earth to Akna. Tata's dead. You can't talk to him."

"But I can. Not like you and I are talking, but in my heart. Kind of like praying."

"You can pray here. You don't have to go outside to pray," Hai said with confidence. "Tell me the truth. Where are you going when you sneak out?"

"I am telling you the truth. Look..." she opened the curtain over the sofa. "Do you see the big old oak tree out in the field? It's hard to see through the fog, but you and Nakia have been there with me before."

Hai nodded. "I know it."

"That's my secret place for reaching Tata. I climb as high as I can go and then I sit on the branch and my heart and mind reach out to the sky and I ask him to talk to me."

Hai's eyes widened. "Does he talk back?"

"Not aloud like we do. But if I'm listening really hard, sometimes I do hear him in my heart. Then my heart tells my brain what he said."

"Really?" Hai tilted her head to one side and held her lips tight together. "You aren't making this up? Pretending again?"

"I know it sounds crazy but Tata taught me how to do it before he died."

"Teach me. I want to talk to Tata, too."

"I'll try, but not right now. I really need to go by myself this morning. That's why I got up so early. I would have been back before you and Nakia woke. I have to make plans for the new year. I have to get some answers, and I have to do it alone."

"How long?" Hai asked.

Akna looked at the faded orange plastic watch on her left wrist; the one Nana had given her before she died. She said it was to help Akna stay on time. It would remind her that a new day would come every twenty-four hours. Whenever a bad day happened, she only had to hang on to make it through the next twenty-four hours. Each day brought the hope and promise that things could change.

"It's 7:10am now." She pointed to the digital display on her watch. "I'll be home before it is eight o'clock. Okay?" She pointed to the old clock on the wall. "Do you know how to read the hands? Do you know when it says eight o'clock?"

"Duh," Hai said, her hands open. "I learned it in first grade."

Akna slapped her forehead. "Sorry, I forgot." She held out her hand as if to shake. "Let's make a deal. If I'm not back by eight, I'll do the dishes by myself for the rest of the week. Okay?"

Hai took her hand and shook on it.

"If Nakia wakes up, what are you going to say?" Akna asked.

"Not to worry, you'll be back by 8:00."

"Thanks." Akna hugged Hai again, zipped up the jacket and quickly slipped out the door. She walked as fast as she could toward the old maple tree in the field.

Fog rippled and billowed in uneven formations before her. The cool mist licked her face like little waves. Near their mobile home it was above the roofline, but the closer she got to the big tree, the more the sky became a big lake enveloping her as if she was walking on the lake bottom.

Finally at the tree, she slowly climbed beyond the first large mossy branches, removing slippery leaves that had decomposed and lodged in nooks and crannies. She had to speak with Tata today. When Mama left this time, she'd had that running-away look that meant things were going to be bad for a long while.

Akna gasped for breath as she climbed higher. She needed to get as close to the sky as possible. She'd had difficulty talking to Tata in her last two attempts, so today she was going to ask Heart of Sky to intervene, to find Tata and tell him to listen.

After another fifteen feet, she found her favorite seat on a large branch that formed a perfect u-shaped spot for her butt. She snuggled into it and took one last look at their home and the entire mobile home park in one direction. Their single-wide, dirty grey mobile home was shrouded in a gauze curtain of fog. The porch light barely illuminated the bright red door and the plastic shutters on either side of the living room windows.

Then she focused in the other direction. Long parallel lines of pruned vines, stakes and wires dipped in and out of visibility as if they were playing hide and seek. Though the vineyard's boundary was a block or two away, there was nothing but low land with scrubby bushes and weeds between this tree and the view of the place where Tata had worked all of Akna's life. He'd loved it there. He'd said the owner treated him like he was one of them.

She felt closest to Tata here. If he was with the Tzuultaq'a', the gods of the K'iche', then he was certainly still paying attention to the vineyard. The Tzuultaq'a' loved farmers, especially those who understood the land and treated it with respect and care. Tata had died in the winter, readying the vines for spring. Nana had followed only three months later.

One of Akna's last conversations with Tata had been about the sadness that always overcame her when all the grapes were harvested and the winter took away the leaves of all the plants, stripping the bright colors of the year. Tata said that the vineyard in winter was the most important part of the growing season. Without the work of the vines during the winter, there would be no harvest in the spring.

It's true, the vines go into dormancy during the cold months, he'd said. But beneath the surface things were not so quiet. Instead of directing their energy toward producing fruit or new leaf growth, in winter the vines expend their energy into their root systems. Roots will grow, soaking up soil nutrients to keep the vine strong. This helps the vine to prepare for spring and the emergence of new shoots. The more the roots prepare, the more likely the next crop of grapes would create excellent wine.

That was why Akna had to come to the tree today. She needed to find a way to grow new roots to make her strong for the spring and the summer. From the time school closed two weeks ago through New Year's Day, Mama had only been home two days. The few days Mama was home, she was hiding in her room with her medicine during the day and then drinking her tequila at night and crying.

Each day Mama was away it felt like she'd scooped out a space in Akna's heart and threw it on the side of the road with other things she no longer had time to care for. Now her heart had a large hole and she didn't know how to make it whole again.

"I'm telling you to forget that past," Mama said when Akna asked her to tell stories about growing up in Guatemala like Tata did. "It is only a story of pain and troubles. You can be Latina, you can be American, but let go of K'iche'. Let go of the Mayan past. It's not worth it. The memories, the promises, the ways of the K'iche' that Tata talked about are impossible—not real—not here or in Guatemala."

Akna leaned into the trunk and closed her eyes, lifting her face to the mist. With every breath she let the fog saturate her with dreams and prayers. "Heart of Sky, who made the world and all the K'iche' people, help me find Tata. Tell him to listen for me. I need to talk to him now. If he is with the Tzuultaq'a', ask them what is to come and how I can prepare. How can I use this time to grow stronger roots when Mama seems to always tear them away?"

She listened for his response with what was left of her heart. But there was only silence.

It used to be easier to speak with him, to explain what was happening in their lives. But lately, she didn't even know the questions to ask. He'd told her if she searched her memory for all of their previous talks, she would find the answers. They were always inside her.

Akna *had* searched her memory for this entire month and could see no answers. He'd helped her understand the powers of sad. She had slowly lost those powers over the past two years. Could he help her find them again?

She squeezed her eyes tighter to hold back the tears of that memory. She could not afford to cry now. She had to remember and listen to Tata once again.

CHAPTER TWO

THE HOLDER OF STORIES

That day, three years ago, came back to her like a movie. Safe in the nook of the tree, she could watch herself and Tata talk again.

Tata motioned Akna to sit on the wooden stool near his rocking chair. "I have to talk to you about something scary," he'd said.

When he said the word scary, he meant awful. There had only been two times Tata had told her scary things before. It was always about Mama.

Once was when Nakia had just been born. Her mother had to go to a special place for people with thinking problems. Tata had explained that Mama's brain sometimes told her to do bad things to herself, and she had to get special medicine and treatment to fix it. Nana took care of Nakia for the first six months of her life while Mama was away getting fixed.

The second time was when Akna was almost eight. Mama went on a trip with a man Tata said was very bad. When she didn't come back after three months, Tata was afraid they would never see her again. She finally came home in time for Christmas, almost a year later. She never talked about where she'd been or what she did. Mama just pretended it never happened. And everyone else pretended too.

"Is Mama leaving again?"

"No," he said. "It's not your Mama." Tata took in a big breath and let it out slowly.

Akna waited, counting the seconds for him to speak. He kept swallowing like he was trying to say something but, when he opened his mouth, nothing would come out.

Finally, she couldn't wait any longer. She grabbed his hand and squeezed hard. "You can tell me, Tata. I'm grown up now. I can take anything. I'm not afraid."

Tata chuckled and mussed the hair on the top of her head. That seemed to break the spell that had stolen his voice.

"You're all grown up?"

"Well, I'm not as old as you. But I'm nine and I know lots of things, and I don't get scared anymore."

"Is that so?"

Akna stood up, pulled her shoulders back, and puffed out her chest. "I'm like Supergirl. Bad news bounces off me like bullets."

Tata cocked his head to one side and smiled. But the smile didn't reach his eyes. He spread his arms wide. "Is Supergirl too old to sit in my lap like she used to when she was seven and eight?"

She eagerly crawled into his lap and his strong arms wrapped around her like a shield against the outside world. She could still smell the sweet grapes and the fresh earth on him. She thought that when Tata was born, God put an extra bit of earth into his skin so that he would always be able to speak to the earth and help it bring forth beautiful plants.

"Do you know it is your strength and determination that is the glue of this family?" He spoke over her head as he held her tight. "Don't ever forget that. They are your super powers, better than the comics because they are real." He quieted and rocked her for a bit. "How will you remember?" he asked. "You need a code. All superheroes have a secret code that makes them strong.

Akna bit her bottom lip as she tried to come up with a secret code. "I know!" she said. "It's easy but secret. It is S.A.D. When I say I'm sad, my powers will become strong."

"No, no, mi amorcita. You misunderstand. I don't want you to be sad to gain your super powers. I only want you to feel your power in here." He tapped his hand on his chest twice.

"Not sad." She made air quotes with her fingers. "I mean S.A.D. Strength. And. Determination. Like you said."

"Ah." Tata nodded his head and smiled broadly. "Clever. You will say you are sad and they will not know you are really S.A.D."

"Yes, I make words to protect us."

He squeezed a little tighter. "Yes, that is the K'iche' way. "Just remember never to make words to lie or to avoid truth, even if it seems like a small thing. That is a bad thing to bring from our culture."

Akna leaned her head on his broad, warm chest again and listened to the strength of each beat of his heart. It was strong, just like hers.

He took a deep breath and she heard a little stutter in his breath as he let it out. "I'm afraid this news isn't something that will easily bounce off your strong heart," he said with a catch in his throat. "It will only settle there. It will be hard at first; but you will eventually learn what to do with it."

Now she was worried. Tata never delivered bad news without a way to deal with it.

"I am sick, Akna. It is the kind of sickness that will take me to be with the Tzuultaq'a'."

Tata had shared many stories of the Tzuultaq'a' over the years. They were the gods of the mountains and valleys. They were in charge of nature and all that it could provide to their people. They lived in caves under the mountains, though nobody ever saw them. She supposed they were like spirits. Like the saints her mother and Nana prayed to after mass or lit candles and asked for help.

"How soon," she finally whispered.

"Depende de dios," he said.

She pounded a fist on his chest. "It's always up to God," she said. "No me trates como una niña"

"But you *are* a child. And it *is* up to God."

Akna gritted her teeth. "You know what I mean. God didn't say this to you. It was a doctor. What did the doctor say?"

He sighed again. "The doctors say maybe a month, maybe three months. It is cancer, a fast-moving and untreatable one."

Akna gasped. This was the worst of the worst. She bit down hard on her lip as moisture filled her eyes and the darkness filled her heart. She would not cry. She would prove she was strong. S.A.D. she whispered to herself. S.A.D. Now she knew she was K'iche'. She was truly sad but also needed her superpowers to get through this—if not for herself, for Tata and her sisters.

"It is a lot to take in," he said as he rocked her again.

Silent tears stained his shirt. She was not the type to moan or cry out like her mother.

"It will be you, now, who must remember and tell the stories. You will be the one to carry them and tell them to your sisters when they are older, and to your children and your grandchildren. That is how the K'iche' stay alive. You hold the stories of your ancestors and your own story in your heart. Together, they make a new story, a strong story for the future."

"I don't know all the stories," she said amidst the hiccups of her heart.

"But you do, Akna. We have told you stories from the time you were born. Stories of how the earth was made and how we live together with love. Good stories of our ancestors."

"Nana said those are made-up stories," Akna said. "They're not real."

"All stories have truth, mi amorcita. It is your job to determine where the truth is and to remember it."

Akna sighed. She didn't want to be the holder of stories. She wasn't ready. She wanted Tata to tell her many, many more stories.

"You can ask me every day, and I will tell you as many stories as you want."

"Tata, the stories you tell are in K'iche'. Should I tell them in K'iche' or Spanish or English?"

"K'iche' is the language of our people. Spanish is the language of those who tried to take away our culture. We must always continue to speak K'iche' to keep our language alive, our culture alive."

"So, I should not speak Spanish anymore?"

Tata sighed and didn't speak for several seconds. "It is important to speak Spanish, too, because many people in the world speak Spanish and it will help you learn new things and communicate with many people. English is the language of our adopted country. And we are grateful to be here. If we were not able to come here, I don't know what would have become of us. It may be that you would never be born."

Akna doubted that. She was here, wasn't she? What a silly idea. But she didn't say it.

"You will be the in-between person. The person who understands all three and can help the rest."

"Is that what you do, Tata? Are you an in-between person, too?"

His face crumpled up a bit, like he was trying to decide how to answer. But then he smiled. "Yes, I guess I am. Learning a new language comes easy to me. But not so to many people. Because I know K'iche' and Spanish and English, sometimes I can help those who came with us from Guatemala to understand how things work here. But K'iche' is especially important. It requires thinking differently."

"You mean because of the Tzuultaq'a'?"

"Yes and more. It is because K'iche' can accept two things at once. Sometimes more than two things. We accept there is more than one good answer. Not everything is only right or only wrong. Do you understand?"

She shook her head slowly, then said, "Perhaps I don't know K'iche' very well."

"If you practice, and tell the stories, you will understand as you grow older. You will see there is never only one right answer."

Akna wrinkled her forehead as she thought about a secret she needed to tell.

"What are you puzzling?" Tata asked.

"Mama said we should never speak K'iche' outside of this house.

So how could I tell the stories to others? She said that speaking K'iche' makes you less of a person, makes you inferior. Inferior means you're not as smart as someone else who speaks Spanish or English."

"Ah," he sighed. "She is speaking the truth as she knows it."

"You can't both be speaking truth," Akna said. "Am I to listen to you or to her?"

"You must listen to both."

"But—"

Tata held up a finger to stop her interruption. "Remember, I said things are not always right or wrong. There is a story I have not told you that is important. It is a story about your Mama. It will help you to understand many things in the past and perhaps in the future."

Akna grew excited. Her Mama would never tell her a story of her past. When she'd asked Nana or Tata, they always said it was Mama's story to tell. She must wait until she is ready to tell it.

"However, I cannot tell you right now. You are too young."

"Tata," she whined. "How can I be the holder of stories if you don't tell me. How old must I be?"

"Fourteen."

She opened her mouth to protest, but closed it again. She couldn't argue she was close to fourteen. That was five years away.

"Maybe thirteen," he added.

"But…you won't be here to tell me the story when I'm thirteen or fourteen. And I don't think Nana would ever tell me. She does not tell stories like you do. She keeps everything inside."

He didn't speak and she was afraid she had hurt him by being so straightforward.

"Nana will tell you. We have talked about this. She will tell you when you are older. We both agreed."

He suddenly sounded tired. Had she just not noticed before? But she still hadn't asked the question she wanted to know most. She clamped her mouth shut. She shouldn't bother him with this. She should let him rest.

"What is troubling you?" he asked, as if he could read her mind.

She laced her fingers in front of her and held them tight, then wet her lips with her tongue to force herself to speak slowly and without emotion. "If you are with the Tzuultaq'a'…" She swallowed the tears, refusing to let them fall. "Will I be able to talk to you like Mama and Nana talk to the saints? Will you be able to answer me? Will you be able to tell me stories then?"

"That is a good question," he said and then remained silent for what seemed like forever.

Akna forced herself to wait. She already felt bad asking it in the first place.

"This is what I know to be true," he finally continued. "You will be able to talk to me at any time. You can ask me questions, tell me what happened in school that day, or anything you like. You can also talk to me when your Mama is having a hard time and tell me how you feel. Even when you are grown and working or married or have your own children you can still talk to me."

"But will you answer?" she asked. "Will I hear you? Tell me the truth, not pretend."

"I don't know for sure. I don't know how hard it will be to talk to you from the afterlife. I think, for some, it is very hard to hear the ancestors because their day is so full of noise and they need a lot of concentration and effort to just make it through the day."

Akna blew out a big breath. "If I can't hear you, then what's the point of talking?"

"When I wish to talk to those in the afterlife, I go to a very quiet place where I can empty my mind of all that noise. Then I talk to them as if they were sitting beside me."

She crinkled her face at him and wondered if the sickness made him a little crazy or he was just trying to make her feel better with pretending. She knew there was no talking to those who died, and especially no hearing back from them.

"Who have you spoken to?" she demanded. "I mean really. No pretending."

"My parents, my sisters and brothers, friends, even your uncles Humberto and Eloy."

"Really?"

"Yes. I speak to them often, even today."

"What do they look like? Are they ghosts or real people? If they are ghosts, how do you know it is really them? Did you hear them speak? What do they say when the speak? Do they talk in English or Spanish or K'iche'? What does it sound like? Do their voices sound like they did when they were alive?"

Tata sighed. "So many questions."

"I need answers," she said. "I need to be prepared. I need to recognize you and if you are going to speak to me only in K'iche' I need to practice more so I can understand. This is important!"

"You do not need to worry about those things, mi amorcita. The talking is not something you can see and hear. It is different, even more special."

Akna frowned. "I thought so. I knew it wasn't real. I told you to tell me the truth and instead you just give me a pretend story."

"Do you only believe what you see with your eyes?" Tata asked. "Do you only believe what you hear in your ears?"

"Yes," she said with certainty. "I know those things are real."

"Do you believe in love?"

"Of course, but we aren't talking about love. We are talking about seeing and hearing real people. People who have passed to the afterlife. I'm asking do you see them? Do you hear them?"

"Do you see love? Do you hear love?" Tata asked with the same determination.

"Yes. No? I...I mean yes. I see love when you hug me. I hear love when you say you love me."

"And if I don't hug you and don't say words, does it mean I don't love you?"

"No, but that's different." She pushed at his chest. "Tata you're trying to confuse me. You are trying to avoid my questions. That's not fair. You promised."

"But it is fair," he countered. "Because these people loved me is why I can hear them. I hear them in my heart. I do not hear a voice like you hear me now. But I hear them in my heart. My heart remembers what they would say when they were with me. When I ask a

16

question of my brother, my heart knows what he is saying now, even though I don't hear him with my ears."

Akna considered what he said. Could all hearts hear or only special hearts like Tata's? She wasn't sure her heart was big enough to hear Tata from the afterlife. Even if her heart could hear, how did it talk to her brain and translate what her heart was saying? She was a child. Tata was an adult. What if it didn't work for children?

Akna scrambled out of his lap and stood facing him. "Let's practice right now. I want to make sure my heart can hear you."

"I'm not sure—"

"If you're telling the truth, then you must prove it to me. I have to practice now because it will be too late when you're gone. What if I do it wrong? What if I can never hear you again?" Tata, we have to practice. Now!"

He held up his hand in surrender. "Okay. We can try. But my powers are not as strong as they will be when I am with the Tzuultaq'a.'"

"If you believe you will be with the Tzuultaq'a,'" she said, "ask them to help you right now. I will concentrate and ask you a question out loud. Then you must answer silently so my heart will hear."

Tata nodded and took a deep breath. He closed his eyes.

Akna copied him. She took a deep breath and slowly walked three paces away from him and turned her back. Then she closed her eyes. *If there really is a God or Tzuultaq'a'*, she prayed, *please help us now. Please help Tata speak in my heart.*

She searched for a question to ask him. A question she had never asked before. A question where he hadn't already given her the answer or told a story. She peeked over her shoulder to see if he was staring at her, or smiling, or what. His eyes were still closed. Perhaps he was praying, too.

With her back to him once again, she concentrated even more. Finally, she had it. A question she had never asked before. She stood straight, her shoulders back and her faced uplifted. She projected her voice so he could hear her. "Tata, what will happen to us after you and Nana are no longer with us."

She squeezed her eyes hard and her heart clutched at even the thought of losing both of them. Nana was not sick, so she might not die until Akna was much older. But this was a question she had never dared to ask Tata.

The more she thought about both of them being gone, the harder the tears worked to fight against her closed eyes. *Please let me hear him. Please God, let Tata speak in my heart.*

She listened and listened for a long time. When the tears began to escape, she knew what his answer was. It was not the answer she wanted, but she knew it was Tata's answer. The answer was something that only he would be brave enough to tell her.

She turned and found Tata standing with tears in his own eyes. He wrapped her once more in his arms and she burrowed into his embrace. "Did your heart hear me?" he asked.

She nodded against his chest.

"What did you hear, mi amorcita?"

She waited a moment to try to catch her breath. She wanted to just cry and push away the thoughts of death. But this was too important.

"You said no one can know the future except God," she started. Her voice stuttered as she talked through her tears. "You said you knew that whatever happened, I would be okay." She held on tighter and waited until she could speak again. "You said you and Nana have taught me all the important things and they will help."

The last part was the hardest. She didn't want to even say it because it meant he knew they would both be gone. He knew there were more hard times ahead.

"Go on," he urged her. "There is more."

She nodded against his chest. "There will be other people I will meet in the future who will help me even if my Mama is not here."

Now Tata renewed his strong hold of her. She wasn't sure if she was holding him or he was holding her.

"Then you said what you told me before. The power of SAD and love would see me through."

He held her for a long time before speaking. "At^h anima' ta'ik kolomal tz'aqat. Tu corazón escuchó exactamente correcta, mi amorcita. Your heart heard exactly right."

Her tears burst beyond the dam made by her squeezed eye lids. She could no longer speak. When she tried, it came out as hiccups of partial words that made no sense. All she could do was hang on tight.

Tata rocked her and waited for her to calm

When there were no tears left, he said quietly, "My story is coming to an end, but yours has barely begun. You must now continue our story and make your own."

Akna opened her eyes to find herself still in the nook of the tree. Why did she still cry two years later? She was in fifth grade now and soon would be heading for middle school. She looked through her tears to the sky. The sun was slowly burning its way through the fog. Perhaps Heart of Sky did listen to her. Perhaps this was a sign that Tata had heard her questions. Perhaps his answer was to remember that story, and remind her about the power of SAD. She needed to work harder on getting that power back.

CHAPTER THREE

THE SICKNESS THAT CHANGED THE WORLD

Mama came home late on New Year's Day, long after Akna had made frozen mini pizzas for dinner, helped Nakia bathe, and got them ready for bed. Just as she was starting to read the bedtime story, Mama came in the door and yelled toward the bedroom.

"I have to talk to you, Akna," she shouted and then slammed the front door shut. "After you've read your story, you need to come talk to me. You won't be happy. But that's life."

Then she heard the thing she dreaded most, Mama pouring a drink. She knew the creak of that high cupboard, the tinkle of a glass to pour into. When the chair scraped at the small dining table, it almost groaned when Mama plopped down. That sound meant she was in for a full bottle.

Anna swallowed and called on her SAD powers. She smiled at Nakia and pulled her and Hai closer as she sat between them with the Unicorn book.

She pointed to a blonde girl about Hai's age. "I think she is eight like you." Then she vowed to read the story with all the voices she could muster. "Mazie always wanted a unicorn, but she knew she could never have one because they lived in an apartment. So, she used her imagination instead."

"¿Que es imaja…imaja…tu sabes?" Nakia asked.

"Imagination is when you pretend. It's not real. See?" She pointed to a drawing of a horse with a horn on it. "See? Mazie drew a picture of a unicorn and then she pretended she could see it and talk to it."

Nakia laughed. "Yegua," she said.

"Unicornio," Akna corrected. "Unicorn. Un yegua con un cuerno."

"Los yeguas no tienen cuernos."

"That's right, horses don't have horns but unicorns do. Correcto, pero los unicornios lo hacen."

Because Nakia was only five, she had barely started school and she was struggling with English. At home they'd always spoken Spanish for Nana and Tata. After they died, Mama didn't want them talking to anyone outside of school. She was always afraid people would snoop around the house and think she wasn't a good mother.

Akna tried to read to her every night in English to help her learn more words and catch up with the other children in kindergarten. She wanted her to at least see the words and pictures.

"I wish I could draw like that," Hai said.

"You will when you get older," Akna assured her.

She put a bookmark in the place where she'd stopped reading and got up from the bed. "Go to sleep now and dream of unicorns and wishes that come true. After you're asleep, Mama will come give you a magical kiss to make sure no monsters visit your dreams."

"Sin monstruos," Nakia echoed.

"That's right," Hai said as she snuggled closer to Nakia. "No monsters."

Akna wished there were no monsters; but tonight she was afraid Mama was going to tell her about one.

She took her time tucking in the well-worn quilt Nana had made when Akna was a child. Nana had said the turquoise background represented the sea they could see from their home in Guatemala. The different shades of brown and greys were to remember the mountains that protected the valley where they lived. The yellows, black, red, and white represented the corn that was sacred to the K'iche' people.

When she crawled into bed with her sisters later tonight, she would share that quilt and know that Nana had shared her heart in it. As long as they had the quilt, they had a part of Nana with them.

She bent to give each of her sisters a kiss on the forehead. This was likely the only magic she could give them right now. Akna would pretend everything was fine for their sake. She would do whatever was needed to make sure they'd never have to worry about Mama.

She carefully placed the book in the drawer next to two others. They didn't have a lot of toys, but Akna always made sure to get three books from the bookmobile each week it came down their road.

Books were her escape to a world where families were whole and pets were magical. Even when someone had troubles, they were able to work it out in the end. In other words, nothing like her real life.

Akna quietly checked her secret money jar. Whenever she did the grocery shopping, Mama would give her money. Depending on how much she'd been drinking it could be as little as fifty dollars or sometimes as much as two hundred. Whatever Akna didn't spend she kept in the jar for the days Mama would disappear. Mama never thought about giving her money then, because she never let them know she was going to disappear. They would go to school one day and she wouldn't be there when they got home.

If Mama was already drinking, it was a sign she would disappear again soon. Akna counted the bills now, one hundred and twenty-three dollars. She'd try to get more from her tonight before she went to bed, just in case.

She looked at her sisters once more and sighed as she closed the door to the bedroom. It was time to find out why Mama was so sad tonight. She forced herself to move toward the kitchen. Her fingers trailed along the wall and landed on the last picture of them as a family taken two years ago. The church had a picture day once every five years. A professional photographer came in. You could get one picture for free. If you wanted more you needed to pay.

Nana had insisted they go because Tata was sick and he may not be around the next time pictures were taken. In addition to the free picture, Nana bought a second one to hang in their own home. The picture was taken near the place where everyone lit candles to the saints and said prayers. Tata, Nana, and Mama stood in the back. Akna, Hai, and Nakia stood in the front.

Akna scrutinized the faces in the dark hall. They all seemed happy. They all smiled. Was it real or was it pretend? She couldn't remember the exact day. She couldn't remember what may have gone wrong that day. She kissed her index finger and then tapped Tata's and Nana's face.

She often wondered if the Catholic God and the Tzuultaq'a" spoke to each other. She worried that perhaps Tata and Nana were not able to be together in the afterlife. When she'd asked Nana if she'd be with Tata, she'd shrugged and said, "I will tell you after I get there."

Akna stood just outside the kitchen, gathering the strength she needed to listen to whatever trouble was visiting them now.

"Come sit with me," Mama said with a wave of her hand from the kitchen. Some of the dark, golden liquid sloshed over the side of the glass she held.

"Sit. Sit," she said again and placed a glass at Akna's seat.

"I'd rather stand." Akna leaned on the back of the chair.

Mama downed the liquid in her own glass and quickly poured another. After downing it she slammed it onto the table.

She pointed at Akna's glass. "Hazlo. You're going to need that to calm your nerves for our little talk."

Akna shook her head.

"¡Hazlo! I can't talk until you've downed it. You gotta be calm for this. Go on now."

Akna slowly raised the glass to her mouth and let it hover without sipping. Sometimes Mama would simply continue to drink and forget what Akna was doing. Her hand trembled a bit as she smelled the sugary sweetness, and the bit of citrus that could fool you into thinking it would be like soda.

But her mom continued to stare at her and wait.

Akna took a small sip and quickly put the glass down as the pepper assailed her throat and the burn worked its way to her stomach.

"Now that's not so bad, is it? Now take another."

"It burns."

"It's supposed to burn, mi cielo. That is what reminds you that you are still alive. The little bit of pain reminds you. We are both still alive today. Tomorrow, no matter what happens, we will still both be alive because we survived the pain today. Go on now."

Akna shook her head again. "Just tell me. I don't need your tequila. You're the one who needs it. I don't want to be sick."

Mama sighed. "When did you get so independent? It used to be you'd do anything I asked."

"My teacher says kids my age aren't supposed to drink alcohol. So, I'm not."

Mama's eyes got wide. "You didn't tell her about drinking with me, did you?"

Akna debated whether to lie and say she did just to get a little back for all the worry she knew Mama would soon put on her. But then she saw Mama's hand shake as she poured another glass for herself.

"No," she finally said. "I didn't want to get in trouble."

"Good. That's good. You would get in trouble, mi Cielo. Bad trouble."

This time Mama drank a little slower. "It's bad this time," she said. "Worse than all the other times."

Akna held tight to the back of the chair, bracing herself. Did Mama even remember all the other times? Her fingernails dug into the chair, and a splinter pushed into her palm. She picked at it until she could get it out and then threw it to the floor.

"Es muy malo. Lo peor que he hecho. Ojalá pudiera recuperarlo, pero es demasiado tarde. Demasiado tarde." Mama poured another drink and downed it all at once.

Akna gritted her teeth so as not to scream and remind her of every time something horrible happened. What could be worse than when her boyfriend, Luis, had suddenly taken Mama away for a week and told Akna to take care of everything while they were gone? What could be worse than Mama being sick for two weeks after she came home and wouldn't talk about what happened? What could be worse than having to make up stories for her sisters every night why Mama couldn't tuck them in or kiss them good night, or greet them in the morning?

What could be worse than all that?

Mama's eyes were starting to water. "*Mi cielo, mi cielo.* How can I tell you this?"

"Then don't tell me," Akna said quickly, backing away from the chair. "I don't want to know." She scampered to the front door and opened it, ready to flee.

Mama grabbed her arm, pulling her back. Then she squeezed between Akna and the door, her back against it, blocking Akna's ability to leave.

Akna's shoulders drooped and she hung her head. She studied every speck of dirt between the cracks of each vinyl plank. Dirt she couldn't control. No matter how often she swept it was always there.

She no longer wanted the truth. She no longer wanted to hear about things she couldn't change. She wanted to go back to her bedroom and pretend just like Mazie did with the unicorn. She wanted to remember better times.

If she didn't listen maybe it couldn't happen.

She took a big breath and let it out slowly. "Let's just go to bed and we can talk about it in the morning," she suggested quietly. "You always feel better in the morning."

Mama shook her head. "It will be too late then. Demasiado tarde."

Then it came to her. Luis was taking Mama away again. But this time it would be for even longer than the one week they did last year. "It's Luis, isn't it?" she said through clenched teeth. "Where are you going this time? How long will you be gone?"

"No." Mama sighed heavily. "Luis is in jail." She leaned against the door as if she couldn't stand without support. "He's in there for a long time. We're through. He wasn't the catch I thought." She fisted her hand and pounded it against the door.

"Oh, *mi cielo,* I've really screwed up this time. It's all my fault and there isn't anything I can do about it." Mama's eyes watered and her voice had a choking stutter when she spoke.

This was bad. Really bad. Akna put her arms around Mama and led her back to the table. "Don't cry, Mama. We'll figure it out. We always do."

"Not this time, bebé." Then her soft cry became a wail as she dropped her head onto the table. Her hands and arms covered her head.

Akna's heart raced faster than a cat on a mouse. The tequila in her stomach churned and she swallowed hard to make sure it didn't come back up.

What did Mama do this time? Was she going to jail, too? If that happened, would Akna and her sisters be left here alone? And for how long? She wasn't sure she had enough money for them to live more than a couple weeks.

With every sob escaping Mama's throat, Akna's heart beat faster and her head felt like it was going to leave her body. She tried to take deep breaths but it was as if her lungs couldn't catch a breath. She had to get out before she exploded…before her body deserted her.

Akna headed for the front door. "I'll be back in a few minutes."

"Don't go…" Mama wailed above the sobs. "I need to talk to you now."

"I'll be back." Akna opened the door and closed it quickly. Then she started running. She ran until her breath was so tight that only a scream could loosen it again. The scream came out like the warning horn of a passing train, at first sounding low and then getting louder and louder as she ran further from their home. She screamed and ran and ran and screamed again until there were no screams left. But she still kept going until her legs and her lungs caught up with her runaway heart. It took three circuits of the park for all three parts of her body to find a pace to work in unison again.

Then she ran to the oak tree in the field. The closer she got, her legs slowed. Her heart and her lungs slowed and she started walking. Finally, she could take some deep breaths and with each breath her brain worked better. She could start to think again.

She stopped at the bottom of the tree, hugging the trunk—though her arms could not encircle it. She closed her eyes. *Tata, I hope you can hear me. I think the world is going to change again. You said I would be okay. This is the time to prove it.*

When Akna opened the door, she was determined to make things right. No matter what trouble Mama was in this time, she'd make sure Hai and Nakia were okay. She'd make sure they made it through. Again.

She stood in the doorway a minute before stepping in. She heard water running in the kitchen and the clink of plates. Was it possible? She closed the door and peered into the kitchen to see Mama at the sink washing the dishes. She hadn't washed dishes for months. Then Mama started singing, "Nobody knows the trouble I've seen. Nobody knows my sorrow."

Akna grabbed a towel from the peg near the sink and stepped beside her. "I'll dry," she said, softly. She took a plate out of the rack, dried it and put it on top the shelf above the counter.

Mama washed each plate, each glass, each piece of silverware slowly, carefully. Then rinsed it and put it in the strainer.

Silently, Akna dried each one. Maybe when they were done Mama will have forgotten what was so horrible and they could just go to bed and forget this trouble had ever happened.

"What are you musing about?" Mama asked, her voice was scratchy but didn't have any more tears in it.

"Nothing. Just doing the dishes."

"You're such a good girl. Always working. Always looking out for me and the babies."

When they were done, Akna wrung out the dishrag and then draped it over the rod that extended from the cupboard.

"When I was your age, I helped my Mama, too. I enjoyed it. It made me feel grown up. Do you like helping me?"

She wanted to scream and say no. She wanted to say that she wished Mama didn't drink all the time and didn't take medicine all the time. She wanted to say that it was too much for an eleven-year-old to handle.

But she didn't say any of it. She took a deep breath and remembered what Tata would say. He'd always said: *give your screams to the ravines, the wind, the water, the fire. Let the ancestors wield them for you. With every whistle of wind in the mountains you will know your screams are heard. With every crash of the waves and burning of the fire the ancestors are sharing your pain for all to hear.*

"Sit." Mama turned the chair next to her so they would face each other. She patted the seat of the chair. "Come. It's time for my confession."

Akna sat slowly, her eyes searching Mama's eyes as if she could figure out the answer and prepare herself first.

Mama took both Akna's hands into hers and squeezed. "You know I'm sick, right?"

Akna shook her head. "No. Just sometimes you are sick. Not all the time."

Mama chewed on her lower lip and Akna furrowed her brow. What had she missed? Even though Tata had tried to explain about Mama's mind sickness, Akna still blamed it on her, like it was her own choice. Maybe she'd been wrong. Maybe she really was sick and Akna didn't want to know because she didn't know how to fix it.

Slowly she forced a question out of her mouth. "Do you have cancer, Mama?"

"Oh no!" Her Mama wrapped her arms around her own shoulders and hugged tight. "No, nothing like that. Nothing that horrible."

"Then what? You're scaring me."

She leaned forward and brushed Akna's hair back. Her fingers lingered as if it would be the last time she would touch her. "*Mi cielo*, I have let you down."

"No Mama. You've not let me down if you're sick. I can help. I can ask to study at home and help you get better."

"*Mi alma, mi tecero*, I do not deserve you."

Akna stood and hugged her tight, promising herself she wouldn't let go so her Mama couldn't leave.

Mama hugged back. "What is this? *Mi cielo*, why are you so scared?"

"Don't leave," Akna pleaded. "Is it another boyfriend? Is it something I did? Please don't leave again. We need you to stay here. We need you to be our Mama."

Mama pulled her back into her chest and Akna went willingly, hoping this was one of many confessions that she just had to get out of her system. Then they could go to bed and wake up the next morning and everything would be the same, pretending nothing happened.

"I'm so sorry," Mama said as she rocked back and forth with her arms surrounding Akna. "Lo siento. Lo siento."

Akna held tight. "Don't go," she said into Mama's chest. "Please don't go. I'll be good. I'll do anything you say."

Mama gently pushed her away and looked into her eyes. "Lo siento." This time she said it as if she really meant it. She really was sorry. Worse, it sounded like there was nothing she could do to make it right. "You remember the social worker who came to our house and talked to you a couple of times?"

Akna nodded. "I didn't tell her anything, like I promised. I didn't tell her about you taking vacation without us or anything."

"I know. I know." She sighed deeply. "This is not your fault, Akna. It is mine."

She knew why social workers came to someone's house. It's usually because a neighbor was a busy body. Someone may have figured out when Mama was gone too long and called. The social worker lady kept asking if Akna always had enough to eat and if they went to school regularly. She could say yes to that without lying. She made sure that she and her sisters were taken care of, no matter what.

"Then what is the social worker going to do? Are they going to take us away?" Akna asked.

"I must leave in order to get well. This is something I must do without you."

"How… long?" Akna asked, her voice barely able to get out.

Mama took a deep breath and took a step back. She looked over Akna's head. "The court order is for six months. Because they do not believe you are safe with me, you must leave while I get well. This is the only way I can keep you. If I don't do this, they will take you away forever and I will go to jail for a long time."

Akna crossed her arms tight across her chest to hold in the *thump, thump...thump, thump* of her heart that was so loud she was afraid it might burst out.

"It's called rehab. I have to do rehab. It takes that long to get well. First, I must spend a month in a place like a hospital. Then I can come home, but I have to go to meetings three times every day and report to a probation officer and take a test to prove I'm clean."

Other kids at school had talked about this process in their family. Usually, it was a father who took bad drugs and beat the kids or the mom. But then he'd go to jail. The kids and the mom would be safe and they'd start over, sometimes in another town or even another state. Her Mama never hit her. Though her boyfriends were sometimes scary, they'd never hurt any of them. Mama didn't act like a drug addict. Certainly, the medicine she took wasn't illegal.

"A policeman and that social worker will come here tomorrow. They will take you and Hai and Nakia to a foster home."

Akna widened her eyes as all the horrible things she'd heard about foster homes ran through her mind. "No!" she pronounced. "I'll run away. I'll take Hai and Nakia and we will hide. We'll run far away so they can't find us. I'll take care of them. I can go find Miguel or Bernardo. They'll take us in."

"You don't even know them and they don't know you."

"I remember them," Akna insisted. "I remember when I was five or six and Miguel took care of me while you went away on vacation. He was very nice. He also helped potty train Hai. I think he had a wife who helped. I don't remember her name but I remember them."

"Querido, that was a long time ago. Miguel's life has changed now."

Akna counted back from eleven years old to five. "Only six years ago. Not that long."

"Miguel lives in Ohio now. That's thousands of miles away."

"We can go to Ohio. Miguel is family. I can take Hai and Nakia on the bus. It's better than foster care."

"He doesn't have room for you. He is in a one-bedroom apartment."

"We can sleep on the floor. We can pretend we're camping."

No matter what Akna suggested, Mama just kept shaking her head no at every option.

"What about Bernardo? I remember him, too." Akna tried again. "He's family. Family takes care of each other."

Mama sighed loudly. "Even I don't know where Bernardo is right now. He's in the army. He could be in Japan or Germany or …"

"Then I'll do it myself. I'll pretend I'm older. Fifteen? Sixteen? I'll stay here with them. I know how to cook and buy groceries and take them to school and everything. I'll keep the house clean. I've been doing it for two years. You know I have. I can do it. If you leave me enough money while you're gone for a month, I will do everything. How old do I have to be to take care of them? I can tell them I'm sixteen. They will believe me."

"Whoa. Whoa. Whoa." Mama reached for her. "Do not start lying. That is the worst thing you can do. Foster care is not what you think. It's not that bad."

"Yes, it is. Tonio said he'd been in foster care for a year and they were awful. They made him work all the time and if he complained they made him stay in his room without dinner. And they wouldn't let him see his Mama. He said it was like prison."

Mama wrapped her arms around Akna once more. "It won't be like that. They promised me they would take you to a good home. They found a home that would take all three of you. Do you know hard it is to get that kind of placement? Most foster kids get separated from their siblings. But that social worker promised me the three of you would never be separated. You can even sleep in the same room like you do now."

Akna's eyes were leaking again. She squeezed them tight. Why was Mama so against helping her? Why was this the only answer? She had five other siblings older than her. True Akna didn't know them, but Tata had told stories about them. Certainly, someone had room for them. Family was everything. Tata told her that family stuck together no matter what.

Mama simply held her and waited. She waited until there were no more tears. She kept rocking Akna back and forth. "Lo siento," she said over and over again.

But sorry didn't help. It never helped.

CHAPTER FOUR

STRENGTH AND DETERMINATION

*P*ound. *Pound. Pound.*

The house shook whenever someone knocked too hard.

She knew who it was because none of the neighbors ever knocked that hard. Akna peaked through the curtain near the door. It was a policeman and the social worker lady she'd met twice before.

"Just a minute," she shouted through the door. "I'll get Mama."

She ran down the narrow hallway to the back of the trailer. "Mama?" she said loudly on the other side of the door. "Wake up, Mama. The people are here."

Hearing nothing, she tried to be quiet opening the door. Mama was sound asleep with the blanket pulled tight over her head.

"They're here!" She shook her hard. "Wake up!"

She didn't want to leave without saying good-bye. And what about Hai and Nakia? She tried to explain to them what was happening during breakfast this morning, but they just started crying and asking too many questions she didn't know how to answer.

She shook Mama again. "Wake up! Wake up!"

Finally, Mama groaned and held her arm over her head. "Go away. Leave me alone."

"Mama, the policeman and the social worker lady are here. You have to get up now."

"Tell them I'm sick. Go on now. I'll be fine. Go on."

"But they are going to take us away and we won't see you for a long time. You have to get up. You have to say goodbye to Hai and Nakia."

"I can't, Akna. I'm too sick to get up. Go away. You'll be fine. I'll see you in six months." Then she pulled the blanket back over her head.

Akna stared. She didn't know what to say. She should be angry, but instead she was numb. She'd spent all night silently packing their things, making sure she had Nana's quilt. She took down the picture in the hall and vowed it would go in her bedroom at the foster home so that all three of them could remember better times.

Before she went to bed last night, she'd tried to talk to Mama about rehab and how they would send letters and how they would get back together in six months; but Mama had already given up. She'd said her piece and then gone to her bedroom and locked the door.

Perhaps the medicine made Mama numb, too. That was the only explanation that made sense. Certainly, Mama would never choose to sleep through the most devastating time in Akna's and her sister's lives.

Akna tried once more, but in a whisper with no emotion. "Don't you want to say goodbye to Hai and Nakia? They will be heartbroken. Don't you want to say something to help them feel better about leaving?

"There is nothing to say," her mother mumbled from beneath the blanket. "The world is a hard place. They need to learn that to survive. Now go. I'm sick."

In the past when she was like this, Akna would just leave her alone until later. But today she couldn't do that. None of them could.

"Turn off the light and close the door," Mama said.

"I love you, Mama," Akna whispered as a rote reply she would say every night. She switched off the light. "Get well soon."

There was no response as her Mama curled into a ball beneath the blanket.

Akna ran the back of her hand across her eyes. She was not going to cry right now. It would change nothing. She'd cried enough to fill all the rivers the Tzuultaq'a" would need. She had to be strong for her sisters. She straightened her spine and kept repeating to herself, *Strength and Determination. Strength and Determination.* She strode back into the small living room and opened the door.

"Sorry to keep you waiting," she said in her best church-going voice. "Mama can't come talk to you because she's sick. You can sit down if you want while I get my sisters."

Akna scanned the living room to make sure there was a clean place to sit. "Oh…" She quickly grabbed the empty tequila bottle off the TV tray and ran into the kitchen to put it in the sink. Then she moved the big suitcase to one end of the sofa to make room for the police officer and the lady to sit. "Sorry, I…uh…forgot to clean up last night. When Mama gets sick I'm supposed to do the cleaning."

The lady nodded. "You are doing a fine job, Akna," she said. "Do you remember me? I'm Mrs. Sleeper. I'll be taking you to your foster home today. You don't have to clean up for us. We won't be staying long."

Mrs. Sleeper turned to the policeman. "Officer, would you mind loading their suitcase into my car while I help get the children?"

"No problem, ma'm." The man easily stuffed the big suitcase under his arm like it was a toy to be delivered. He stepped out of the house quickly.

The lady stood. "Where are your sisters?"

"I…uh…think it's better if I get them by myself," Akna said. "Nakia's only five. When she gets scared, she mostly speaks Spanish. And she's already freaked out by everything. Do you speak Spanish?"

Mrs. Sleeper shook her head. "Only a word here and there. Are you sure, honey? I'm good at handling crying children."

"I'm sure," Akna said. "I'll be right back."

She darted to the back of the mobile home where their bedroom was. She was still trying to think of a way to sneak them out the back and run to a neighbor's house or perhaps grab a passing bus to anywhere but here. She probably had enough money to get the three of them to Ohio. She didn't care if they all had to sleep on the floor in a living room. It would be better than being with strangers. Certainly, someone would take them in. Someone they knew.

Hai appeared in the doorway. She had her rainbow backpack already on and held tight to a ragdoll Nana had made for her fifth birthday.

"Is the foster care lady here?"

Akna nodded, not knowing what to say to make this easier.

Hai turned back toward the bedroom. "Nakia, vamos. Es hora de irse ahora. ¿Tienes tu mochila y tu conejito?"

"Si." Nakia appeared with the stuffed bunny Tata had won at the State Faire before he died. She took Akna's hand and peered around her. "¿Es simpática o da miedo?"

"She's not scary at all. She seems nice. Want to find out for yourself?"

Nakia nodded.

Akna held her hand tight and Hai followed behind. She couldn't help but feel she was leading her sisters to their execution. Not a real one, but the end of life as they knew it. At least, at eleven, Akna was pretty old and had lots of memories of life with Tata and Nana and Mama. Nakia was still too little to really understand. She'd barely started kindergarten this year. She was just beginning to understand English.

But Hai was old enough to understand and to be really hurt. She was only eight. When Akna was eight, Tata and Nana died and she thought her life was over. It wasn't but it was a lot harder, especially with Mama's sickness. She didn't want Hai to have that horrible feeling right now.

Akna decided then and there she would make sure Hai could still be a child. Tata always said Akna had lots of love, more than most people. And she believed him. From now on she would find a way to give her Tata's love and Nana's love and Mama's love along with her own.

"Oh! There you are," Mrs. Sleeper said a bit too brightly when they entered the living room. "I was worried you might sneak out the back door."

Akna looked straight at her. Did she know she'd been thinking that? Did other kids do that when social services came to get them?

Akna chuckled uneasily and shook her head. "No, we wouldn't do that. Mama told us you had a very nice place for us to go." And if it wasn't, Akna had the means to get everyone away she reminded herself.

"That's right." Mrs. Sleeper said with a genuine smile. "It is a very nice place. Mr. and Mrs. Bohn are one of our best foster parents."

Bone? Akna rolled the name around in her head. Who would have a name like the bones in your body? It was not a name she'd ever heard before. Most of the people in their park had Spanish last names. Some of the kids in school had other kinds of last names like Marsh and Smith and Lee and Bhangu. But not Bone. She wondered what country that name was from.

She took one last look around the mobile home before closing the door.

The tomato plants. She'd forgotten about the tomato plants. Empty tequila bottles stood in the kitchen window with tomato plant starters she'd planned to put in the ground in the spring. It was the only thing Akna knew how to grow. Tata said they could grow anywhere, even in a landfill where garbage was all around.

Her eyes misted. There was nothing she could do for them. Perhaps the foster home would allow her to grow tomatoes there. She closed the door and stared at the car with her sisters waiting for her signal. She took in a deep breath, swallowed hard, lifted her chin and marched to the car like an aristocrat awaiting the guillotine. They may imprison her in this new home, but they would never take her soul.

Akna opened the door and each of her sisters slid into the backseat ahead of her. First Hai, then Nakia in the middle, and finally Akna. They each held their backpack in front of them. She double-checked Nakia's seat belt around the booster chair. As Mrs. Sleeper started up the car, Akna checked her backpack for the umpteenth time, making sure she had her money-clip still hidden in a box Tata had made for her small rock collection. She dug her fingers through the rocks until she felt the clip. It was still there.

Before she and Mama went to bed last night, Mama had given her $100. She'd told her to put it in her wallet and keep it hidden. It was her emergency money. If anyone was mean to them or tried to hurt them, Akna could use the emergency money to get bus tickets and bring them all home. Akna also had a key to get back into the house even if Mama wasn't there.

She hadn't told Mama that she also had more money she'd stashed since the last time Mama had disappeared. If they had to come home early, she wasn't sure how long the money would last before the six months for rehab were up. But she wouldn't worry about that now. She'd figure out a way to make it last if she had to.

Mama said she expected everyone to be really nice, because the social worker had promised. But she admitted that once in a while there was a bad one, like the home Tonio had been sent to. If that happened it was up to Akna to take care of all of them.

"Wouldn't you like to sit up front with me, Akna?" Mrs. Sleeper interrupted her thoughts.

"No thank you. I want to stay with my sisters in case they need me."

"I understand." Then she slowly backed away from the house. "This is your chance to say goodbye to your house."

"Goodbye house," Hai said, waving her hand.

"Adios casa," Nakia echoed.

"I'm not saying goodbye because we will be back in six months," Akna said louder than she'd planned. Then she added with more confidence than she felt, "Mama's rehab is six months. Then she'll be back to get us."

"I understand," Mrs. Sleeper said again. After the car left their park, she added, "Of course, your Mama would like to come get you when she's well. But sometimes these things take longer than planned."

"She'll come in six months," Akna said again. She wasn't pretending this time. She had to believe it or it wouldn't come true.

Mrs. Sleeper didn't correct her.

Akna doubted Mrs. Sleeper understood anything. How could she? Did she ever have to leave her house and go live with people she didn't even know? Did she ever have to take care of her mother? Did she ever have to take care of her little sisters? She doubted it, not with this big fancy car and her perfect dress and shoes, and her neatly styled short blonde hair. She certainly didn't look old enough to even be a mother.

No, she'd bet that Mrs. Sleeper didn't know anything about this. She was just a government person who got paid to take children away from their parents. Well, Akna wasn't going to let her keep them anywhere past six months. No matter what happened with her mother.

"How long 'til we get there?" Hai asked.

"It's only about an hour. We'll be there sooner than you think."

"Conejito quiere saber dónde está el baño," Nakia said.

"Baño is bathroom, right?" Mrs. Sleeper said. "Didn't she go before we left?"

Akna toyed with the idea of making her stop several times along the way, but discarded the idea. She really wanted to get this over with. The sooner they got to the foster home, the sooner they could leave it.

"She's just asking for her bunny. Her bunny asks lots of questions when she's nervous. We all went before we left. We will last an hour."

"Good. Sometimes getting off the freeway can add lots of time to the trip. Traffic can be a beast."

"No hay paradas de baño. Así que dile a conejito que lo sostenga," Akna said.

Hai giggled. Then Nakia giggled.

Akna couldn't help but laugh with them.

She saw Mrs. Sleeper look in the rearview mirror with one eyebrow quirked.

"We just told her bunny to hold it," Akna said.

"Ah, good idea."

They traveled in silence for a while. The scenery wasn't anything special to keep Akna's attention. Lots of buildings and signs and cars and freeways intersecting each other. After about half an hour Akna had started to formulate a brilliant plan for escape. Only if needed of course.

"Do our foster parents speak Spanish," Akna asked.

"I don't know. I don't think so. I didn't realize Nakia didn't speak English."

"She does when she has to. She just started kindergarten. At home she doesn't have to, so she doesn't practice a lot. I've been reading her English stories at night to help her learn faster."

"You're a good sister, Akna. I bet she'll learn English a lot faster when everyone around her is speaking it. I'll be sure to let your foster parents know so they are prepared to help, too."

For the first time since yesterday, Akna believed that maybe she really did have some super power. Mrs. Sleeper didn't speak Spanish. She'd bet the foster parents didn't speak Spanish. That meant she and her sisters could have all kinds of private conversations and no one would know what they were saying, or thinking, or doing.

And that meant Akna and her sisters could easily make any secret plans they needed.

CHAPTER FIVE

IT'S A HARD KNOCK LIFE

*W*ithin no time they were in a neighborhood with real houses and streets.

Mrs. Sleeper pulled off and pointed at a brick building. "That's where you'll all be going to school," she said. "It's only a few blocks away from where you'll be living, so it's a short walk."

Akna searched for a sign. "Margarita Elementary School," she read aloud. "That's interesting. That's a Spanish name."

"Yes!" Mrs. Sleeper sounded very pleased with herself. "This town is close to fifty percent Hispanic. You'll likely have friends who speak Spanish just like you."

Akna wasn't sure whether to be happy or sad about that. It could mean that her secret escape plan was in jeopardy. On the other hand, it could mean that she wouldn't feel so different from everyone. She'd just have to make sure she never shared the plan with anyone except Hai and Nakia.

About seven blocks later Mrs. Sleeper pulled into a driveway. A big mailbox at the curb said Bohn on it. So, the name was not written like it sounded. B O H N was bone.

The address was 204 Mariposa Lane. Akna said that over several times in her mind so she would memorize it in case she ever got lost. She wondered if they knew that Mariposa was Spanish for butterfly. She would love to turn herself and her sisters into a butterfly and perhaps they could fly into the clouds and see Tata and Nana again.

The two-story house appeared welcoming with a nice wooden door in the front and a big side-light window to the right of it. On the left was a two-car garage. No one even had a garage where they lived. A few people had carports, but many mobile homes simply had a small slab of cement for one car and that was it.

The first thing she noticed was a leafless tree, about as tall as the roofline, with a fiery-red bark. It stood out even more because there were lots of low bushes in other parts of the front yard that were green and spready. There was even a lawn big enough to play on, probably as long as their mobile home and the same width. Peaking over the roof from the backyard was a very large tree, also without leaves. It wasn't close enough for Akna to know if it would be a good climbing tree, but it looked promising.

Attached to the roof in the front, she could see three small windows. It didn't look like a full story. More like a half-story or an attic because the windows were sticking out of little triangular shaped sections. She'd seen houses like that in a couple of books she'd read where people lived in New England. But she'd never seen them like that in Oregon.

The fanciest thing she'd ever seen in Oregon was the winery where her Tata had worked. The building was built to resemble a castle, but nobody lived there. It was a pretend castle so rich people would buy lots of wine.

Mrs. Sleeper turned off the car and the locks clicked open. "This is it. Time to meet your new family."

Suddenly, Akna wasn't so sure about getting out of the car. Maybe she should have asked for those bathroom stops after all.

"Let's go," Hai said as she unbuckled her seatbelt. "I want to see our bedroom and everything. It looks like a nice place."

Yeah, too nice, Akna thought, as she helped unbuckle Nakia from the car seat. They would never fit in here. This was nicer than the fanciest mobile home in their park. She bet everyone here was fancy like Mrs. Sleeper.

They all stood in a straight line staring at the house as Mrs. sleeper wrestled their big suitcase out of the trunk.

Akna closely examined that second story. Was that where she and her sisters would be sleeping? In the attic? Probably where it was hot in the summer and cold in the winter. Just like the story about Annie and the orphanage.

She'd seen that movie on TV. She remembered the song, *It's a hard knock life*, and how all the orphans had to work all the time scrubbing floors and washing clothes. The orphans often didn't have much to eat and Mrs. Hannigan, the lady who ran the orphanage, was really mean and took all the money. She remembered how the beds were lined up and the room was cold and the kids wore rags all the time.

Yup. She bet that's what was going on here. Probably the rich people's kids lived downstairs in big rooms, and the three foster kids lived upstairs in the attic and did all the work.

She was really glad she had more than $200 now. They'd just get some food and sleep a couple nights, maybe a week, tops. Then they'd be out of here. They could escape while walking to school. No one would ever know. No way was she staying if they were going to be treated like orphans in that movie.

Mrs. Sleeper was now lugging their suitcase up the driveway. It was nearly half her size and didn't have rollers because they'd broken off long ago.

"Here we go," she said as she passed them, grunting a bit with the weight. "You'll love it here."

Each of them wearing their backpacks, Nakia latched onto Akna's hand on her left and Hai held almost as tight to Akna's hand on her right. However, it was Hai who was pulling them forward. She wasn't scared at all. But Akna was the oldest and she knew that life wasn't always friendly.

Akna put on her meet-the-teacher smile and they all marched together up the driveway and stood behind Mrs. Sleeper. She hoped the woman who owned this house didn't look like Mrs. Hannigan.

Mrs. Sleeper pressed the doorbell and Akna heard it sound inside with a pretty tune. Yep, fancy.

She stood like a soldier and held even tighter to Hai and Nakia.

"Ouch," Hai said.

"Lo siento," Akna said. "Un poco nerviosa."

Mrs. Sleeper smiled. "It's natural to be a bit nervous. It's okay."

Busted. Maybe Mrs. Sleeper knew more Spanish than she let on.

"It's the word nerviosa," she said. "It's very close to nervous. Hmm…I wonder how many other Spanish words are a lot like English or vice versa."

Akna let out her breath. Okay, it was just coincidence.

The wooden door opened and a petite, strawberry-blonde haired woman smiled. "Oh, hello. You must be the Sales girls."

Akna was surprised the woman pronounced their last name correctly—saw-less. Whenever she went to a new class in school, they would say her name like a sale at a store instead of the correct sound and accent.

Mrs. Bohn was not much taller than Akna. Her face was very pale with some freckles like Susie at her old school. As she turned to one side, Akna could see her strawberry-blonde hair was wrapped in a messy bun in the back. It had streaks of white barely showing in some of the strands. She was definitely older than Mama but not as old as Nana. Her smile seemed genuine. Maybe she wasn't as bad as Mrs. Hannigan in the movie.

"We are here," Mrs. Sleeper said. She pointed at the woman in the doorway. "May I introduce your foster mother, Mrs. Bohn." Then she pointed to Akna and her sisters in turn as she made their introductions. "The oldest here is Akna, age eleven and a half. Next is Hai, age eight. Last is Nakia, age five."

Mrs. Bohn stepped back from the door and gestured for them to enter. "Come in, come in. Welcome to your new home, Akna, Hai, and Nakia. You come in, too, Mrs. Sleeper. I've assembled all the girls in the living room."

Other girls? How many other kids lived here? Any boys? Were the other girls going to hate them for taking time away from their mother?

Akna and her sisters walked slowly behind Mrs. Sleeper. The entry way was quite small considering the size of the house from the outside. But then she looked to the right and a large living room came into view. The pale walls had lots of pictures of people having fun together. There were so many different children and ages and adults it was hard to know who belonged to who.

The largest sectional sofa Akna had ever seen was along one wall and then the angled part was dividing the living room from the dining room. She guessed it could easily hold fifteen or twenty people. It was very bright in bold pink and purple flowers on a creamy white background. It didn't look brand new, but it didn't look all scratched up either.

On the end of the sofa furthest away sat three girls each spaced about a foot apart. None of them appeared to be part of the same family. Nor did they have any of the features of Mrs. Bohn.

"Sit. Sit." Mrs. Bohn gestured to the sofa. "I'm just finishing up getting lunch together for everyone. Why don't you all introduce yourselves, and we can talk more over lunch." Then she bustled off toward the dining room and disappeared around a corner. Soon Akna heard what sounded like doors being opened and closed and dishes being stacked or moved.

Mrs. Sleeper sat in the middle of the sofa like she was the umpire in a football game. Perhaps she would make sure no one attacked each other.

Akna led Hai and Nakia to the other end for them to sit. She pointed Hai and Nakia toward the end and Akna sat on the side closest to Mrs. Sleeper. Anyone with bad intent would have to go through her to get to her sisters.

"Hello girls," Mrs. Sleeper said to the three who were on the other end. "How about you introduce yourself while Mrs. Bohn is getting lunch together."

The tallest one said, "I'm Sandra. I'm fifteen. I'm a sophomore in high school and the oldest. I came to this home when I was ten and I'll be staying until I graduate from high school. Then I'm going to college and then I'm going to become a missionary. I don't know where but it will be somewhere far away where no one speaks English. I want to help people come to know and love Jesus like I do."

She had pale skin, but medium brown hair down to her shoulders, styled with a flip up at the end. Her brown eyes appeared to be too big for her slender face. The multi-colored leggings she wore showed a slender figure like some teen models Akna had seen on TV. The white pull-over sweater came to her knees more like a dress. It seemed too big for her body. The front of it said Carpe Diem in bright pink cursive lettering. Akna stared for a moment trying to figure out what that might mean.

Sandra smiled. "It's Latin. It means seize the day. Like make each day the best you can. That's what I always try to do."

"Oh. Thanks," Akna said. "That's a good thought."

The short, curly-haired, sandy-blonde with a round face spoke next. "I'm Polly. I'm twelve."

Akna was surprised she was twelve, because she was closer to Hai's size. Her hair was so curly that if it wasn't blonde and her face white, Akna would have thought it was an afro.

"So, here's my sad story," she started off dramatically. "My mom's in the crazy house, my dad is in jail," Polly spoke in a sing-songy way. "This is my second foster home; but it's just swell. The first one sent me back because I was way too pale. I had an adoption that only lasted a spell. If I ever got mad, they believed I was unwell. So, they sent me back like I was stale. Mrs. Sleeper found another place for me to dwell. I've been here a year and I haven't turned unwell. I'm not schizo as others might foretell. At eighteen the Bohns will have to say farewell. Then I think I'll go and win a Nobel."

Akna laughed aloud at how well Polly pulled all those rhymes together. She had to respond. She thought for a moment and then had it. "Sorry about all the pell-mell, but at rhyming you excel."

Polly gave her an air high five from her side of the couch.

Sandra pointed and shook her finger at Polly. "You know you're not supposed to say schizo. You either say she is mentally ill or she has schizophrenia which is a mental illness."

Polly stuck out her tongue and raised her hand near her mouth with the thumb and three fingers going up and down in the talk-talk-talk gesture.

Akna stifled another laugh. She was surprised Polly shared so much, even though she tried to make it funny. Akna sure wasn't planning to say why they were in foster care. At least not all the bad things. What did it mean to have a mom with schizophrenia? Was her own Mama crazy? She didn't think so. Tata never called her that. If she was crazy, they couldn't fix her, right?

Polly elbowed the third girl and said, "It's your turn, Gianna."

Instead of speaking, the girl simply stared at Sandra like she was putting some kind of spell on her. She was dressed in a long black sack of a dress. She wore hiking boots. Her hair was also very black and it was probably to her waist. Half of it covered one side of her face completely, and that side was several shades of blue.

"I'm Gianna," the girl spoke slowly and quietly. "I'm thirteen. You don't need to know why I'm here. I can leave whenever I feel like it. This isn't a jail. At the moment this is an okay place to live. That's all I have to say."

"Thank you, girls," Mrs. Sleeper said almost immediately after Gianna stopped speaking. "Akna, would you like to introduce yourself?"

Well not really, Akna thought. She didn't want to make friends with these other girls. They obviously all had problems—more problems than she and her sisters did. It didn't sound like any of them were ever going home. But she guessed, if she didn't play nice, Mrs. Sleeper might say too much about their Mama or why they had to come here.

"I'm Akna. I'm eleven and a half." She turned to her sisters and pointed to each one. "This is my sister Hai. She's eight. The youngest is Nakia. She's five."

"Why are you here?" Polly asked. "I mean none of us came here because we wanted to."

"Our mom is sick," Akna responded. "But she will be well in about six months and then we will go home and be together again. So, we are only here for a short time."

"Rehab," Gianna said in a whisper just loud enough for everyone to hear. "I know all about that."

Akna blanched. How would she know that?

Should she lie and say she really was sick like cancer? Mrs. Sleeper would probably call her on it. She sat unsure of what to say.

"I don't know what rehab is," Hai piped up. "I know that Mama is sad a lot, and the rehab place is going to fix her. She loves us and if Akna says she will come get us in six months, then that is the truth."

Gianna dropped her head and said quietly, "You're lucky then. You have a *real* family."

Akna hugged Hai to her side. She was so proud of her and happy that she believed. At the same moment she wondered what she would tell Hai and Nakia *if* Mama didn't come back in six months. She shook that thought away. Mama *would* come back. This rehab would definitely fix her.

"How about you, Nakia?" Sandra asked. "Are you scared?"

Nakia looked over to Akna and cocked her head.

"Ella preguntó si estás feliz de estar aquí o tienes miedo," Akna said.

Nakia's eyes grew wide. ¿Asustado? ¿Están sus monstruos aquí?

Sandra answered before Akna could. "Sin monstruos. Somos buenas personas y nos cuidamos unos a otros aquí."

Nakia stood and smiled broadly. "Maravilloso. Entonces estoy feliz de estar aquí."

"You know Spanish?" Akna asked, realizing her language super power may have just been blown.

"I'm not a native speaker," Sandra said. "But one of my mother's boyfriends spoke Spanish—mostly when he was throwing a hissy fit. So, when I came here, I started taking Spanish classes so I'd know what all those words meant if I should ever run into him again. I have a thing or two to tell him." Sandra smiled in that way that meant someone was in trouble. "I learned all the bad words too," she said and winked. "I'll catch you if you're swearing."

Akna nodded. Everyone here definitely had problems. She wasn't the only one with a screwed-up family.

"Sandra and Gianna, please come help me set the table and put out the food," Mrs. Bohn called from behind the wall.

The two girls scurried in her direction. As Gianna rose from the sofa she said, "There's a calendar for chores. We all take turns. Sandra and Polly made all the stuff for lunch earlier."

Lunch was delicious and there was plenty of food. Enough bread and fixings that each person could make a whole sandwich. Sandra explained that every Saturday they all got together and made the bread for the entire week. They would choose the bread for that week from a bag of bread names. That helped them learn many different recipes. It was always a surprise to find out what each person chose. Sandra's favorite to eat was honey wheat. Gianna's favorite was sourdough. Polly's favorite was rye. Mrs. Bohn said she liked all of them, but the one that was the most fun to make was focaccia. Outside of wheat, Akna hadn't heard of the others.

Today's bread was the honey wheat. There was also lettuce, tomatoes, pickles, mustard, mayonnaise, sliced avocados and three kinds of lunchmeat—ham, turkey, and roast beef. They could choose whatever they wanted. On top of that, they could choose what they wanted to drink—water, ice tea, lemonade, or strawberry lemonade. Mrs. Bohn didn't allow any soda in the house. And for dessert they could each have one homemade chocolate chip or oatmeal cookie.

Akna marveled at the amount of food available. Was this just to impress Mrs. Sleeper that this was a great home? Or was this the norm for meals?

At the end of lunch, Hai exclaimed, "I could stay here forever with this kind of food!"

Everyone laughed. Mrs. Bohn said it wasn't always sandwiches but they ate well enough.

When Mrs. Sleeper left, she gave Akna a business card and said, "If you ever have a problem, you can call me at this number. If I don't answer it means I'm busy but I will definitely get back to you. Okay?"

Akna took the card and nodded. Was Mrs. Sleeper suggesting maybe this home wasn't all that great after all?

"I believe you will be happy here," Mrs. Sleeper said as if reading her mind. "But if you have any questions—even if it's about your mama or anything else—you can call me."

Yes, her Mama. In all that had happened over the past few hours she'd almost forgotten about her. Was she still asleep at home? Had the policeman forced her to wake up and go to rehab wherever that was?

Akna followed Mrs. Sleeper to the door as Hai and Nakia talked with the other girls. "I do have a question," she said. "When do you think we will get to phone Mama in rehab? I want to let her know we are here safe and the Bohns are very nice so she won't worry."

"Oh honey, did she not explain to you how rehab works?"

Akna shook her head.

"Oh dear. Why don't you follow me out to the car so no big ears hear us talking?"

Akna stepped outside and made sure the front door was closed.

Mrs. Sleeper leaned one hip against the front fender of her car. "During the first month—the time she is in the residential treatment —you won't be able to talk to her. In order to work out her problems and the way she's made choices in the past, she won't be able to talk to anyone—boyfriends, children, friends, not anyone. In that way nothing can distract her from doing the hard work she needs to do to make better choices about her life. Do you understand?"

Akna was surprised. She thought it was like going to the hospital and getting some medication and coming home only it lasted a day or two. Mama had done that a few times when Tata and Nana were alive. They always got to visit her in the hospital. Tata said it was important to visit to remind her of all the love she had at home. Once Mama was gone for a whole month in the hospital and they visited every other day.

"So, it's like jail," Akna said.

Mrs. Sleeper held her hand lightly. "No, honey. It's not jail. She's not a prisoner. No one in Oregon is forced to go to rehab or stay there. She can walk away whenever she wants. But if she stays there it will help her to learn some important things about why she thinks drugs are the answer."

"After the first month then we can call her?" Akna asked.

"Once she gets out of residential treatment, she will be living back at home. Then she will be allowed to *arrange* for phone conversations. But remember, even though she will be living at home, she will be very busy with meetings and doctor appointments and counseling and checking in with the court regularly. So, you'll probably only hear from her once every couple of weeks, maybe only once per month. She has to call me and set up a time. Then I call Mrs. Bohn to let her know your mother will be calling.

"Because of her conviction, the court sentence says if she doesn't do everything required of her for six months, she will go to jail for five years. If she finishes the full six months of rehab, there is no jail and she can get you back."

Akna swallowed hard. Jail? Conviction? Mama did say something about jail if she didn't do rehab, but Akna thought she was exaggerating.

"What did she do?" Akna asked. "She only said she was sick and there was a court order for rehab. She didn't say anything about jail for five years. What did she do?"

"Oh dear." Mrs. Sleeper raised her eyes to the sky as if asking for God's help. "She didn't tell you anything?"

Akna shook her head.

"Oh dear. Oh dear. Oh dear." Mrs. Sleeper shook her head from side to side. "I'm afraid I can't tell you. But I'll talk to my supervisor about it and see what can be done. If you were fourteen, we are allowed to tell you, but not at eleven. Eleven is just too young."

"I may be eleven but I might as well be fourteen," Akna said angrily. "Or even fifteen or sixteen. I've been taking care of everyone for the last two years since Nana and Tata died. I know more about the real world than most eleven-year-olds. You tell your supervisor that. You tell her that I can take anything. You tell her I have a right to know. I'm the mother now for my sisters."

"Technically, Mrs. Bohn is the mother figure right now," Mrs. Sleeper said quietly. "You don't need to be the mother, anymore, Akna. You can just be an eleven-year-old now."

Akna shook her head vigorously. "Mrs. Bohn will never be our mother."

"I know that, Akna, but—"

"I promised Tata and Nana that I would always take care of them," Akna continued, even though tears kept leaking out of her eyes. "I have to know how to plan for the future. I have to know what hopes to have. When I was only eight, before Tata died, he said I am strong. I am determined. I am eleven now and I am even stronger and more determined. You tell your supervisor that."

Mrs. Sleeper hugged her tightly. "I will honey. I will."

As she scurried away, Akna noticed a tear slip down Mrs. Sleeper's cheek. Maybe she really did care. Maybe she understood at least a little.

CHAPTER SIX

THE ROOM AT THE TOP OF THE STAIRS

kna took her time joining everyone back in the house. All she could think about was what thing her Mama did to be sent to jail. She knew about the drinking. She knew about the disappearing. But she didn't think either of those were the kind of thing that puts someone in jail.

Maybe it was time to get to know these other girls better. They all seemed to know more about their own situations than she did, and they were all older—especially Sandra. Though Sandra already seemed a bit standoffish. She really hadn't shared her situation except to say how long she was there. And if Sandra was going to be a missionary it might be all she would do is pray with Akna.

No, she'd start with Polly. She seemed okay with talking about hard stuff. Maybe they knew what kind of things put mothers in jail. Also, Gianna knew about rehab. Even though she seemed kind of quiet, somehow Akna trusted her. Maybe because she didn't share everything. Maybe she had more in common with Akna than anyone in the house.

As she made her way back to the living room, the only person there was Mrs. Bohn.

"Where are Hai and Nakia?"

"They're upstairs getting settled into the room. Would you like to do that, too?"

Akna nodded.

"Good. All the girls sleep upstairs," Mrs. Bohn said as she led the way. "You all share one very big bedroom."

Uh huh. Now the truth came out. The attic, just as she suspected.

"I find it to be a nice way for all six of you to get to know each other, help each other, and maybe even to share state secrets." Mrs. Bohn twittered at her cleverness. Then she stopped at the top of the stairs and made a sweeping gesture. "Welcome to your bedroom."

Akna stepped next to her. It wasn't an attic! The vaulted ceiling was a lot higher than the ceiling downstairs in the living room and dining room. She was sure even the tallest man in the world couldn't touch the peak.

Those small windows she'd noticed from the outside were normal size from the inside. Beneath each one was a single bed. Three on one side and three on the other. Each bed had a window above the headboard, a small table with a little drawer on one side, and a desk on the other side. At the foot of each bed was a large trunk.

"Akna! Akna!" Hai squealed and ran to her with a big hug. "Isn't it the best? It's so pretty and there is a place for everything. And look!" She held up a doll that was probably two feet tall. She pressed a button on the doll's stomach.

The doll said, "Hola. Mi nombre es Teresa. ¿Cómo te llamas?"

"And she speaks English, too." Hai said. She pressed another button.

The doll said, "Hello. My name is Teresa. What is your name?"

Akna couldn't believe it. She'd never heard or seen a doll like that. She joined Nakia. "¿Tu muñeca también habla español e inglés?"

"Si!" Nakia answered. "Now I learn English...um *mejor*."

Akna turned to Mrs. Bohn. "Thank you. Thank you for thinking of them."

"Of course, dear. We want you all to feel welcome. It is important to keep your native language and English."

"Our native language is actually K'iche' not Spanish," Akna said.

"My Tata told me that the Spanish conquered Guatemala and forced everyone to learn their language. I'm pretty sure there are no dolls that speak K'iche'."

Mrs. Bohn looked like she was confused and Akna felt a little bit bad for bringing it up. The truth was she was the only one who really spoke K'iche' at all. Hai hadn't spoken it in two years, and Nakia almost never. Mama didn't like them speaking it and refused to speak it after Nana and Tata died.

She didn't know why she made a big deal of it. She just didn't want to like it here at all. Everything here was too good to be true. Almost like everyone was trying too hard. It didn't feel real. She knew when things seemed too good, then something bad always happened. How long would it take here?

"Can you write that down for me?" Mrs. Bohn asked. "I'd like to look it up and learn more about it."

Akna nodded. "I don't have any paper at the moment."

"Look in the drawer in your desk."

Akna opened it and there was a pad of yellow paper with lines. They really did try to think of everything here. She quickly wrote it down in big letters K'iche'

Mrs. Bohn looked at it. "Do those two apostrophes mean something special?" she asked.

"It's like a little breath. Like when you say uh-oh, the part in the middle is a little bit of air that comes out before the next syllable."

"Like an accent?" Mrs. Bohn asked.

"No." Akna shook her hand in frustration. "I don't know how to explain it. I just speak it. I don't know how to spell all the words and write them down either. And I've never seen a book written in K'iche'."

"Thank you," Mrs. Bohn said. "I'll look it up later tonight and see if I can understand more."

Akna couldn't help but be surprised. Maybe Mrs. Bohn was genuine. But she wouldn't start trusting yet. For now, she would focus on trying to be grateful for just today. She'd learn to do that whenever

Mama was well for a while. Focus on that one day or that one week and be happy.

Nana had always said, "Don't borrow trouble." That meant, don't start being sad and worry about what bad things *might* happen. Take whatever good the day offers you. There will be plenty of time to be sad and worried later.

Mrs. Bohn pointed to the bed next to the drawer where the paper had been. "As your sisters have already chosen their beds, this one is left for you. I hope that is okay."

Akna looked across the room. Hai and Nakia were straight across on the other side along with Gianna who was closest to the stairs. On her side, Akna was sandwiched between Polly and Sandra. With Sandra being closest to the stairs. For a moment she was sad that she wouldn't be sleeping in the same bed with Hai and Nakia. But they didn't seem to be upset about it at all.

"It's fine," Akna finally answered.

Mrs. Bohn opened the trunk at the end of the bed. "Here is where we keep extra blankets and a change of sheets. Each girl washes her bedding once per week. Because we only have one washer and dryer we have a schedule. Three girls do their bedding on Tuesday and three more do it on Thursday. You and your sisters will be on Thursdays.

When you change the bed, you get fresh sheets and then the used sheets can be washed." Then she pulled out a drawer beneath the bed. "We don't have room for dressers, but each bed has a long drawer on each side where you can keep all folded clothing." She closed the drawer.

"Follow me." She walked back toward the stairs to what appeared to be a wall. Then she pointed to a pull and placed her fingers in and pulled toward her. "This is a shared bathroom."

Akna entered the door. It was the biggest bathroom she'd ever seen, except for the one at school. There was a very long counter along one wall with three sinks in it. Next to the sinks along the back wall was a large shower. Maybe five feet. Next to that was an old-fashioned tub with feet that resembled cat paws. Opposite the sink were two doors. Each led to a private toilet room with a small window above the toilet.

Akna wasn't sure about sharing a bathroom with six people, especially everyone being able to watch her take a shower. At least she could poop in private.

This home was nothing like what Mrs. Hannigan provided the orphans in that movie. It wasn't Daddy Warbucks rich either, but it was much more than they'd ever had at home.

"One more thing," Mrs. Bohn said. "Follow."

At the other end of the bedroom was a wall similar to the one they had just left. But this had six doors that blended into the wood with a number on the handle. "This was is yours, number two," Mrs. Bohn said as she opened the second door from the right. It was a three-foot closet for hanging clothes. It contained two rows of rods and a shelf on top. Near the floor was a box with some kind of wooden lid.

Mrs. Bohn pulled up on the box and it folded out into a small step ladder. "This is for those who may be too short to reach the top rod or the shelf," she said. She stepped on the ladder and could reach the rod, but still couldn't reach the shelf. "Or, if you are short like me, you ask someone taller, like Sandra, to help you."

It seemed like the Bohns had really planned for everything. Akna didn't know anyone in her life, except maybe Tata, who could have even thought of these things.

"Do you always have six foster children living here?" Akna finally asked.

Mrs. Bohn nodded. "Most of the time. We are licensed for six girls. Girls only. When someone leaves, we usually have a replacement within a couple weeks."

"So did three people leave all at once so you could take us?"

"Not all at once. One person graduated this summer. One person went home to live with her father just before you came."

Akna waited to hear about the third person. But Mrs. Bohn didn't say anything more.

"And the third person?" Akna asked.

"She died almost a year ago," Mrs. Bohn finally said. "She was very sick. I'd rather not talk about it right now. Maybe at another time."

Akna let it go, but she couldn't help but wonder how someone could die at this amazing place where everyone seemed pretty happy to be here. Things weren't always as they seemed. She would keep her guard up just in case. Maybe someone poisoned her because they didn't like her. Or maybe Mr. Bohn did something to hurt her.

"My husband, Mr. Bohn, used to be a house builder," Mrs. Bohn continued as if nothing sad had been said. "When we knew we were accepted as foster parents and were licensed for six, we planned for this bedroom up here." She waved her hand toward the roof. "He built this entire second story in about six months. We planned everything together. He did bring in other professionals for plumbing and electricity, but he did all the framing and carpentry work."

"Wow," Akna said. She really was impressed. She didn't know anyone who could build a whole house. "Where is Mr. Bohn? I haven't met him yet."

"He'll be home about 6:00, just in time to wash up for dinner. He works in a metal shop now. He doesn't like climbing up on roofs and doing so much heavy labor anymore."

Akna nodded.

"You're probably wondering what's next."

"Tomorrow's Monday, so I guess we go to school," Akna said.

"It's not quite that easy. Monday we have a doctor appointment for all three of you to get checked out and to get any vaccinations you may have missed. Mrs. Sleeper got your school records, so I already have those. Tuesday we'll get you registered in school, and then go shop for a few more clothes. If everything goes well, you will start on Wednesday.

"You get one week of reprieve from chores. That means that by next Sunday all three of you will be on the chore schedule. That includes dishes, cooking, laundry, setting the table, helping out in the yard, and house cleaning."

Akna nodded again. She'd never known such an organized person.

She knew how hard it was just trying to keep things straight for herself and her sisters.

"I can do all those chores," Akna said. "I've done all that before."

"Good. I'll leave you to get settled, then. If you have any questions about the room, or anything else, you can ask the other girls. Dinner is at 7:00. There's a big clock up there." She pointed to the end of the bedroom where the bathroom was. "Happy to have you and your sisters here, Akna." Then she gave Akna a quick hug and started down the stairs.

Akna sat gingerly on her new bed, then popped up and ran toward the stairs. "Um, Mrs. Bohn?"

"Yes, dear?" she said turning sideways on a stair.

"Are we supposed to call you Mrs. Bohn all the time or something else?"

"What would you feel comfortable with, Akna?"

"I don't know. I've never been in a foster home before. I just don't want to make you mad or anything."

"I'm hard to make angry. Gianna and Polly call me Mama Lois. Lois is my middle name and the one I use. Sandra just calls me Lois. Either of those or Mrs. Bohn is fine. I'll answer to all of them."

No way was Akna going to call her Mama anything. That would be like saying she didn't have a Mama. She didn't like that at all. Maybe the other girls didn't like their mothers or were trying to get back at them for being bad. But she loved her Mama and no one could ever replace her.

"I think I'll call you Mrs. Bohn, then," she said.

"Okay. You get settled now. If you need anything you'll find me downstairs."

Akna watched Mrs. Bohn as she went all the way down the stairs and then turned toward the living room. She'd never met anyone like her. She laid flat on her back and stared at the smaller peak above the bed.

Gianna slowly approached. Her hair still covering half of her face. "Mama Lois can go on and on in the beginning. But she's a good person," she said. Then she drew her hand from behind her back and thrust some kind of book at Akna. "This is for you. It's a diary. It has a key so you can lock it. Shari gave me one when I came here, because I was so angry all the time. Shari is the one who graduated early and left. She's going to college."

"But I'm not angry," Akna said. It seemed strange that Gianna was giving her a gift and they barely knew each other.

Gianna thrust it at her again. "Take it. You don't have to be angry to write stuff."

Akna took it. It had a beautiful cover that looked like a water color painting. In the center was a butterfly with four different wings. Each wing was a different color and the largest wing had a pattern against a white background that she'd never seen in any butterfly. At the bottom were water-colored Easter eggs. The entire background was a wash of oranges and greens and pinks. It looked like someone had spilled the paints by accident and they all had blurred together.

Below the butterfly were words printed in a black color. The first two words looked like an old typewriter printed them. The last word was written in cursive. It read: Allow the unfolding.

Akna wasn't sure what unfolding meant but it seemed like an important word. Maybe it meant writing or telling or explaining. That would make sense. She ran her fingers over the words. "Thank you," she finally said. "It's beautiful."

"Shari said it would help me to write things down and she was right. It helps me to think things out and to plan."

"I need to plan lots of things," Akna said.

"Be sure to lock it up and keep the key with you. It will keep out any snoopers, especially Sandra. She likes to rat on people. Think of a place to hide it with your personal stuff. The rule is we can't touch anything in another girl's space. So, your trunk or the drawers under your bed are safe. But if you leave it sitting around, you know who would pick it up and peek."

Akna nodded, though she was thinking those two places were too obvious. Just because people weren't allowed to do something didn't stop some people. She'd think about it and what would be the best hiding place.

Gianna backed away. "I'll…I'll let you unpack."

"Thanks," Akna said again.

"I guess I'll see you at dinner." Gianna backed further toward the stairs. "Bye."

Akna wriggled her fingers in a half wave. "Bye."

Gianna hung at the top of the stairs like she didn't really want to go. Then she turned and Akna heard the clip clop of her boots on every stair.

Only she and her sisters were left in the bedroom. She headed to their section.

Hai had already put away all of her things and she was now helping Nakia. None of them had a lot of clothes. They each had brought three sets of shirts and pants and underwear. They each had one sweater and one jacket.

Dresses had not been part of their wardrobe for two years. When Nana and Tata were alive, they only wore dresses to church or special celebrations. She had to admit she didn't really miss it. It was hard to play in a dress or run or do anything fun really.

"So, what do you think?"

"I think it's wonderful," Hai said. "Everyone is so nice. We get our own space. I think this will be fine for six months."

"Yo también," Nakia said.

Hai hugged Akna. "I think things will be easier for you, too."

"Yeah. I guess."

"Do you miss Mama?" Hai asked.

"Sure, I do. I'm worried about her. I feel like I should be there to make sure she's safe."

"I'm happy not to worry about her," Hai said. "Is that bad?"

Akna felt that way too, but she would have never said it aloud. She was afraid that saying it would make something bad happen to Mama.

"Mama has been sick for a long time," she finally said. "I am happy she is getting help. That is what's important."

"Right," Hai echoed. "I'm done with my stuff. Do you need help unpacking?"

Akna laughed. "Well, let's see." She picked up each of her folded things from the almost empty suitcase. "One, two, three..." She counted to eight all the things she had, then marched them to her bed, open the drawer beneath and put them in there.

She marched back. "Now, the only things we have to hang are the three coats."

Hai and Nakia both took their jackets and marched like toy soldiers to the closet. Hai easily hung her jacket. Nakia slowly opened the door to her closet. She expertly pulled down the small ladder and climbed the two stairs. She fumbled with managing the coat and the hanger and balancing on the stair.

"Es dificil," she said as the jacket slipped off twice.

"You did a good job," Akna said. "Let me show you a trick." She took the empty hanger and placed it on the rod. "First you put on the hanger, so you don't have to hold it. Then you put the coat on by opening it up and folding it over the hanger like this." She demonstrated then translated her instructions to Spanish and did it again. "See?"

Nakia took the small jacket, opened it behind the hanger and then wrapped it over. "¡Funcionó!" She clapped her hands at her achievement.

Akna hugged her tight. "¡Excelente!"

Hai joined in the group hug.

Akna returned to the suitcase and picked up the picture she'd brought from home. The one that had hung in the hallway and showed all of them together. She stared at it and wondered how so much could go wrong in two years.

Hai pointed to herself. "How old was I, then?"

"Six," Akna replied. "Do you remember going to the church and waiting in line with Nana and Tata?"

Hai wrinkled her nose and pushed her lips together as she thought. "I think so. I think Mama didn't want to go but Nana kept saying she had to."

Akna had forgotten about that. Hai was right. Mama said she was sick, as usual. But Nana didn't listen. She insisted they go and make this memory together for everyone.

Now that she remembered more clearly, she realized Mama rarely went to mass. It had always been Nana and Tata who took them. Mama professed to be a good Catholic. She had placed the crucifix to the side of the front door. She had the rosary in her bedroom on a table next to the bed and all her medicine bottles. Akna had frequently heard her saying the rosary. Mama did go to confession nearly every week, but she rarely made time for mass.

How could Akna believe in anything anymore? At least Tata had many gods to converse with. Mama had only one God that stood off to the side and looked down on humans making horrible mistakes and then confessing on a weekly basis but not ever changing. At least Tata's gods all had a specific purpose--rain, wind, sun, mountains, farming.

She shook her head. She didn't want to remember Mama and all the things that went wrong. She wanted to remember the good things.

Nakia put her hand on the picture to pull it down so she could see it. "Where am I? How old was I?"

Akna pointed to the toddler in the picture with her arms wrapped around Akna's leg. "Here. You were only two, maybe two and a half years old."

Nakia smiled. "I like this picture."

"Me too," Akna said. "Where shall I put it. Who wants it near their bed?"

"You should have it," Hai said. "It is most important to you."

"It's for all of us. We all need to remember. Perhaps I should put it between your two beds." Akna held it up to the wall to show them.

"No, you should have it," Hai repeated. "You need to remember more than us. We can come look by your bed whenever we want."

Akna pulled the picture to her and hugged it to her body. "We all need to remember," she said quietly. "All of us."

Hai nodded but didn't say anything.

Why were Hai and Nakia so eager to put everything behind them? They'd barely arrived. How could they so easily accept this new home? She would not let them forget Mama. She would look harder for stories, good stories about Mama that she could share. Perhaps they only had sad stories about Mama in their head now.

Akna placed the picture on the desk next to her bed. She would ask Mrs. Bohn if she could hang it on the wall. She stared at it again. Perhaps she could try a little harder to like it here. For now. Perhaps she could look harder for the good things, for Hai and Nakia's sake.

It had been an amazing day. So much sadness in the beginning and yet so much acceptance from Mrs. Bohn when they arrived. She was nothing like Mrs. Hannigan. They had a home for the next six months that was more than comfortable, and everyone really did seem nice. What little she knew already of the other girls told her that none of them had made it through their life unscathed. Yet, they had all found their way here.

Akna thought of Tata and the last conversations they had. She was sure he was talking in her heart right now. He was saying: "See, I was right. You will thrive no matter what obstacles you face. You are the light because you have SAD superpowers, and more love than many people muster in a lifetime."

CHAPTER SEVEN

DINNER WITH THE LOVE BOHNS

At a little after six that evening, Akna and her sisters were upstairs still talking about their new home when they all heard heavy steps come in the front door.

"Papa Bohn's home," Polly said loudly for everyone to hear. "How was your work today?"

"Same as always," a deep voice answered with a bit of a tired sound. "Lots of things to make today. What time is dinner?"

Polly giggled. "It's at seven, like always."

"Right. Right," the deep voice answered. "Off to clean up. I'll see everyone at dinner." Then the sound of heavy shoes moved under the bedroom. A door opened and closed.

"He sounds nice," Hai said.

"Uh huh," Akna responded, unsure if he was nice. Some of Mama's boyfriends started out nice but then they weren't. "He has a deep voice."

"That doesn't mean he's like Luis," Hai said. "They wouldn't let a man like Luis be the father in a foster home with all girls."

Akna looked Hai in the eye. "Did Luis ever hurt you?"

Hai shook her head. "No. But I remember him hurting Mama. I didn't like him. I never want to see him again."

Akna hugged her. "You won't. None of us will. Mama said he's in jail for a long time and she doesn't like him anymore."

"Good!"

"Akna, Hai, Nakia," Mrs. Bohn's voice floated up the stairs. "Why don't you wash up and come down now. You don't have to help, but the girls can show you how we set the table and put out the food so you know what to do when it's your turn."

"Yay! We get to help," Hai said. "You never let me help at home."

"I didn't want to burden you," Akna said as they walked downstairs with Nakia in front of them."

"I think you just like being in charge," Hai said. "And I wasn't going to fight you about it."

"Oh…" Akna wondered if she'd made a mistake. She just wanted Hai and Nakia to just be little girls. She didn't ever want them to have to grow up too fast. "I'm sorry. I guess I was just used to doing it."

"Now I'll learn everything and when we get home, I can help."

Akna smiled. "Okay."

The kitchen and dining room was a flurry of activity.

Mrs. Bohn said, "Akna why don't you shadow Sandra as she sets out the meal on the table. And Hai why don't you go with Polly to see how we set the table."

"Me?" Nakia I asked.

Mrs. Bohn bent low to look her in the eye. "You have the most important job of all. The napkins." She pulled out a basket with napkins already rolled up and a band holding each one together. She handed the basket to Nakia. "Will you carefully put one to the left of each plate?"

Nakia nodded her head and stepped to the table. She stood in front of the plate with one napkin in her hand. "¿Cuál es la izquierda?"

Akna watched Mrs. Bohn step behind Nakia. She took Nakia's left hand and put it to the left of the plate. "Left," she said. Then she took Nakia's right hand and put it to the right of the plate. "Right," she said. "Now put the napkin to the left of the plate."

Nakia took the napkin from her right hand and passed it to her left hand and then set it down.

"Very good!" Mrs. Bohn said. "Now let's do the next one."

Akna watched for a minute as Nakia easily placed the napkin in the correct place for the next two plates.

Something caught in Akna's throat. She quickly turned away and disappeared into the kitchen.

It was quite a sight. There were two bowls on the counter. Akna inspected each one. Something like spaghetti was in one. Another was obviously salad.

Sandra had a large loaf of bread in her hand and then pulled out a board from a cupboard. "This is where we keep cutting boards," she said as she plopped the bread on top of it. She pointed to a drawer to the left. "That is where we keep sharp knives." Then she pulled out a knife with a kind of wavy design and laid it on the cutting board. "Have you ever seen this kind of knife?"

Akna shook her head.

"It's called serrated. That means the blade is like a saw. Look."

Akna picked it up. "Oh, I see. Like teeth."

"Right. This is the best knife to cut bread because it doesn't mash it down and it doesn't make you work too hard. Do you want try it?"

"Sure." Akna had never cut bread before. They always bought bread in the store already sliced. Even when Nana and Tata were alive, they didn't buy bread you had to cut. Actually, they didn't have bread all that often. Most of the time they had tortillas as bread. A lot of the bread type things that Nana made were sweet, for breakfast or dessert. The only thing she remembered Nana making like bread to eat at dinner was coronas, a kind of roll.

"How thick should I cut?" Akna asked.

Sandra held up her thumb. "About that thick. It doesn't have to be exact."

Akna placed her own thumb on one end if the bread and then placed the knife next to it. She made a sawing motion and the knife went through more quickly than she anticipated.

"That's great," Sandra said. "Do you want to do the rest of the loaf?"

Akna smiled big and nodded her head. "I've never cut bread before."

"You're a natural." Sandra picked up the two main bowls. "I'm taking these out while you finish it up."

"Thanks!" Akna waited until Sandra left the room to start again. She repeated the same technique again. First butting her thumb to measure, then placing the knife and then moving her hand further down the bread while she was cutting. Within a minute, Akna had cut the entire loaf. "Ta da!" she said aloud, proud of herself. "Nana, maybe I'll learn to cook better like you."

Sandra came back in and handed her a basket. "We put a cloth napkin in the bottom." She pulled a napkin from the drawer and unfurled it. Then she placed it in the bottom with the ends hanging out. "Then we take all the pieces and cut them in half, in case someone doesn't want a whole slice."

She stacked what Akna had cut in two stacks. "You want to cut down the middle of each stack."

Akna picked up the knife again. Sandra sure was trusting of a newbie.

She eyeballed the size and put the knife in what seemed to be the middle. "I'm going for it." This time it easily slipped through all the slices. With renewed confidence she did the other stack.

"Perfect," Sandra said again. "Now you arrange them in the basket so it's easy for people to pick one out.

Akna placed them one by one, carefully making sure they were all easy to get. "You guys really do everything fancy around here, don't you?"

Sandra chuckled. "It does feel fancy when you first get here," she said. "I remember when I came, I'd never seen bread that wasn't in a bag with a twist tie from the grocery store."

"Me too," Akna said, glad to know she wasn't the only one.

"Lois thinks bread is an important staple, and the only kind of bread she wants in the house is homemade. Soon enough you'll be learning how to make your own bread. And pretty soon, it will seem like this is the way you've always eaten."

Akna wasn't sure she'd exactly feel that way. But she was interested in learning how to make bread. Maybe, when they got home, she could surprise Mama with her new skills.

When she placed the bread on the table, she stood back in awe. The table was set like something you would see on TV where a rich family celebrates a special holiday. Everything was perfect. Every spot had two plates, a large one and a smaller one to the left. Every spot had a beautiful napkin and *four* pieces of silverware—a knife and spoon on the right and two forks on the left. In the middle was the food and a vase filled with roses.

It felt like she was in a movie. It didn't seem real. How would she ever get Hai and Nakia to go home after living here for six months? Compared to home, this was like a palace.

Everyone scurried to the table, each one standing behind a chair. She and her sisters stood together waiting.

"Here you are." Polly pointed to three seats between her and Gianna. "You're against the wall with me because we're not on cleanup duty."

Hai and Nakia worked their way onto the bench against the wall. As Akna began to follow, she heard heavy footsteps behind her.

"Beautiful," a low voice boomed.

She turned and a tall man with salt and pepper hair filled the kitchen doorway. The skin around his eyes wrinkled as he smiled. He looked strong, in spite of his somewhat slender frame

"You've all presented a beautiful meal," he continued. Then he reached out a hand toward Akna as if to shake hers. "You must be Akna. Lois told me what a wonderful helper you are already. She also told me about how much you love and protect your sisters."

Akna grasped his hand as hard as she could and gave a single hard shake, then withdrew.

"Good strong handshake," he said approvingly. "I like that. It means you are determined."

"You must be Mr. Bohn," Akna said. "Yes, I am strong and determined."

"I can see that already."

"Let's get settled and say grace," Mrs. Bohn suggested.

Akna scooted next to Nakia on the bench. She wondered what kind of prayers this family said. She wasn't sure everyone was the same religion.

"We like to take turns," Mrs. Bohn said as she grasped Mr. Bohn's hand and then Sandra to her left. In turn each girl did the same so they all held hands around the table.

"Is there a special prayer you would like to offer, Akna?"

Akna searched her mind for anything she knew. They never said a prayer before a meal at home. Much of the time Mama was away or sick or didn't feel like eating. But she wanted to say something. She didn't want anyone to think she didn't know how to pray. She closed her eyes and it came to her.

"This is one Tata used to say at a special meal," she said. "It is a Catholic prayer, I think. Is that okay?"

"Of course, dear. Any prayer is okay, even one you make up."

She closed her eyes again. "Bless us, O Lord, and these Thy gifts which we are about to receive from Thy bounty, through Christ our Lord. Amen."

Then Nakia repeated it in Spanish. "Bendicenos, Señor, y bendice estos alimentos que por tu bondad vamos a tomar. Te lo pedimos por Cristo Nuestro Señor. Amen."

"And bless all the hands that made the meal, set the table, and provided love for the meal," Mrs. Bohn added.

All the girls said "Amen" together and squeezed each other's hands.

"Let's eat," Polly said and reached for the bowl of pasta to start it around the table.

Each person reached for the bowl closest to them, took their share and then passed it to the left. Akna helped Nakia by holding each bowl as Nakia dished out her own servings. They were too unwieldly to hold and dish it out at the same time.

"Oops," Mrs. Bohn said as a bit of spaghetti flew across the table.

Gianna picked it up and put it on her plate. "Thanks for the extra, Mama Lois."

Polly giggled. "Nothing is going to waste, except your waist."

"Polly, apologize. That is not nice," Mrs. Bohn said. "Everyone grows differently."

"It's okay," Gianna said. "I don't care that I'm solid. My mother is solid and so am I."

"You are still going to apologize." Mrs. Bohn looked straight at Polly.

"I just meant to be funny. I didn't mean anything by it."

"But it isn't funny to some people," Mrs. Bohn insisted.

"I'm sorry," Polly said with a frown. "I didn't mean anything by it."

"All of it is going to my waist," Mr. Bohn jumped in and patted his stomach.

"Virgil, you are *not* helping," Mrs. Bohn's lips clamped together as she stared at him.

He sighed. "You're right. You're right. I apologize. Let's pass some more and enjoy this meal." He then held the pasta bowl to make it easier for Mrs. Bohn to get her spaghetti out, and soon they were all eating.

After everyone had a chance for a few bites, Mr. Bohn asked, "What's the exciting news of the day?"

"Duh," Gianna said. "We have three new sisters."

Akna's eyes opened wide. Sisters? Did they already consider them family? Or was Gianna just saying that because it was expected?

"Of course," he said and smiled, taking in all three of them from across the table. "Is everything okay with your room?"

"It's amazing!" Hai jumped in. "It's the best room ever."

Mr. Bohn's smile was broad and he leaned forward. "What's your favorite part?"

"My own bed. I don't have to share with Akna and Nakia anymore."

"I can see how that might be nice. What about you, Nakia? Are you happy to have your own bed?"

Nakia nodded. Then she shook her head. Then she nodded again.

"Hmm...I'm not sure what that means," Mr. Bohn said.

Sandra jumped in. "¿Estás contenta de dormir sola en tu propio ser?"

"Aún no lo sé. Si me asusto voy a saltar a la cama de Akna," Nakia replied.

Sandra translated. "She said she doesn't know yet and she'll jump in Akna's bed if she gets scared."

Akna clamped her mouth shut before she said something wrong. She didn't like Sandra showing off her Spanish all the time. It was Akna's job to take care of Nakia. It was Akna's job to interpret as needed. Sandra was not the mother or the sister.

"That's a good plan, Nakia," Mr. Bohn said with a smile. "I'm very lucky because I sleep with Mrs. Bohn and she makes sure no monsters get me."

Nakia giggled at that. "You scare monsters," she said. "You big."

Mr. Bohn nodded. "I guess I am big enough to scare most monsters."

Mrs. Bohn elbowed him in the side. "He just makes it up so he can snuggle."

He nodded. "True. And get free kisses." Then he kissed Mrs. Bohn on the cheek.

"TMI!" Sandra said.

Polly and Gianna giggled.

"They do this a lot," Gianna offered. "But it's kind of cute, in a Hallmark movie kind of way."

"On Valentine's Day, he pulled Lois onto his lap and gave her a big kiss," Sandra said. "It was disgusting for someone their age."

Mr. Bohn laughed aloud. "Wasn't disgusting to me."

Mrs. Bohn beamed. "Me either."

"Life isn't all about being proper all the time," Mr. Bohn said. "Keeping the child in you alive is important as you get older. In the case of Mrs. Bohn, her love is an amazing gift. She gives it away to everyone. You girls already know that. But she even gives that love to a big oaf like me. You know you are in love with the right person when you can be serious with them *and* be silly with them and never worry about how you look."

Mrs. Bohn bumped her shoulder against his. "Sooo right, my one and only oaf."

"I'm never going to marry," Sandra said with confidence.

"Me either," Polly agreed.

"I'm too young to think about it." Gianna said.

Akna hadn't really thought about it either. She'd also never seen a married couple act so in love—especially not people this old. She knew her grandparents had loved each other, but they didn't talk about it or show much affection except in times of tragedy like when Tata was sick and Nana didn't leave his side for several weeks before he died.

Akna had no idea who her father was. When she'd asked her mother, she said it wasn't important and she refused to answer any questions about the past. Mama's boyfriends never stuck around longer than a few months, and she never talked about marrying any of them.

"How long have you been married?" Akna asked.

"Forty-one years!" the other girls all answered at once.

"I remember when they had their fortieth anniversary," Sandra said. "They had to get permission for Mrs. Fraley to stay with us for a week while they took an Alaskan cruise."

"That was a treat," Mrs. Bohn said. "We saw so many amazing things."

"That was the only time, they took a vacation without us in all the time I've been here," Sandra said. "That's been—"

"Five years." Polly and Gianna said together. "Jinx."

"It was a special trip," Mrs. Bohn said again. "It's hard to get away on your own, but we are blessed to have such a big family to help us and they all live within easy driving distance. Before adding foster children to our family, we raised four girls and a boy. They are all married and have their own children now, and some of those grandchildren have children, too. I'm sure I've lost count of the grandchildren and great grands."

Wow, they must be ancient then, Akna thought. She quickly did some math in her head. If they got married at eighteen and they'd been married for forty-one years that meant they were at least fifty-nine and maybe even older. They both definitely had some wrinkles, but not a lot. Though they had some grey hairs, it wasn't all over. Who would want to be taking care of kids—especially foster kids—when they were old? Yikes! Tata was seventy-one when he died, and Nana was only seventy.

She hoped they didn't die in the six months while she and her sisters were here. That would be just too much to take. She couldn't take going to another foster home.

The rest of the meal, Akna didn't talk much. The conversation went back and forth about homework, school, and memories of things she couldn't imagine in her own life. It was a lot to think about. In fact, it was too much. Her brain hurt with all that happened today.

After helping carry dishes into the kitchen Akna asked if it was okay if she went to bed. Nakia and Hai quickly echoed her request.

"Of course, dear," Mrs. Bohn said. "I'm sure you are all very tired. A lot of new things to see and do all in one day. A lot of confusing emotions, I bet." She leaned in and gave Akna a hug and then a kiss on the forehead. She did the same with Nakia and Hai.

Nakia hung on Mrs. Bohn's leg for a little longer. "Gracias," she said. "Gracias Mama Bohn."

Akna's heart sunk. Nakia had already adopted a new Mama. In just one day she'd changed her loyalty. How hard will it be to go home after six months? Nakia and Hai hadn't really cried about leaving Mama. They'd been mostly worried about meeting strangers and if they would be nice.

The Bohns were nice all right. Too nice. In six months, would Nakia be crying and holding onto Mrs. Bohn and asking to stay?

Don't borrow trouble, her Nana's voice echoed in Akna's heart.

She couldn't help worrying. This day didn't turn out at all how she thought it would. She didn't know what to think anymore.

CHAPTER EIGHT

NEW SCHOOL

The doctor visit was okay. Dr. Desk was a woman doctor and according to Mrs. Bohn, she treated all the foster girls in their home. Even though Desk was a weird name she was really nice. She wondered if the doctor had been teased as a child.

Nakia was thrilled the doctor spoke both Spanish and English. The best part of the visit was they didn't have to get any shots, which was great.

Evidently, whenever they got a shot at home, it was put in a big computer that could share information with other doctors and nurses. So, the new doctor was able to find it and read it before they arrived.

Akna checked herself in the bathroom mirror for the umpteenth time. Mrs. Bohn had taken them to the biggest Goodwill store Akna had ever seen. They each picked out five slacks and five shirts. So, she now had eight pairs instead of three. She'd gone back and forth the night before deciding what to wear.

She'd finally settled on her new light, stone-washed jeans and a long-sleeved, lightweight coral sweater that felt more like a t-shirt. On the sides it had little drawstrings that you could pull to make it cinch up a bit. Mostly she liked how soft it felt on her skin. The drawstrings were just a little bit of fanciness.

Gianna came in behind her and peered over Akna's shoulder in the mirror. "You look good, Akna. That shirt color looks good with your dark brown hair. I'd die for hair like yours, a little bit of curl but not too much."

Her look was completely the opposite of Akna. She wore another all-black outfit. This one was charcoal jeans with accordion like rips on the calf from the knee to the cuffed ankle where her jet-black ankle-high boots began. Her top was a black scoop neck t-shirt, with a zip front jacket that looked like leather.

Today, instead of hair covering half her face, it was braided so that the blue streak wound all the way down the braid. She'd pulled it over her left shoulder to rest in front. Unlike when they first met, she seemed confident and ready to take on the world.

"Do you wear any color besides black?" Akna asked.

"No. I like black."

"Why?"

"Because I don't want to be like anyone else. I don't want to waste time figuring out what is the latest fashion, or what the cool kids are wearing. I hate that stuff. I can wear black to be invisible if I feel like it and don't want people to see me. Or I can wear it like today, and dare people to question me. Just like you did."

"You must have some clothes that aren't black."

"Nope. Even my underwear is black."

"Wow." Akna couldn't conceive of making that choice. It seemed so limiting. Wearing all black would feel sad, and not the good kind of sad. Akna would feel like she was suffocating all the time.

"You like color," Gianna said. "You feel happy when you wear colors. I feel happy when I wear black. Color makes me feel chaotic. Black makes me feel in control. At least that's what the shrink says. I think I just like black. Nothing wrong with that."

Akna thought about that. Tata said bright colors were part of their heritage. Lots of bright colors like yellows and oranges and pinks and blues. Nana always said that if nature puts orange and purple wild-flowers next to each other, then why not wear them together in clothing or use them on walls and drapes and furniture in the home.

Gianna looked at her watch and yelped. "Oops, the bus is almost here. Have a good first day, Akna. Don't let the dirtbags get you down." Then she bounded down the stairs.

Akna primped her hair again. Gianna loved Akna's waves, but Akna preferred Gianna's straight hair. Why was it people always wanted something they didn't already have?

She turned from the mirror and walked out. "Hai, Nakia, are you ready to walk to school now?"

"Yes!" They screamed in unison.

"I don't want to be late on our first day," Hai said.

The three put on backpacks. Nakia got down the stairs first, then Hai, and Akna at the back. She was happy her sisters were excited. Akna, on the other hand, dreaded starting over again. She didn't make friends easily and she didn't really want to make friends here and then have to leave them later.

Mrs. Bohn was at the front door. "You all look wonderful. I know we filled those backpacks last night. Did you take anything out?"

"No," they all said together, and Nakia giggled.

"Water bottles?"

They each stepped to one side to show a water bottle fitted in the netting of the backpack.

"Good. Now don't forget to drink a little all day."

"We won't," they said in unison.

"Can I give you a hug?" Mrs. Bohn asked. "It's your first day and there will be so many new things to see and learn. I want to give you a hug to carry with you all day."

Nakia reached her hands out first and Mrs. Bohn bent to hug her and whispered something in her ear that Akna couldn't hear. Nakia smiled very big and nodded.

Hai stepped in and hugged Mrs. Bohn first. "It will be a wonderful day. I just know it."

Mrs. Bohn hugged her back. "That's right. If anyone gives you any guff you tell the teacher or the principal. No bullying allowed."

Akna felt hugging wasn't for someone her age, but she didn't want Hai and Nakia to think she didn't like Mrs. Bohn. She gave her a quick hug and stepped back. "Thanks. For, uh, everything."

"You are so very welcome, Akna," Mrs. Bohn replied. "It's natural to feel nervous when you are going to a new school. Just take it slow and remember, all the teachers there want to help. They all want to help you feel comfortable and learn."

Akna wasn't sure that was always true. At her last school she liked her fifth-grade teacher, but she didn't like her fourth-grade teacher at all.

"What was it you told Mr. Bohn at dinner last night?" Mrs. Bohn asked Akna. "Something about determination, I think. Yes, that's what you need."

"Strength and determination," Akna replied. She'd been so worried about fitting in that she'd forgotten about her SAD superpowers.

Mrs. Bohn opened the front door. "I guess you're ready then."

Nakia rushed out first, then Hai, and finally Akna.

Mrs. Bohn waved from the front door. "Bye. See you all after school, then you can tell me all about your first day."

Akna waved and then hurried down the path to the street. She looked up to the sky for a moment. It was overcast and the sun hadn't burned through the fog yet. The sun made it easier to pull on her SAD powers. Instead, she said in her heart, *here we go Tata. Help us put on our SAD powers today.*

"I lead," Nakia said as they started down the block.

"You know the way?" Akna asked.

"Si, soy la buscadora de caminos."

"Okay, we will follow."

All three had practiced the route with Mrs. Bohn on Monday. Then she had Hai lead on Tuesday when they went to register for school. This would be a great test for Nakia. No one would ever want her to walk home alone from school, but it was good for her to know the way.

The good news was that Margarita School was kindergarten through fifth Grade. It was a little over a mile away which meant Hai, Nakia, and Akna could walk together. Unfortunately, Polly and Gianna went to the Serrano Middle School which was further. Akna would have liked to have at least one friend at the school.

Nakia started off running, but tired after about three blocks. Akna had no problem keeping up. In fact, she'd missed her running. In the past three days, nothing had happened to compel her to run like circumstances did at home. She shook the thought out of her head. They just hadn't lived at the Mariposa house long enough for things to go wrong yet. It would. That was normal life.

Hai caught up last and bent over taking deep breaths. "Let's just walk, Nakia. I don't want to be all sweaty when we get there."

"Okay, just walk," Nakia agreed. "I was fast. No?"

"Yes, very fast." Hai started walking ahead. "Let's walk only this fast the rest of the way, Okay?"

Nakia caught up to her and grabbed her hand. "Okay."

Akna put herself on the other side of Nakia and they walked three abreast.

"Isn't that sweet," a stocky boy with blond hair said, dripping with sarcasm as he slowly rolled passed them on a bicycle. "You wouldn't catch me with my little sister or brother."

Akna straightened her back. She would not say anything, she would just walk. She squeezed Nakia's hand.

The boy then rode in a large circle and came alongside them again. "Yo, girl. Are you afraid to talk to boys?"

Hai stopped and turned. "Yo, boy! We don't talk to jerks." Then she grabbed Nakia's hand again and started forward.

"Whoa, whoa, whoa," the boy said as he continued to follow them. "I wasn't talking to you pipsqueak. I was talking to your big sister. Let her speak for herself."

Akna kept walking. "Digas nada más," she said between her teeth to her sisters.

She saw another boy who looked Hispanic riding from the other direction. He stopped directly across the street from them.

"The blond boy stopped his bike in front of them on the sidewalk. "Ha blah es pan old, big sister?" he said without any correct pronunciation. "I can speak some Spanish, too. I know some *sweet* words." He circled his hips in a suggestive manner.

It was obvious he was going to bother them all the way to school. Akna stopped abruptly and turned with a stomp. Her hands made a fist and she pointed at him to animate her meaning. "¿Puedes hablar español? ¿Entiendes lo que significa ir al infierno? Porque ahí es donde te enviaré si no nos dejas en paz."

"Whoa, I don't know what you said but no need to get snippy."

Nakia and Hai froze and stared at Akna with their mouths wide open.

The boy across the street started laughing loudly.

"What's so funny, man?"

"She told you if you didn't leave her alone she was sending you to hell, dude. I wouldn't mess with her. I think she's bruja. She has the power to curse your life. You may wake up tomorrow with boils on your dick, or diarrhea shooting out your backside, or even worse."

"Are you a voodoo princess or something?"

Akna said nothing. Instead, she used the Gianna stare with one finger pointing at him and drawing his form in the air.

He cocked his head, then turned his bike around and left without a word.

The boy across the street came a little closer but not all the way.

"Thanks," Akna said

"He's a jerk. He goes to Serrano and hangs out with some sketchy dudes. But I don't think he'd hurt you or anything." He came the rest of the way across the street. "I'm Jorge. I don't think I've seen you before."

"I'm Akna. We're new. This is our first day."

Nakia was still staring at Akna and clutching her leg. "Eres una bruja? ¿De verdad enviarías a ese chico al infierno?"

Akna bent to her sister and gave her a hug. "No, Nakia. I was just trying to scare him and make him go away. I was pretending."

"Fingiendo como en Halloween. Lo entiende?" Jorge said.

Nakia smiled and clapped her hands. "Estupenda!"

"We have a community theater here. You should try out for a show."

"I don't think so," Akna said. "We're…uh…really busy." She was going to say they wouldn't be here for long, but decided that was TMI.

"All three of you go to Margarita School?" Jorge asked.

"Yes," Hai said. "Akna's in fifth grade. She'll be graduating this year. I'm in third grade."

"I'm in kindergarten," Nakia said with pride.

"I'm in fifth grade, too." Jorge smiled at Akna. "Is it okay if I walk my bike with you to school?"

"I guess," Akna said.

For about a block no one said anything. Akna felt a little strange. She was kind of happy to meet someone at her new school. But she didn't really like boys. In her other school, if she got to know a boy, they started off nice but then became stupid.

She glanced at Jorge in her peripheral vision. He seemed okay, but she wasn't going to really count on him or anything.

"What's your main teacher's name?"

"Ms. Hollinrake," Nakia said quickly.

"Mrs. Berg," Hai answered.

Akna didn't say anything. She'd let her sisters do all the talking.

Jorge smiled. "Mine is Mrs. Omenma. She's nice, but fifth graders have way too much homework."

"All teachers give too much homework," Hai said.

"At this school, they don't believe in homework until fifth grade," Jorge said. "You work on projects during study time. But in fifth grade they start giving homework so you can prepare for middle school. It's a bummer."

Akna didn't remember the principal talking about that when they registered and met her.

After walking another block, Jorge asked, "How about you, Akna? Who is your home room teacher?"

"Um, Mr. Serna. I've never had a man teacher before."

"You're so lucky," Jorge enthused. "Everyone likes him. I think you'll get along fine."

The next block they made a turn and the school was in front of them. Nakia clapped her hands. "We're here! We're here! See, I knew the way."

"Good job!" Akna held her hand up for a high five.

Nakia jumped up and hit her hand easily. "I knew I could do it. I knew it."

Akna checked her watch. They were fifteen minutes early. They had to check-in at the office and then someone would take each person to their classroom and introduce them. She dreaded that part where everyone in the class would know she was the new girl.

She sighed. It was time to get it over with. "I guess I'll see you around, Jorge." She knew she'd probably never see him at all. It was nice of him to walk with them, but he probably had his own group of friends.

"I'll look for you at lunch if you want," he said.

"Um, maybe… Okay…We'll see." Geez, she sounded like a dweeb. What was wrong with her?

He waved and jumped back on his bicycle and pedaled fast for that last block to the school.

On the way to the office, Akna noticed him again hanging out near the bike stand. A group crowded around him and they were slapping backs and punching arms like best friends. Then the whole group moved together toward the front door.

Yup. Already had plenty of friends.

"Come on," she said to her sisters. "It's time to have fun." She put on her best smile for them. "Are you excited?"

"Yes!" they said simultaneously and she could tell they meant it.

Soon they were in the office and the secretary greeted them. "Hello Sales sisters. Good to see you again. Are you excited about getting in your classes?"

"Yes!" Nakia said again and Hai nodded and smiled.

Akna didn't say anything. She was afraid if she did, she might admit she was kind of scared and she couldn't do that in front of her sisters.

"Take a seat. I know that the principal wants to meet you and take each of you to your classes." Then she disappeared into the principal's office.

They hadn't met the principal when they registered. The admin assistant had done all the paperwork for them. Akna silently read the name on the door, Mrs. Barker, and giggled to herself.

Then a tall woman with medium brown hair in a shoulder length bob came out. She wasn't dressed fancy at all. She wore jeans and a bright pink pullover sweater. She came around the front desk and said, "Hello. I'm Mrs. Barker. I'm very happy to meet the three of you. Now let me guess." She pointed to Nakia. "You're Nakia and you're in kindergarten."

Nakia smiled big and immediately stood and gave her a hug.

"Thank you, Nakia. I bet you'll make friends without a problem. We'll get going to your class in a minute." Then she turned her gaze to Hai, and held out her hand. "You're Hai and you're in third grade."

Hai smiled, stood, and shook the principal's hand. "We met a boy on the way to school and he said only fifth graders have to do homework."

"That's true. We have a no homework rule at this school for kindergarten through fourth grade."

"Are you kidding?" Hai asked.

"I'm serious. Last year, we did the research and found that parents hated homework as much as kids did. They didn't have the time to help kids with homework and the kids who didn't get help, couldn't keep up. So, we banned homework."

"But not for fifth graders?" Akna asked "That sounds unfair."

"We do give a little homework for fifth graders because we want to prepare them for middle school. We want to be sure they know how to organize and prioritize. It's not a lot, and most fifth graders finish almost all of it in their study hall period."

This was all very different for Akna. Her other school had homework through all the grades and fifth grade only had one teacher like all the other grades.

"At our school, we have many students with parents who can't help them with homework. So, all the teachers decided to do something different. To teach in a way that helps everyone do better in the classroom. Of course, we would like you to read and practice at home. But what we want more than anything else is for you to be playing, and enjoying time with your family, and getting lots of time outdoors and having fun."

"Mama couldn't help us at our other school because she was sick a lot," Hai said. "But I think Mrs. Bohn could help us."

Akna wasn't sure everything Mrs. Barker said was real. It seemed really crazy to her that most kids in elementary school didn't have homework or that Akna would be able to finish most of her homework in her study period. She'd wait and see if it was true or an exaggeration.

"Shall we get going to meet your new teachers and see your classrooms?"

"Yes!" Nakia said. "Me first."

Mrs. Barker chuckled. "Can I hold your hand then?"

Nakia immediately offered her hand.

"Hai and Akna, you can follow us so you know where to meet Nakia at the end of the school day. We wouldn't want anyone to get lost before heading home."

Nakia's classroom was closest to the office, only a few feet away. Mrs. Baker knocked on the door and waved through the window. She instructed Akna and Hai to wait in the hall. Once they went inside, Akna stood on tiptoes to look in the window and listen through the door. All the children were in a circle on the floor with the teacher.

Mrs. Baker took Nakia to the front of the class near the teacher and said, "Hello, class."

"Hello, Mrs. Baker," they all answered.

"I have a new student for you. Her name is Nakia Sales. Can you say her name?"

"Nakia Sales," they all echoed, pronouncing both names correctly.

"Very good! Who is going to be Nakia's buddy?"

"Me!" A girl with very curly chestnut-brown hair and a light brown face jumped up and danced from side to side. A navy-blue tunic, with a picture of a kitten topped cherry-red leggings. Beneath the kitten was the word meow with whiskers on either side.

The girl ran to the principal and gave her a big hug. Then she took Nakia's hand and said, "Come sit by me. I'll show you how to do everything."

Without even looking back, Nakia followed her and sat next to her in the circle as Mrs. Baker backed out the door.

Akna quickly stepped out of her way. "She seems pretty happy," she said to Hai.

Next, they went to Hai's classroom. It worked in much of the same way, only the students sat at round tables with four students to each table. They were working on multiplication word problems when Mrs. Baker and Hai entered the classroom. Hai was introduced and another student "buddy" brought Hai to her table. Hai didn't look scared at all.

Mrs. Baker came into the hall. "Your turn. Your class is the furthest away."

As they walked Akna's heart started to jackhammer in her chest. What was wrong with her? Her sisters were fine. This was no big deal.

"Do all new students get a buddy assigned?" Akna asked, as she tried to push back her fear.

"That's right."

"Do they volunteer? Or are they forced to do it?"

"They volunteer." Mrs. Baker made a turn down another long hallway.

Blood thudded in her ears and her head started to get foggy.

"Do they get extra credit?"

"No, they volunteer because they like to help." Mrs. Baker stopped in front of the room.

"Are they forced to be friends? What if we don't like each other? Can I ask for a different buddy?" Akna kept thinking of questions. She knew she was putting off going in, but unlike her sisters she wasn't excited to be meeting new people. "I don't feel very good."

Mrs. Baker pointed to an alcove with a short wooden bench at the corner of another hallway. "Let's sit over here before we go in and rest. You must be exhausted. It's been a very busy few days for you arriving in town, getting to know a new family, and now a new school."

Akna made her way to the bench.

Mrs. Baker sat next to her. Then she leaned over at her waist and took in a deep breath. "When everything is fighting for attention inside me, I lean over like this and look at the floor." She took in another deep breath. "That helps to focus my brain on just one thing."

Akna copied her, matching her slow breaths. She counted the dots directly in her eyesight.

"When my brain has cleared a little, I sit up very slowly and close my eyes," Mrs. Baker said.

Akna did the same after checking that Mrs. Baker really had her eyes closed.

She could hear Mrs. Baker taking big slow breaths and copied her again.

It seemed like a long time without talking. Akna peeked at Mrs. Baker a couple of times, but her eyes were still closed and she was sitting very still and breathing slowly. So Akna did, too. She wasn't sure how long they did that together, but she was feeling better.

"When I think I'm ready, I open my eyes very slowly," Mrs. Baker said.

Akna did that and looked straight ahead at a big cork board. At the top it said: *What is your word for the day?* Beneath it there were hundreds of different words not in any order.

Akna moved toward the board and started to look at them. Decisive. Helpful. Animated. Gutsy. Sensible. Patient. Fun. Clever. Inventive. There were so many, she could stay here until lunch just reading them.

"Do you see one that describes you?" Mrs. Baker asked.

"I don't know if I could pick just one."

"What's the first one you noticed that seemed true for you?"

Akna looked again. "Committed. I'm committed to making sure my sisters are okay."

"That's a good one. I can tell that they are the most important thing to you right now."

Mrs. Baker was quiet for a while and Akna kept reading.

"The second word I like is Determined. It is one of my favorite words because my Tata, my grandfather, said I was determined."

"That's a good word," Mrs. Baker confirmed. "That sounds like a word that's just for you, not for anyone else. Is there another one you think is better?"

Akna searched the board again. There were lots of words she wished described her like Confident and Worthy and Secure. But those weren't true words for her. She should be able to find at least one more word among hundreds that described her.

Finally, she spotted it. "I think Reflective is a good word because I think a lot about stuff after it happens and even before it happens." She paused and rolled the word around in her head. "I am reflective but I don't think it's a good word because it makes me worry. I don't want that word."

"You want to stick with determined?"

"Yes," Akna said with as much confidence as she could.

"How are you going to use that word today to make it to the end of the school day?"

"I'm determined to walk in that door without my heart pounding in my head."

"Good." Mrs. Baker slowly started back toward the classroom and Akna followed alongside her. "What else?"

"I'm determined to give my assigned buddy a chance for at least a week."

"Good plan."

"I'm determined to find a person I met on the way to school who said we could have lunch together." Akna was surprised that came out of her mouth. But now she realized that Jorge probably really did want her to sit with him. If she could actually find him, she would.

They were already back at the door. Mrs. Baker put her hand on the door. "One more determination?"

Akna nodded. "I'm determined not to borrow trouble like my Nana always said."

Mrs. Baker opened the door and Akna stepped in front of her to enter the room first.

CHAPTER NINE

LUNCH AND MUSIC CLASS

The first half of the day went okay. Unlike her previous school, fifth graders had more than one classroom. She had a total of five different teachers. Mrs. Baker explained it was designed so they had lots of practice in changing rooms before they got to middle school. Every class was forty-five minutes long, and then there was a fifteen-minute break before the next class. You could get to the next room or if you were staying in a room, you could stand up and move around or go to the bathroom.

Every morning they had Mr. Serna in home room for thirty minutes. She'd arrived with only ten minutes left before the bell rang and the whole class shifted to Mrs. Feldman for math. Her assigned buddy said not to worry, she didn't miss much. Homeroom was mostly to take attendance and make sure you were organized for the day. Mr. Serna would make any general announcements and put the schedule on the board for the different periods in case someone forgot their paper schedule or didn't have it memorized. She said that homeroom was also a time to wish Happy Birthday to whoever had a birthday that week.

She carried her schedule in a notebook where it was easy to find.

Times	Monday, Wednesday, Friday	Tuesday, Thursday
8:15am – 8:45am	Home Room Mr. Serna, Room 52	Home Room Mr. Serna, Room 52
9:00am – 9:45am	Math Mrs. Feldman, Room 61	Reading/Writing (Lang. Arts) Mr. Serna, Room 52
10:00am – 10:45am	Vocabulary and Spelling Mr. Serna, Room 52	Science Mrs. James, Room 36
11:00am – 11:45am	Technology / Computers Mr. Kramer, Room 47	Health and Emotional Learning Mrs. Gomez, Room 28
12:00pm – 12:45pm	Recess / Lunch	Recess / Lunch
1:00pm – 1:45pm	Music Mrs. Cosgrave, Room 10	Social Studies Mr. Tanaka, Room 22
2:00pm – 2:45pm	Library Study Time	Physical Education Mrs. Lewandowski

Her assigned buddy was named Jessica Smythe, but she went by Jessa. She was tall for a fifth grader and had hair even longer than Gianna, except it was blonde. Instead of wearing it loose, Jessa had it all braided and then coiled on top of her head like a crown, which made her tower even more over every student in the class. At five foot two inches, Akna's head only came up to Jessa's chin. With her hair piled on top, Akna was sure from the floor to the top of her bun Jessa was close to six feet.

Jessa also talked really fast and her thoughts seemed to flit from one subject to the next without much connection. During the walk to math class, Jessa said both her father and mother had been basketball players at Oregon State University, so she didn't have any choice except to be tall. She had a brother too, but he was sixteen and he was already on the varsity basketball team in high school. Even though Jessa started playing basketball at home with her parents and brother, she didn't really like basketball. Her favorite sport was volleyball and she was already on an intramural team.

Jessa was the perfect assigned buddy, because Akna didn't really have to talk if she didn't want. Jessa wasn't rude, she just couldn't keep her mind from going a mile a minute and she shared everything her mind was thinking. She seemed to take her buddy job very seriously, always checking with Akna to make sure she wasn't lost. Also, when she ran out of things to comment on, she would pepper Akna with questions all at once. Where did she live? Did she have brothers or sisters? What school did she go to before moving here? Why did her family move in the middle of the year? Why didn't she wait until the summer and then start middle school?

Fortunately, Jessa didn't seem to notice when Akna only answered every third or fourth question. But whatever Akna told her, she remembered and would ask another related question later. It was amazing how her mind worked so fast all the time!

Math was pretty easy for Akna. When she would do the shopping at home, she had to do all the calculations herself. How much money she had, how long it would last, what everything cost. She had to make sure she didn't spend it all in one week and then have nothing in another week. The hardest part about math was understanding the word problems. Sometimes the things they talked about used a different number system and she got confused.

Today one of the problems used centimeters instead of inches. Even worse, you had to tell the answer in meters. It seemed silly that they had to learn metric math when nobody really used centimeters, did they?

When she and Jessa were walking back to Mr. Serna's room, after math class, Akna commented on it. Jessa explained that the whole world used the metric system except for three countries—the United States, Myanmar, and Liberia.

Akna didn't even know where Myanmar and Liberia were. But what most interested her was that it meant Guatemala used the metric system. Right then she vowed she would learn this metric math because one day she wanted to go to Guatemala and see where Tata and Nana and Mama came from. When she had a chance to travel there, she wanted to know how to measure things correctly and make them proud.

When the bell rang for lunch, Akna was ready.

"Do you have someone to sit with already?" Jessa asked as they ambled toward the cafeteria.

"Maybe. I'm not sure."

"We can go through the line and then look for your friend after we have our food."

Akna followed Jessa, not knowing what else to say. She didn't want to be the reason Jessa couldn't see her friends for a whole week.

"Really, you don't have to do that. I'm going to look for my sisters anyway."

"You have sisters here? What grades?"

"Kindergarten and third."

"Kindergarteners eat in their room. First through third eats before us. Our lunch time is for fourth and fifth graders only."

"Oh." Akna scrutinized the ground as they walked. She wasn't sure what to do. She'd been looking forward to reconnecting with her sisters and hearing their excitement about their classes. She really didn't want to eat with a bunch of strangers.

Jessa gestured toward the door. "Here we are. What's your friend's name? Maybe I know her already and where she sits. Being tall has its advantages."

Akna didn't respond. Instead, she pretended to concentrate on the food choices. It was between a hamburger and a vegetarian sandwich. She chose the hamburger because Jessa told her the vegetarian sandwich was like eating a *boring* salad and nothing else. If you liked salad, the hamburger came with a little salad on the side and a choice of chocolate milk or regular milk.

When they exited the line, Akna scanned the room. There were a lot of people. How would she ever find Jorge in here. Then she saw an arm waving and heard shouting, "Akna over here. Over here."

Jessica's eyes widened and she said, "Jorge Rodrigues? Jorge Rodrigues is your friend?"

"Well, yes. I guess. I mean…I just met him. Why? Is there something wrong with him?"

"Um *No*! Good looking. Rides a cool metallic-blue bike. Has a great laugh. Is easy to talk to. Super smart. What's not to like?" She was making a beeline toward the table now. "Do you mind if I join you?"

"Don't you want to sit with your friends?"

"I could sit with them any time. I mean Jorge Rodrigues, now that's something special."

Akna knew she shouldn't be jealous. It wasn't like she really knew him. They just met this morning. For all she knew he didn't really like her. He was just being nice to the new girl walking with her sisters.

"If you don't want me to horn in, I understand," Jessa said, though her feet continued to move in a straight line to Jorge's table. "I'll just say hi and then leave."

"No, it's okay."

"Are you sure?"

Not sure at all, Akna nodded.

As they both approached, Jorge stood and smiled just like he did when they first met. "I'm glad you saw me waving. I wanted to make sure not to miss you. Have a seat."

Jorge stood and offered a hand to Jessa. "Hi, Jessa, I'm Jorge. Are you a new friend, too?"

The previously talkative and confident Jessa, suddenly froze and didn't move.

Akna gave her a little shove. "Jessa's my assigned buddy for the week."

That seemed to unfreeze her. Jessa shook Jorge's hand multiple times but didn't let go. "I'm Akna's buddy for the week." Suddenly she let go. "Wait! How did you know my name?"

"You are the tallest girl in the class and I think everyone knows your name."

"Oh. Yeah, there's that." She stared at Jorge like he had two heads or something.

"Have a seat." Jorge gestured across from him.

What was happening here? Up until now, Jessa had been pretty normal. She was acting soooo weird now.

"I'm surprised you aren't sitting with all the popular guys," Jessa said.

Jorge laughed. "To tell the truth, I'm really not a group kind of guy. I prefer just sitting with two or three people, not a big group. It's too exhausting."

Akna raised her brows. She felt that way, too. Maybe because she'd always been afraid to reveal anything about her family, she tended to avoid cliques.

"But I've seen you hanging out with other guys sometimes," Jessa pressed. "Like Joe and Randy and..."

"Peter, Paul, and Mary?" Jorge asked.

Jessa swallowed. "Well...I don't know who they are. I mean the popular ones."

"I don't care who's popular and who's not," he said. "I just like people, that's all. There are a few guys, like Joe and Randy and Mateo and Danny, who are real true friends. And there's a lot of people I talk to but are more just people I like."

Jorge looked directly at Akna. "How was your morning?"

Akna couldn't help but beam. He wasn't going to let Jessa do *all* the talking.

"It wasn't as bad as I expected. Mrs. Baker was really nice. I like Mr. Serna. He's my home room teacher and social studies and language arts."

"You're lucky to have him for home room," Jorge said. "I have him for those other classes too, but on a different schedule from you. Did you know he got teacher of the year last year?"

"No. That must mean he's *really* good."

"He is. He gets the whole not-knowing-which-culture thing."

Akna cocked her head to one side. She knew her culture. She was American, Spanish, K'iche'. That's what Tata said.

"What I mean is you can talk to him about stuff," Jorge added, placing his hand over hers for a moment, then quickly withdrawing it.

"That's true," Jessa chimed in. "He's my favorite teacher of all time.

I guess not all time because I don't know *all* the teachers. I might meet an even more favorite teacher in middle school next year. Maybe I should have said for this time."

"He seems nice," Akna agreed. "I don't know him very well yet. He did make learning vocabulary fun just before lunch and he picked really hard words for spelling. I like learning lots and lots of new words."

"Writing and reading is my favorite class with Mr. Serna," Jorge said. "Just before Christmas we had to write about our family traditions and read it aloud. There were some really interesting stories."

Akna gulped. She was glad that was last semester. The last thing she wanted to read aloud to a whole class was about family. Her family and Christmas usually meant Mama was gone for a few days. After Nana died, Akna was the one who put up their fake tree and decorated it and made sure that Hai and Nakia had a good time. When they asked about Mama, she would always say that Santa had a sick elf and asked Mama to come to the North Pole and help. Nakia believed her. Hai stopped believing last year.

"No one was forced to read their story," Jorge continued, as if he'd read her mind. "Some people just turned in their papers and didn't read them. Mr. Serna said that was okay, too. It's good to keep some things private."

Akna didn't say anything. People would eventually figure out she was a foster kid soon enough. And then they would probably be asking why. But she wasn't going to broadcast it. She was going to put it off as long as she could.

"So, what do you have after lunch?" Jorge asked.

"Music with Mrs. Cosgrave."

"I have theater," Jessa said.

"Great! I'm in that music class, too. You'll love Mrs. Cosgrave. She finds really interesting music for us to sing. We do classics, but she picks a cool way to do it. Like, instead of the classic "Little Drummer Boy," we did the Alicia Keys version of "Little Drummer Girl." Instead of the old-fashioned "Let it Snow," we did the version they did on that movie, *Glee.* Really up tempo."

The bell rang, signaling they had to turn in their trays and get to the next class within fifteen minutes.

As they dropped trays near the door, Jorge said, "Hey Jessa, I can show Akna where the next class is and you can have a break."

"I'll walk with both of you. My job is to make sure that Akna never gets lost this week. I wouldn't want to get in trouble if something happened to her."

"I'm good," Akna said. "I'm sure Jorge will take good care of me."

Jorge made an x sign on his heart. "Atraviesa mi corazón y espera morir."

Akna giggled. "No need to die."

Jessa sighed. "Well, okay. I guess you're trustworthy. Nice meeting you in person." She started walking away then turned back. "Hope to see you again."

"Same," Jorge said as Jessa quickly put space between them with big, long steps. "She seems nice."

"She is. I think she has a crush on you."

"That's only because she doesn't really know me. If she did, she wouldn't think so highly of me."

"Really? I can't believe that. Were you in juvvie or something?"

"No. Not that bad. Long story. No time. Maybe another day." He pointed at the music room. "Ready to sing your heart out?"

Akna smiled as he gestured for her to walk in ahead of him. She would love to learn some happy songs. Whenever her mother was unhappy or drunk, she often sang *Échame la culpa* – Put the blame on me. Then it would go round and round in her head. Akna knew all the words, even though she hated them.

Jorge took it upon himself to introduce her to Mrs. Cosgrave and to the class.

Jessa was right. Everyone paid attention to Jorge when he spoke. They respected him. His introduction made her blush. Not that he said anything embarrassing. He just said nice things about her even though he barely knew her.

Mrs. Cosgrave had the class start with their scales and then they did voice exercises. Then she played and sang the song "Lean on Me" by Bill Withers. The class had already been practicing the chorus, so that was what they did next.

Akna didn't know the song, but the chorus was easy to pick up.

Then Mrs. Cosgrave added a side-to-side step and a handclap with each step to the beat.

By the end of the class, Akna had it down and sang her heart out, just as Jorge said she should. The song ended with each side of the room doing a call and response. "Call me (Call me). Call me (Call me) about eight times.

Now she had a new song stuck in her head as she strolled toward her final class period—library. This was a time set aside for students to work on things or review exercises or get reading done for the next day.

Akna didn't do any of those. Instead, she found a table by herself and pulled out a piece of paper. At the top she carefully wrote: *Who to Call*. Then she drew a line down the middle of the page. On the right hand she wrote names of people who said she could contact them if she ever needed anything. On the right she wrote what might happen if she did call on them. Then, after thinking about what she wrote, she would put a mark next to each person's name. She wrote an X for definitely not, an O for maybe, and a check mark for definitely yes.

Mrs. Sleeper **X**

She might put me in a different foster home if she thinks things aren't working out.

Mrs. Bohn. **O**

Maybe. She doesn't expect me to be perfect. But one person with troubles may take too much of her time with other kids living here.

Mrs. Baker **X**

She seems nice. But she's the principal. There may be rules that she has to tell someone else certain kinds of stuff. Probably Not.

Mr. Serna **O**

Jorge said you could talk to him about anything. But he was a teacher and maybe he would have to tell the principal. Maybe.

Gianna **O**

I think she understands more about my Mama than I do, even

though I haven't told her anything. And she's not a follower. Mostly Yes. A little bit of Maybe.

Polly **O**

She talks straight. But I think she's kind of flighty. Need more investigation.

Sandra **X**

Definitely not!! She's all about rules.

Hai and Nakia. **X**

~~Hai, maybe. Nakia is too little.~~ No. It's my job to help them. Not their job to help me.

Jorge **O**

??????????????????????

When she was done writing, she reviewed it one more time. Satisfied, she folded the paper into fourths and stuck it in her pants pocket. She didn't want anyone to find this. When she got home, it would be locked in her diary. This was her preliminary thinking. She had some investigating to do first. She didn't need help right now, but she wanted a plan for when a bad change came along.

CHAPTER TEN

BINDING BREAD

*S*aturday was bread-making day with the Bohns. Everyone gathered around the big dining room table. Even Mr. Bohn was there. The entire table was covered in parchment paper. Akna bent to look under the table to see why it wasn't curling up. It had been secured beneath the table edge with flat tacks.

In front of each of the eight spots was a large mixing bowl, a glass measuring cup marked in fourths up to two cups, a set of measuring spoons, and a set of six tiny glass bowls that Mr. Bohn called pinch cups. There was also a very large wooden spoon at each spot. Akna marveled at the set up. She thought this must be like a real bakery would work with many people helping.

"Time to pick the bread," Mrs. Bohn announced and drew a velvet bag out of her pocket. She undid the drawstring and then bent to offer it to Nakia. "As you and I are working together, you get to pick one for me and one for you."

Nakia's eyes widened as she put her hand into the bag. She withdrew a large wooden coin and put it on the table in front of her. Then she did it again.

"May I read the names?" Mrs. Bohn asked her.

Nakia nodded her head several times.

Mrs. Bohn peered at the first coin. "We are baking honey wheat bread." She placed it on the table and picked up the other one. "Rye bread." She placed it on the table in front of Nakia. "Those are two yummy choices, Nakia. Good pick."

Then she passed the bag to Mr. Bohn on her right. He held it open for Hai. "You and I are going to bake together, too. Pick two really good ones."

Hai quickly put her hand in and withdrew two wooden coins at once. She read aloud: "Dutch oven cinnamon raisin bread and peasant bread." She looked up at Mr. Bohn. "Peasant bread? That sounds like something you'd see in a movie from a long time ago."

"It is," he said. "It's a kind of bread poor people made, which means it doesn't have a lot of fancy ingredients. The best part is we don't have to do any kneading."

"What's that?"

"It's when you push and pull on the bread to distribute all the gas bubbles from the yeast throughout the dough. It builds up muscles." He raised his arm at an angle and fisted his hand to show his muscles. "Peasant bread and most breads with fruit, like raisins, don't use yeast. So, no gas bubbles to worry about spreading around." Then he passed the bag again.

The bag continued around the circle, and each person chose a wooden coin and announced their choice. There were no two alike. Gianna and Akna were the last two in the circle. Gianna got the bag first.

"I'll be helping you with your bread, Akna, unless you already know how to do this."

"I've never made bread before."

"Then you pick first." She held the bag toward Akna.

When Akna put her hand in the bag she was surprised to find there were more than two rounds left. She counted at least eight still left in the bag and hadn't touched all of them. She finally withdrew one. "Coo...um..roun?" She showed it to Gianna.

"Couronne. It's French for crown. Like *corona* but without the A. That's a fun one because you make a circle with the dough.

Gianna picked last. "Pumpernickel sandwich bread."

"Ready. Set. Bake!" Mr. Bohn shouted.

People were moving back and forth between the table, a refrigerator in the garage, and the pantry at the other end of the kitchen. They all talked at once about what they were baking. Akna simply followed Gianna to the big fridge in the garage.

"A lot of these recipes use the same kind of base and depending on what base you are making you might add an extra egg or extra honey or grains or garlic," Gianna said as they got in line for the refrigerator. "We call it starter bread. Every two weeks we all make different starter breads. We bake half of them and then store the rest of the dough in here." She reached in and pulled out a large white tub with her name on it. "This is what I made last week. It's a multigrain with two pounds left to bake."

Next, they went to the pantry and got a ribbed basket called a brotform. Akna had never seen such a thing. It had two pieces, the main basket and then a small basket turned upside down in the middle.

Back at the table, Gianna showed her how to measure out one pound using the scale. And then she had to take that and make eight equal-sized balls. Gianna said the trick was that it had to be soft and bouncy, but still strong enough to hold together.

Akna rolled out one of the balls into a flat disk and then brushed a little oil around the edges. That was to make sure it would hold the little basket on the bottom when they had to turn it over. The seven other balls had to stick together to form the ring, but the disk in the center would disappear.

Akna then followed the instructions to flour the brotform, including the little basket inside. Then she placed the flat disk over the upside-down basket in the middle and spread out the oiled-edges just a little bit to the sides on the bottom. Finally, she placed the eight balls in a circle around the edges of the larger basket.

The last step was to use a small knife to cut the disk over the little basket. She carefully cut seven equal pie slices—well close to equal. No matter how hard she tried, they weren't exactly the same. Some were a little fatter than others. Then she carefully curled each slice back onto one of the balls.

When Gianna first explained it, Akna thought it was really complicated. But it was easy to do in the end and it turned out really pretty.

Then she had to wait for the dough to rise a bit. This rising wasn't going to be a lot, just enough to have a springiness. She had to wait for sixty whole minutes before she could do the final step.

So, she watched Gianna make her pumpernickel bread. It was another kind of bread she'd never heard of before. Gianna said it would be a dark brown when it was cooked, and they would use it for sandwiches and to go with salads.

They didn't talk a lot while she watched Gianna do each step. That was something she liked about her. Gianna didn't talk unless she had something important to say. That was how Akna was, too. She hated small talk. She didn't mind silence when hanging out with someone. It gave her time to think, instead of having to always answer back to questions that didn't really matter.

When the sixty minutes were up, the hard part came. Akna had to turn the basket over and have it land perfectly on the baking stone she'd placed to the left of the basket. Once it was on the stone, Akna could remove the basket.

Gianna showed her how to put a piece of parchment paper over the top of the basket. Then in one, graceful motion Akna had to turn the basket upside down and remove her hand, so the parchment paper and the basket would be on the stone.

"Fast or slow?" she asked before turning.

"Whatever's the most comfortable for you," Gianna responded.

Akna decided fast was the best way. She placed a hand on top the parchment paper and drew in a breath. "Here it goes." She raised her hands in the air and flipped, then screamed, "noooooooo" as the parchment paper went flying off the table in one direction and the basket went in the opposite direction.

Everyone looked up and it felt like someone with the power to slow time snapped their fingers and it all happened in agonizing slow motion. Everyone stared at the basket with their mouths open in a big o-shape until it landed at an angle, wobbled like a spinning top, and then tipped over right in front of Sandra.

Akna couldn't believe her bad luck. Right in front of perfect Sandra.

Then Mrs. Bohn started clapping. Then Mr. Bohn joined in. Soon everyone except Akna was clapping and laughing.

She didn't know what to do. She wanted to cry or scream, or better yet run out the door like she did at home when she was all pent up with emotions and needed to let them out. But she didn't know where to run unless she ran to the school and back. She didn't really know this neighborhood yet.

Instead, she bowed low from the waist. "And for my next circus trick I'll juggle all seven rolls into the oven. That is if the bread didn't fall out and roll under the table already."

"It's still in there," Sandra said as she tore off another piece of parchment and placed the upside-down basket over it. "Bring your stone over here and I'll help you get it on."

Akna picked up her stone and scooted past four other seats to get to where Sandra had the basket and paper. She braced herself for some kind of comment about how clutzy she was.

"It really is miraculous," Sandra said. "When I first tried something like that, the bread went flying out of the basket and all over the floor. It was because I put too much oil on the disk."

"Really?" Akna asked. She couldn't believe that perfect-Sandra would ever make a mistake.

Sandra nodded. "That wasn't the worst one. The worst one was when—"

"She dumped a bowl of eggs on Mama Lois' lap," Polly said.

"Then she ran to get a rag to clean up, but it had been soaking in the sink and she didn't wring it out," Gianna added.

"And Lois' pants turned kind of brownish-yellow like she'd peed in them," Sandra finished.

Everyone was laughing now, even Sandra.

"See yours *was* a miracle," Sandra said. "Only one little mistake, instead of making it worse and worse like I did." She pointed to the parchment paper with the overturned brotform. "I think everything is still fine inside. Just put your stone down, then pull at this paper while lightly holding the basket down until they are both over your stone."

"Slowly," everyone said all at once.

Akna smiled. "Right."

They all watched her every move as she slowly dragged the paper and the basket onto her stone. Then she let out the breath she was holding.

"Now tap around the bottom of the basket to loosen everything."

Akna did as Sandra said.

"Lift the basket *very* slowly. Try not to shake it so that you don't break any of the rolls."

Again, Akna followed Sandra's directions exactly. The basket came off and all eight of the bread rolls were still attached. Then she removed the little basket in the middle.

She smiled. It looked pretty good considering it flew across the room.

"Oven is ready," Mrs. Bohn said after checking the temperature. "There's still enough water in the pan for steam. Bring your stone over here and put it on the middle shelf."

Akna moved cautiously with the stone and her crown of bread. She placed it on the shelf and Mrs. Bohn closed the oven.

"Now set the timer."

"Gianna," Akna yelled across the room. "What's the time?"

"Twenty minutes and then check."

Akna tapped the word "timer" on the oven. Then she tapped the number two and zero and zero, zero.

"That's twenty hours," Mrs. Bohn said softly. "This oven starts with minutes, not seconds."

Akna flung her hands out to each side. "How do I stop it?"

"Tap the timer again."

She did and it cleared. This time she tapped only a two and a zero, then tapped timer again. It immediately showed the seconds as it counted down.

"That was close," Akna said. "It would have been burnt."

"Someone would have caught it," Mrs. Bohn said. That's why we all do this together. You'll remember next time. You did a good job. The best part is we all get to sample it when it comes out of the oven."

"Yeah," Akna agreed, not sure she wanted to be around when that happened. "I hope it tastes good."

Mrs. Bohn patted her on the back. "It will. With Gianna's starter bread and your beautiful creation, there's no doubt it will be a great addition to lunch."

Akna hoped so. She didn't want to let Gianna down. She didn't want to let anyone down.

Everything about this bread making required practice and patience. She didn't mind the practice. She could do that every day if they'd let her. But patience was not her superpower. Mama had always told her that Akna wanted everything to happen at the snap of a finger, when the world wasn't like that. It moved very slowly.

To make the time pass, Akna immediately cleaned up her mess and was already helping Gianna in the kitchen. She was hand washing all the bread-making paraphernalia.

When the oven alarm went off, Akna jumped a little. She opened the door and peered into the oven. The golden-brown crust looked really good, just like the picture.

"Turn off the oven," Gianna instructed as she tossed an oven mitt to Akna. "Pull out the stone and place it on the counter if you can find an empty space.

Akna carefully pulled the slightly heavy stone out slowly. She found a spot between the refrigerator and the oven that was just big enough to put the stone down.

"It's still in the shape of a crown," Gianna commented. "That's not easy to do."

"Now what? Do I cut it up or put it on the table like this?"

Gianna pulled out a small rack from a lower drawer and placed it on the counter next to the stone. "It needs to cool a bit. Slide it off the stone and onto the rack." She pointed to a metal spatula in a large jar of spatulas and big spoons, whisks and other stuff.

Akna placed a spatula under the bread and slowly worked it under the first part and then scraped under every part of the circle. It appeared she left only a few small pieces of crust on the stone. She sized up the distance between the stone and the rack. She contemplated using two spatulas to move it, but she wasn't sure she could manage that. Instead, she picked up the crown with both hands and scooted it over quickly. Her held breath whooshed out. Fortunately, that transfer did not repeat the earlier flying bread high jinks.

Gianna and she worked together getting all of the cooking implements washed and dried and put away. Then Gianna washed the stone, too, and Akna dried it.

"Put it next to your bread," she instructed. "I think it's cool enough now you can move the bread back to the stone."

As Akna positioned it back on the stone, the kitchen suddenly became crowded. Mrs. Bohn stood over a giant pot of green pea and ham soup she'd made earlier in the week and had been stirring and simmering while they were all working on making the bread dough or baking bread earlier.

Hai and Nakia were helping set the table, moving back and forth from the kitchen to the dining room with plates and napkins and silverware. Gianna showed them where to find all those parts. Akna could hear the occasional correction from Polly. "No, put those over there. That's right."

Mrs. Bohn took a soup spoon and dipped in the pot, then took a taste. "Mmm...just right. Nice hearty consistency and the ham added the perfect amount of saltiness." She set the spoon in the sink. "Gianna, it's time you joined the others. Akna and I will be out in a minute."

Akna stood close to her bread. "Should I take this out or cut it or what?"

"Just a minute," Mrs. Bohn said as she placed her hand in an apron pocket and pulled out her cell phone. "I want to take your picture with your first baked bread for a meal. Can you hold the stone in front of you?"

Akna easily held it firm with both hands in front of her.

Mrs. Bohn raised the cell phone to eye level. "That is such a beautiful crown. You did a great job on your first bread baking day."

Akna couldn't help but smile. Just then Mrs. Bohn took the picture.

She leaned over and showed it to Akna. "Look at what you did today. You made bread from scratch." Then she pointed to Akna's eyes. "I can see you are proud of your accomplishment. See that smile and the twinkle in your eyes? I've been waiting for that twinkle all week."

Akna stared at the picture. She did look really happy and proud. Her hair was a bit wild, the way it curled every which way, but it was mostly in the bun she'd done after breakfast this morning to keep it from falling into the batter.

Outside of the annual school pictures with her class, Akna couldn't remember when her Mama had last taken a picture of her or her sisters. The one in the hallway at home was more than two years old. Nana had a scrapbook with pictures of them that Tata often took. She suddenly realized that she didn't think about bringing those scrapbooks. Would they be okay at home if Mama was there? What if someone broke in? What if the place caught fire when no one was there? Who would save those pictures?

Akna frowned. She should have thought of that when she packed for them. Hai and Nakia would want to see all those pictures, too.

Mrs. Bohn looked at Akna with her lips pressed together. "Are you okay? Do you not like the picture? I can take another one."

Akna shook her head. "No. I love it. Thank you. Is there a way to print it out? I'd like to tape it in my diary, so I can look it at again and again."

"Good idea!" Mrs. Bohn said. "I'll transfer it to my computer and print it out on photo paper after dinner."

"Thank you. Um…what should I do with the bread now?"

"Oops, I almost forgot." She dropped the phone back in her pocket. "Take the stone and bread out to your seat at the table and I'll join you in a minute when I get this soup into the tureen."

As Akna carefully placed her bread and stone in front of her seat, she noticed there were a stack of bowls and a small plate to one side. Everyone had a large plate already at their seat.

"That's a perfect crown," Mr. Bohn said. "That golden color looks like you could wear it on your head right now."

"Yes, Akna," Nakia giggled. "You would be a queen with a golden crown. Why don't you put it on?"

"I don't think we want another bread flying contest," Akna said.

"A cape. We need a cape for the queen," Polly said as she hurried back into the kitchen. She came out with a red gingham table cloth and placed it over Akna's shoulders. "Tie the ends together so it doesn't fall off."

Akna grabbed the two ends and made a knot at her throat. She felt kind of silly but no one was looking at her like she was a dweeb.

Soon, Mrs. Bohn was at her side with a large blue bowl with a ladle inside. "I see you are queen for a day," she said with a smile. "Well deserved for this beautiful Couronna bread. Let's all stand and hold hands while Gianna says grace and asks for blessings for this meal."

"Thank you for this wonderful meal prepared by Mrs. Bohn and Akna Sales. Thank you for bringing Akna and Hai and Nakia into our home. We are truly blessed by their presence. Amen."

Akna took an extra few moments before she raised her head. She hadn't been called a blessing since her Nana died. Though she said it to her sisters all the time, she didn't think she would ever hear someone say that about her again.

"Akna, it's time for you to cut the bread into slices," Mrs. Bohn interrupted her thoughts.

Using two fingers to measure a width like she'd learned last time she cut bread, she easily cut eight slices out of the ring.

Mrs. Bohn passed her a bowl of soup. "Let's start the soup to the left. After passing the bowl, put a piece of your nice warm bread on the plate and pass that next."

Akna did that until everyone, including Mrs. Bohn was served. Then she received her bowl of soup, and took the final piece of bread she had cut for herself. Everyone had waited patiently until Akna was seated and ready. For a few minutes, the only sound was that of soup spoons dipping into each bowl.

"Mmmmmm…it's good, Akna," Hai said with her mouth half full of a piece of her bread.

"¡Excelente!" Sandra said at the other end of the table and Nakia clapped and repeated Sandra's praise.

Akna smiled so big she was afraid her cheeks might crack. "Gracias. Lo aprecio más de lo que puedas imaginnar. ¡Gracias!" She thought for a moment and then added, "And in K'iche' maltiox. Maltiox, Sandra."

Sandra nodded, then dropped her head and quickly wiped a hand across her eyes. Then she shook her head from side to side like she was trying to shake off something.

Even though Akna still believed they would be going home in six months, she was starting to feel like maybe this could be a really good pretend family for now. She wanted to be a part of this family, to know how it felt when everyone worked together every week. With six months of practice, then maybe—just maybe—she and her sisters could recreate it again when they got home.

That evening, after Hai and Nakia were asleep, Akna sat at the small desk next to her bed with the lamp down as low as she could turn it and still see the page. Sandra, Polly, and Gianna were still downstairs doing homework. It was a good time to write her first entry into the diary Gianna had given her.

She carefully wrote the date and then titled it, *First Week on Mariposa Lane.*

I know I should have written every day, but so much was happening I couldn't even think straight most of the time. At home I would come home from school and have so much to do with making food and cleaning and taking care of Hai and Nakia and sometimes taking care of Mama, *that I would crash at night. That's kind of how it feels here, except I'm not taking care of everybody but everything is so new that I'm tired all the time.*

School is so so. Mr. Serna is a good teacher. I like all the classes I have with him. Math is okay but I don't think the teacher likes me. Science is interesting, I can't wait until we get to go on a field trip. PE is kind of embarrassing, but Jessa said to get over it.

Jessa was my assigned buddy. She's really tall. She's lived here forever and knows pretty much everyone. She's a nice person but I don't know if we have anything in common. Her friends are all boy crazy. I think she is too because of the way she got all red when she talked to Jorge. I'll wait and see if we still talk to each other when she doesn't have to be my buddy anymore.

Jorge is this boy we met on the first day of school. He's nice. I guess he's super popular. We ate lunch on Wednesday, but he didn't ask me to eat with him on Thursday and Friday. That was okay because Jessa had me eat with her friends. I tried not to pay attention to him, but I couldn't help it when I was leaving the cafeteria. He kind of hangs out with these other boys I think are his friends. That's okay with me.

My favorite class of all is Music. Jorge is in that class with me. The only one we have together. The teacher says I have a good voice. I used to love singing with Nana and Tata but I stopped.

Akna put her pen down for a moment. The night Mama told her they would be going to foster care was the only time she'd heard her Mama sing since Nana died. Mama seemed in a good mood when she was singing. But now Akna wasn't so sure. She wasn't sure about anything anymore when it came to Mama. She'd thought she knew everything. But obviously she didn't.

She twisted the diary around and then wrote in the margin, *Ask Gianna about why Mama would go to jail if she doesn't do rehab.* She'd forgotten about that just in the past four days. She turned the book back to normal and started writing again.

I think Jorge could be my friend. He seems to understand a lot of stuff without me saying anything. But I'm not sure. On Friday, after school was out, he walked with me and Hai and Nakia half way home. He stopped and pointed to his right and said that was his turn for home. Then something weird happened. He asked where we lived. When I said Mariposa Lane, he frowned for just a second and bit his lip. Then he said it was a nice neighbor-

hood. But it didn't look like he liked that neighborhood. He got on his bike kind of fast and rode away. He didn't wave goodbye or anything.

Maybe he knows about the foster home and now he doesn't want to be my friend anymore. I hope that's not true. But I don't know if I can ask him. I guess I'll have to try to be patient and see what happens next week.

CHAPTER ELEVEN

LEARNING TO SWIM IN DEEP WATER

Sunday morning was reserved as a time for worship. Mr. and Mrs. Bohn did not attend a specific church because they often had children from different backgrounds. So, every child had a choice to choose to stay home with Mr. and Mrs. Bohn and hear a Bible story and talk about it. Or they could go to a church they wanted.

Sandra went to the Lutheran church three blocks away. She always met up with friends on Sunday. Polly and Gianna stayed at home. Gianna said she was pagan and Polly said she didn't know what she was.

During breakfast Mrs. Bohn said, "Akna, you and your sisters will stay home with me today. However, if you would prefer to go to a Catholic church on Sundays, I can make arrangements with someone in the neighborhood to take you to St. Mary's and bring you home. They are a good parish and do a lot of good things in the community. I understand they also have mass in Spanish if you want to go then."

Akna hung her head and ground one foot into the carpet. "I don't know. I haven't gone to confession in two years. We stopped going to mass after Nana died."

"I'm sure God will forgive you for not going. He understands all you've been through. The question is if you want to go or not."

"I don't know," Akna repeated. "I...it's just that...the truth is...I don't know what I believe. Tata believed in a different god then the Catholic god. He called the creator god Heart of Sky and from that came many other gods called the Tzuultaq'a". And those gods helped create the K'iche' and helped them throughout their lives. Nana was the one who believed in the Catholic god."

"And your mother? What did she believe?"

"I think she believed in the Catholic god, too. But I'm not sure, because when Nana died, she stopped going to mass. We all did."

"How about you, Hai?" Mrs. Bohn asked.

"I'll stay here. There are too many rules at Nana's church. I may not remember them."

"Me too," Nakia said, nodding her head vigorously with her eyes wide.

"I guess we will all stay here then," Akna answered. "Which God will we be talking about?"

"I was raised in the Methodist Church," Mrs. Bohn said. "I guess that means it's the same God your Nana believed in."

Akna sighed. Now that the decision was made, she realized she'd kind of hoped they would talk about the Tzuultaq'a". After a few Sundays, maybe she could get enough courage to ask Mrs. Bohn to talk about the other gods at least one time.

Mrs. Bohn read from a very large book called *The Children's Bible in 365 Stories*. She said it was written so one could read a story every day for a whole year. The story this Sunday morning was about the Good Samaritan.

Akna knew this story. It seemed to be a favorite of Nana and Tata to teach how people should always help others. It was about a Jewish man who is robbed and beaten and left to die on the road. First a Jewish priest passes by but doesn't stop to help. Then a Levite, also Jewish and of high status, passes by and doesn't stop to help. A third person, a Samaritan, stops to help the man. He even goes as far as to take him to an inn and stay with him a while and then he pays the innkeeper to continue taking care of him.

Mrs. Bohn also explained something Akna had never heard. That is that in ancient times Jews and Samaritans were enemies. People knew this because they looked different. Even today there are people who are afraid of anyone who looks different from them.

Even though the hurt man was not of the same religion or race, the Samaritan still helped the man. He didn't have to. No one would ever know if he helped or not. In olden days, it was easy to pass by and no one would know if you were even there.

In today's world it could happen too. But some people would take pictures with their phone and maybe even put them on social media and talk about the poor man but still not render aid.

Then Mrs. Bohn asked if it is a sin to ignore someone in need when you know you can help.

Gianna said she didn't believe in sin. But that she would help if she could, and it didn't have anything to do with God. It was a human thing to do.

Polly said she would call the police but see if she could maybe offer some water or cover the person to keep them warm. She said her mother called that good karma.

Both Hai and Nakia said they would run home and tell Mrs. Bohn to come help.

Akna said she would do the same. If she saw an adult coming, she would ask them to help, too, while she ran home. What she didn't say is she would also be very afraid of the man, even if he was hurt. Her mother had warned her many times about men and how evil they could be, telling her to always stay far away.

Akna realized that even with the power of SAD, she was still scared about a lot of things deep inside. More than anything she was scared of not knowing what was to come and how to plan for it.

After the Bible story, Polly was assigned to help Mrs. Bohn get lunch ready. Akna took that chance to find Gianna. She wanted to ask her questions about rehab and jail. She found her in the backyard, half way up a big oak tree. She was writing in a book—probably her own diary.

Akna wandered over to the tree and stood there not saying anything for a while. She didn't want to disturb her, but she also really wanted to know the answer and couldn't talk in front of others.

"I see you hanging down there with a dog-faced look," Gianna said.

"I don't have a dog-face. No one has ever called me that before."

"I mean a hang-dog, you know feeling guilty about something. Are you worrying about that Samaritan story?"

"No, not that. I'm worried about disturbing you. You're busy. I should go."

"Stop right there. If I didn't like my diary so much, I'd throw it at you. You are the most self-effacing foster kid I've ever met."

"What does that mean?" Akna hated it when Gianna used so many big words she didn't understand. She wondered if she would know that many when she turned thirteen.

"It means you try not to call attention to yourself. It means you are always afraid to know the answer because it might not be what you want. It means you get hurt easy."

"I don't get hurt easy," Akna said. "I've just seen a lot of hurt all my life, that's all. And I have plenty of fight. You just haven't seen it yet."

"Me too, girl." Gianna waved her hand to beckon her up the tree. She pointed to a nook in a nearby branch. "You better come up here before I change my mind."

Akna quickly climbed, easily choosing the right nooks and crannies and branches. There weren't a lot of trees back home, but she knew all the ones big enough to climb and to provide a safe haven to get away and not be found until she was ready.

Once she got to the place across from Gianna, she settled herself into the curve of the branch and braced her feet against the trunk. She guessed she was maybe fifteen feet off the ground. Being January, it wasn't exactly warm, but her new jacket with a pullover sweater underneath was doing its job. She wished the leaves were still on the tree. She preferred being in a tree where no one could easily see her.

"So, what's going on?" Gianna asked. "You lookin' to confess your sins to someone?"

Akna crooked her lip a little. "Nah. I don't have those kinds of sins. Even when I went to confession it was always small stuff like yelling at my Mama, running away when I was mad, not turning in my homework because I didn't understand it. That kind of stuff."

"You really are a goody-two-shoes, aren't you?"

Akna shrugged.

They both sat without speaking for a while. Akna worried her bottom lip, gathering her courage. She wanted to talk but she was afraid to know the truth, and Gianna wasn't the kind to force her. That's why she felt comfortable asking…but it would help if Gianna did force her.

Finally, she took in a deep breath and blew it out with an audible sound. "So…you seem to know about rehab."

"Yep. Lots of experience."

"Do you mean you or someone you know."

Gianna laughed. "Ya think I'm a junkie? Just 'cause I dress in black and wear long hair with a white streak doesn't mean I take drugs."

"I know. I just mean…you mentioned it when I said my mom was going to be back in six months. You immediately said rehab. How did you know? I didn't tell anybody. Not even Mrs. Bohn, though she probably has a file all about my mom."

"Yeah, she does," Gianna agreed. "She has information on all of us and our parents. I don't know if she keeps files, but she knows stuff for sure."

"So?"

"My mom's been in rehab five times that I know of. Twice while I was living with her and three times since I've been here. She goes in to clean up. Sometimes she stays, most of the time she quits before six months. The deal is she can't get me back until she finishes rehab *and* stays clean for six months. It seems to be too long for her."

"Really? That's harsh."

"Not really. The truth is I don't see her ever makin' it, you know. It's just too hard for her and what she…uh…does for a living."

"What does she do that's so hard?"

Gianna pressed her lips together for several seconds. "She hooks to pay for drugs," she whispered.

Akna swallowed hard. She didn't know what to say to that. She'd heard of such a thing but never knew someone who knew someone who really did it.

Gianna looked back. "No big deal. I'm used to saying it now."

Neither talked for a bit.

"So, what do you wanna know about rehab?"

"Well…I thought I could call Mama and talk to her and like tell her I love her and we'll be here when she's done that kind of stuff. But Mrs. Sleeper said she can't have any contact at all for a month. And then, after that she can only talk to us maybe every two weeks or once a month. She also said if Mama doesn't do the whole six months she'll go to jail."

"Is she a drug addict?" Gianna asked matter of fact like.

"No…I mean yes. I mean…I'm not sure. She drinks a lot and she feels sick a lot. She takes a lot of medicine when she feels sick. It could just be rehab for alcohol, right?"

"I hate to tell you this, but you have the right to know. Sounds like a drug addict to me."

Akna swung her head from side to side in denial. "I've never seen drugs. I've never seen needles. I really don't think so."

"A lot of drugs are just pills. And if she's doing something like heroin she's gonna hide it from you. Sorry, kid. I'm just being honest. What she calls medicine is probably not prescribed by a doctor."

"But…" Akna couldn't think of anything to say to make it not true.

Gianna tapped Akna's foot a bit. "Look, I may be wrong. I don't know your mom. Maybe I just see it because that's the way my family is. I didn't know it for a long time either. It took going in and out of foster care and going home several times for me to finally get a clue."

"Thanks," Akna said. But the more she thought about it, she was afraid Gianna was right. It was more than alcohol. "Tata used to tell me Mama was mind-sick. Do you know what that means?"

"Tata's a weird name, what does it mean?"

"It's what I called my grandfather, *mi abuelo*. It's common where they come from in Guatemala. Like some people call their grandfather Pops in English, I guess."

"Oh, I see. 'Cause the first thing that came to my mind when you said that were titties. I wouldn't exactly say it around kids at school, you'll get teased endlessly."

"Titties?" Akna looked down at her chest which hadn't yet grown any breasts. "Like girls' breasts?"

"Yup, a lot of guys call it tatas."

"Oh brother."

"So, back to your question. Usually mind-sick is a nice way of saying mental illness."

"Like Polly's mom? Schizophrenic?" Surely Tata would have said something about that if it were the case. Akna knew what that was—it was like hearing voices, not knowing reality sometimes. That kind of stuff.

"There's lots of different mental illness things. Could just mean depressed a lot—like things in life really get her down and she can't deal. Could be she suffers from some kind of PTSD—that's like when something really bad happens and screws up your life forever. Soldiers get that sometimes from being in a war. I watched a movie about that and it makes it so sometimes they hear like a loud noise that reminds them of a gunshot. And then that noise triggers bad memories and they don't cope very well. It could be lots of things. Women who had boyfriends or husbands who beat them get it. Women who've been raped get it. You'd be surprised how any different kinds of crazy there are."

Akna listened and weighed each one in her mind. The one about something really bad happens and screws up your life she could believe the most. Lots of bad things had happened to Mama in her life. She was pretty sure something bad happened on their way to America but no one ever talked about it. Then there were all the bad men in her life. She'd look up the PTSD one at school tomorrow during her study period.

"Sorry, Akna. I shouldn't have said your mom was crazy. I know that's not a good word to use. Sandra would be correcting me up the ying yang if she heard me say that."

"You didn't say it about my mom. You just said there were a lot of different kinds of crazy."

"Yeah. Well still…"

Akna sat in silence again gathering courage for the hardest question of all.

"You don't have to answer this, but has your mom ever been jail?"

"Yeah, a couple of times. Once for having drugs in the car, heroin it turns out. The other time for trying to … well never mind, let's just say it was illegal. She usually gets out after a week or two because the jails are so full and she isn't violent herself."

"Mrs. Sleeper said the court agreement was if Mama didn't do the whole rehab she would go to jail. I'm thinking six months of rehab might *feel* like jail to her. So, what would she have done to get a five-year jail sentence?"

"Oh man, I'm not a judge or anything. It's not like I know everything about drugs and jail and stuff."

Akna started swinging her feet back and forth below the branch. She couldn't sit still. Her feet had to let the worry out. "That's okay," she whispered. "I just thought maybe you'd know."

"I can ask around if you want. I bet someone at school knows this stuff."

Akna's feet swung faster and harder.

Gianna placed a leg on either side of Akna's swinging feet and braced against the branch where Akna sat. "You're going to worry yourself to death about this aren't you?"

Akna stopped her feet and braced them against Gianna's branch, she stared at them as she kept pressing down so they wouldn't swing. "I can't help it. I need a plan. I need to know what's going to happen to us. I promised Hai and Nakia that Mama would come get us in six months. I can't break their heart. They are too young. It's my fault. I shouldn't have left Mama when she was sick. I should have refused to go with Mrs. Sleeper. I should have—"

"Akna, look at me. It is not your fault. All these things were not in your control."

Akna slowly raised her head. She could feel the tension moving from her planted feet all the way up her body.

"You are not alone. You don't have to do this alone."

Gianna's voice sounded garbled, as if she was traveling through a time warp and getting further and further away from the signal. She was alone. She'd always been alone in the last two years.

Her stomach started to cramp and her chest closed in to compensate.

"Akna, breathe!"

Her heart pounded louder and louder. The blood in her ears rushed to her head. The only thing she wanted to do was RUN! RUN!

She shimmied down the tree and took off.

Gianna followed, matching her pace step-by-step at her side.

Akna noticed her but kept running. She wasn't sure where she was running to or from, she just needed to run. She pushed herself faster and faster, hoping that Gianna would give up and leave her alone. That's what she needed now, to be alone.

At the end of the block, she took a corner to the right and ran until she could run no further. She made another turn, then another. She looked to the side and Gianna was no longer there. She didn't dare look back. She still had to run.

The slap-sound of her feet on pavement was familiar. Every step reminded her of home. It reminded her that she shouldn't be here with the Bohn family. It reminded her that she shouldn't have left Mama while she was sick. She should have put up a fight instead of going with Mrs. Sleeper so easily. Where had her powers of SAD been then? Why didn't she stop everything?

She pushed harder. She knew if she ran hard enough, long enough, her body would start hurting and that hurt would obliterate every-thing else. She had to stop the thinking. She had to stop the worrying. She had to stop wishing for something better. She had to stop wishing for a life and a Mama she and her sisters could never have.

She concentrated on the pain of each step. She wanted it to burn like the tequila going down her throat when Mama forced her to drink. Mama always said pain is what proves you are alive. Akna was too alive. She wanted to be numb.

She slowed her stride as she realized that was what Mama wanted, too. To be numb. Maybe she was more like Mama than she thought.

At the next corner a large park, filled with tall trees everywhere, opened in front of her. Not the kind she could climb, but the kind that could give shelter—big fir trees with long branches. She ran into one where the branches came all the way to the ground. Gnarled wood reached for her with twisted arms.

Akna fought her way to the giant trunk and wrapped her arms as far as she could around the tree and held tight. If only she could step inside this trunk, maybe she could find Tata's spirit. Maybe she could talk to him again.

"Tata, I need to know the truth. I need to know about Mama. What happened? Am I like her? Am I going to turn into her? Where is Mama's SAD powers now?"

She reached out with her heart, calling to him and listened but she couldn't hear anything.

Akna yelled between racking sobs. "Tata I can't hear you. Where are you?"

Nothing.

No one.

She sobbed into the tree. Waterfalls filled her eyes as her misery soaked into the trunk.

She was truly alone.

She gripped the tree harder. "Tata, please. I need you. I need you. Please."

As if he'd heard her, she felt arms close around her.

But they weren't his. These were smaller arms but they held tight.

"I've got you, Akna. I've got you," Gianna said.

Akna turned in Gianna's arms and they gripped each other around the waist.

Gianna hung on and rocked her slightly back and forth until Akna quieted.

After what seemed like forever, Akna finally let go.

"Sorry for messing up your shirt," she said.

"No problem. Now I don't have to wash it."

Akna smiled but she couldn't bring forth the chuckle Gianna deserved.

The trees enveloped the two of them. She really couldn't see out and she doubted anyone could see in. For a moment, Akna wondered if they could stay there and pretend, just for a while, that this was a magical place where anything could happen—a place where Mamas were healed and families were put back together.

"I've gotta tell ya something about the Bohns and the whole foster family," Gianna interrupted her fantasy. "We've all kind of agreed to never let anyone be gone alone for too long. It's kind of a protection club, so no one gets hurt and no one tries to do something stupid."

"Like what kind of stupid?" Akna asked.

"Get lost and run into a bad dude. Get too depressed and think about hurting yourself, that kind of stuff."

"I can take care of myself," Akna said. "I wouldn't hurt myself because I have to take care of my sisters."

"Yeah…well…it's a thing anyway."

"So, you called them?"

"Not exactly. Let's just say they know where I am."

Akna wasn't sure if she liked that or not. How long being alone was too long?

"Sometimes it feels like a pimple on your butt that just keeps growing and itching," Gianna continued. "But most of the time it actually feels good. Like when you pop the pimple and all the ugly stuff drains out."

"Gross," Akna said.

"But effective," Gianna parried. "I mean you got a lot of ugly stuff out just now, right?"

"I guess. But it doesn't make it feel any better."

"I hear you. It's not like there will never be ugly stuff again. 'Cause there will. And maybe whatever ugly stuff is still there will wait underground and then just when you definitely don't want it to show up—like on prom night—the next pimple will make a big blackhead that everyone will point at you and laugh."

"Yuck!" Akna shook her head. "Don't ever become a therapist. You'd scare away all your patients."

"Now that's something to consider. A goth therapist talking about pimples. I could have my own TV deal just for teens."

Akna couldn't help but laugh a little. The funny thing was, if anyone could make that happen, for real, it would likely be Gianna.

"You sure are a good runner," Gianna said. "If you hadn't stopped pretty soon, I might have collapsed and given up. Ever considered going out for a team?"

Akna shook her head.

"I run the 5K on the team for Serrano. I also do the 200 meters to get me working on sprints for the end of the 5K push."

"I'm sure Margarita Elementary doesn't have a track team," Akna said.

"Nope, doesn't have a team," Gianna verified. "But if you want to train with me, you'd be a sure bet to get on the Serrano team if your still around next fall. And if not, you could probably get on any team you want wherever you live. You really are that good. I wouldn't be surprised if you could beat me."

"Really?" Akna considered that it might be a great way to get out all her tension every day.

"Yeah, really." Gianna held out her hand for a shake. "You train with me until you leave or join the Serrano Team. Deal?"

Akna shook her hand firmly. "Deal."

Gianna blew out a loud breath. "We probably should be heading home."

"I don't really know where I am," Akna admitted.

"Not a problem. I pretty much know everything in about a ten square mile area around the house. You ran about three miles in a circuitous route."

"Wow, I don't think I've ever run that far before. We can walk back though."

"Um...warning."

"About what?"

She dropped her voice to a whisper. "When we walk out of this nice hiding place, there're going to be six people waiting on the other side. And there're all going to crowd around you and stuff. It's kind of a Bohn tradition when someone goes rogue."

"Rogue? Me?" She considered that. She'd never been the one to be considered the bad girl. The rogue.

Gianna nodded, then took Akna's hand. "Ready to be royally squashed?"

Akna nodded and they walked out together hand and hand.

Hai and Nakia were the first ones to run to her, each one grabbing a part of her body and hugging her tight.

"We thought you ran away forever," Hai said.

"Who would read to me with you gone?" Nakia asked.

Then all at once the rest of the family closed in.

Everyone talked at once.

"You're never alone with us, Akna."

"We're a family. We're always here for you."

"You can't run away from us no matter how hard you try."

Hugging.

Squeezing.

She was pretty sure that at any moment they'd all be singing the theme song to Annie.

It was a cheesy thought, but it made Akna smile really big as she sang the chorus silently in her head as they piled into the Bohn family minivan. On the way home, she couldn't help herself as bits of the music hummed from her head to her mouth. Gianna was the first to pick it up and started singing the words. Then Polly came in singing rather loudly, and slightly off key.

As they pulled into the driveway, there were all singing at the top of their lungs, "Tomorrow. Tomorrow. I love ya tomorrow. You're always a day away."

CHAPTER TWELVE

EVERYONE HAS PROBLEMS

Monday, Akna woke actually excited to get to school. She'd survived that first week pretty well and she was determined to get caught up and excel in her classes so she could graduate and be proud of herself. Whether she stayed with the Bohns or went home, she wanted to be well-prepared for middle school in the fall.

In math, Mrs. Feldman introduced this silly phrase, "Please Excuse My Dear Aunt Sally." It was what she called a mnemonic—a way to remember the order in which to perform math operations (parentheses, exponents, multiplication, division, addition, subtraction). It worked really well. The first problem she asked Akna to solve in front of the whole class was $(7 \times 8 - 4) \div (6 - 2)$ Somehow, it wasn't surprising that the answer was thirteen, the most unlucky number in the world.

In vocabulary and spelling with Mr. Serna her favorite word for the day was immigrate which means to come to live permanently in a foreign country just like her mother and Tata and Nana did when they came from Guatemala. She also asked Mr. Serna for the Spanish spelling which is *inmigrar*. She wished she knew how to say it in

K'iche'. She couldn't remember Tata ever telling a story of migration in K'iche'. Perhaps they did not have such a word.

Mr. Kramer's technology and computer class was about using Google search to look things up and how to tell which answers could be trusted. Akna learned how to type in questions she wanted to research and how to tell Google the words she didn't want to see. The first thing she tried was to look for the K'iche' word for immigrate. Unfortunately, no matter how much she used different combinations of questions she couldn't get Google to give her that answer. Mr. Kramer tried, too.

He showed her how to find out the total number of languages in the world—about 6,500. Then she looked up how many people in the world spoke Spanish—572 million. English was 1.5 billion! Then he showed her how the Google translator worked. She could type in an English word or sentence and it would translate it to Spanish or vice versa. Because she already spoke both languages. Then Mr. Kramer asked her to see if she thought the translations were correct. If they weren't, he wanted her to write them down in the way she would say it. Most of the time Akna said it was probably correct. But there were a few times she said she would say it differently depending on who she was talking to.

When she found the stats on how many people spoke K'iche', it was only about one million people. And Google didn't have a translator for that language. She'd have to find another way to learn.

The good news was that in all her searching she found a lot of articles about K'iche' people and history and culture. Some were for college professors. When she tried to read them, they were hard to understand. So, she skipped those. But there were many other articles written for newspapers and elementary history teachers that were easier. She printed off all of those to take home and read when she had time.

She would keep her promise to Tata. Akna would not only tell the stories of their ancestors, but she would learn more about the K'iche' people of today, too. Tomorrow, she would ask Mr. Serna if her big essay project for Language Arts could be about the K'iche' people.

Finally, it was lunch and Akna was STARVING! Usually, she went to lunch not caring if she ate or not. Today she was learning so many things so quickly that her breakfast was already long gone in her stomach.

In the cafeteria line she was deciding between the chicken patty sandwich and the street tacos when Jorge stepped beside her, cutting in line.

"Never the street tacos," he said. "It is too little and microwaved. You deserve something special."

"Right," she answered with a big smile. "But they don't have tamales, ever. I haven't even seen tortillas for wraps. It's a pretty boring menu in general."

"They do some different dishes in the fall to celebrate Hispanic Heritage month. I think it's a taco bar though, nothing really hard to make. I guess that means you'll have to stick around for next fall and see if Serrano has it on the menu."

"Or I'll make them myself at home," she said. Her stomach dropped a little. When did she decide Mariposa Lane was home? She shook her head hard. Not now. She wouldn't think about this now.

How was your weekend?" Akna asked, her voice a little too bright.

"Hmmm," he responded as he picked up the apple juice and water to drink. "Same ol', same ol'."

"Who are you eating lunch with?" she asked, not sure if it was too forward, but she was in a good mood today.

He poked her in the shoulder. "You, of course. Do you think I would have run to catch up with you and then put my life on the line to cut in front of this brute?"

His friend Randy, snickered behind him. "Yep, he dumped me for you. Not that I'm complaining. After seeing him all weekend, I'm tired of the guy."

"Yeah, yeah," Jorge said. "You're just jealous I got a solo in the choir performance."

"Really?" Akna asked. "I hadn't heard yet. Not that I had a chance."

Jorge pressed his hand against her back to keep her moving. "I'll tell you all about it over lunch."

Soon, they found an uncrowded corner at the back of the cafeteria. It was kind of an unwritten rule that people who sat far away from the crowd weren't to be interrupted. It was usually best friends or whatever they called boy-girl friends that weren't in love or anything.

They sat directly across from each other, their trays touching in the middle.

"So, anything earth shattering happen this weekend?" Jorge asked.

"I baked my first ever loaf of bread and it was shaped like a crown, called a couranne. I never learned to bake back home."

"Back home?" he asked. "Oh right, you just moved. So, your mom suddenly decided to start baking or she decided you were old enough to learn?"

"Um. Kind of like that."

"That's not an exact answer. Did I say something wrong? I didn't mean I didn't think you were old enough."

"No. Nothing you said."

"I don't get it."

"There's nothing to get."

"Oooo-kay." He drew it out like he didn't believe her.

"Why did you ride away so fast last Friday when I said I lived on Mariposa Lane," she asked to change the subject. The last thing she wanted to talk about was being a foster kid. "Do you know something about Mariposa Lane that made you suddenly not like me?"

"No. It's a nice neighborhood."

"Then, what happened?"

"Do you really want to know?"

"Yes!"

"First, I apologize." Jorge let out a big breath. He tapped a finger on the edge of the tray, his face looking down. "I shouldn't have done that. It's just that…I was afraid, if you knew where I lived, we wouldn't be friends."

"That's crazy. I don't judge people by where they live. Believe me, where I lived before was nothing anyone would choose. Not only that, even if you told me your address, I probably wouldn't know where it is. I don't know very many places around here yet."

Jorge squinted his eyes at her without speaking, like he wasn't sure he believed her. "Nobody wants to come to my side of town."

Where Akna lived before was out in the country so there wasn't a right side and a wrong side. It was just where you lived. Some rich people had more property, like the vineyard owners but it still wasn't right or wrong.

"What do you mean *your* side of town?" she asked.

"Across the tracks."

"Come on, what does that mean?"

"You are west of the railroad tracks. That means you are in the nice part of town."

"Okay, and you're not?"

"I'm on the east side of town. The railroad tracks divide the town and our side is the wrong side. The poor side."

"The railroad tracks are only three blocks away from my house," Akna said. "Are you saying if I step across the tracks, I'm suddenly on the poor side? That doesn't make sense."

Jorge shrugged. "Mis padres dicen it is bad because we live in Section 8 housing. We never invite people over, not even my friends because they are embarrassed."

Akna frowned. "What does section eight mean?"

"It means we rent an apartment that no one wants to live in and that the government pays part of the rent for us. My parents work hard but they don't make a lot of money. My mom is a seamstress for the cleaners and my dad is a janitor for the shopping mall on your side of town."

"Okay, so I still don't know why it matters," Akna said. "Lots of people are poor. I used to be poor."

"I doubt it," he said. "Not if you can afford to live on Mariposa Lane. You don't move from Section 8 housing to that kind of home unless you win the lottery or get an inheritance or something."

"There are other ways to live in that kind of house," Akna said, unwilling to say how she could live there.

"My parents say those are good middle-class houses. Houses they could never afford. Did your dad move here and get a really good job or something?"

"I don't have a dad," she said quietly. "I mean, obviously I had a dad but I never met him and Mama isn't sure who my dad is."

"Oh." Jorge looked down at the table for a moment. "I'm sorry, I didn't—"

Akna waved her hand at him. "Not your fault. I'm used to it, but I don't talk about it with people."

Jorge swallowed and looked away for a minute. When his gaze returned to her, he spoke slowly. "Then I guess your mom is a single mom. Lots of moms are, you know. She must be making good money at her job so you could afford that kind of house. You're very lucky."

Akna rolled her eyes and gazed toward the ceiling for guidance. She was going to spill it. She didn't want to, but she liked Jorge and she wanted to still be friends. She didn't want him thinking she was a rich girl who wouldn't ever consider being his friend because he was poor. That was just stupid.

"I'm a foster kid," she spit out quickly and then the words started spilling out faster and faster like a freight train with no brakes going down a steep hill. "My mom is in rehab and I used to live in a broken-down mobile home with my mom and two sisters. And, if she doesn't stay in rehab, she's probably going to jail for five years. The truth is I really don't know if I'm going to live here for six months or six years."

Jorge's eyes widened and he leaned back in his chair without saying anything.

Akna was out of breath and shocked she said all that out loud to someone. She waited for the sadness or confusion to take over, but it didn't. It was just the truth. A fact of life.

"That was uh…" He seemed tongue tied, then simply said nothing.

Or did he now decide she wasn't good enough for *him*? She told him because being poor wasn't so bad. But maybe having a mom who did drugs was really bad. Maybe it was something that would make his parents not allow them to be friends. Bad mom. Bad daughter.

"If you don't want to be my friend now, I understand," Akna said slowly as she gathered her tray and started to stand.

"Whoa, whoa." He lightly pulled on her hand to sit again. "That was just a mouthful of words I didn't expect. Give me a moment to take it all in."

She slowly returned to her seat and tentatively set her tray back down. "Yeah. Well, I didn't exactly plan to say them either."

After a long pause, he covered one hand with his. "Lo siento, Akna. Lo siento."

She withdrew her hand from his. "No reason to be sorry, it's not your fault my mom is who she is. Just like it's not your fault you live on the poor side of town."

"I guess," he agreed. "You seem so okay about everything. That's amazing."

"You should have seen me yesterday. I was a mess. It comes and goes."

"Being as your sharing your situation, there is another reason I rode off so quickly."

She cocked her head and looked straight into his eyes. "I'm listening."

"It's kind of embarrassing."

"And having a mom in rehab and being a foster kid isn't?"

"Good point." Jorge sat up straight in his chair and rubbed his hands on his thighs. He took in a deep breath and let it out. "After your friend, Jessa, being all googly-eyed about me and then you being so nice, I was kind of worried that you were thinking of me like in a boyfriend way."

Akna's mouth formed an O but she couldn't make anything come out. She kind of, maybe, started thinking of him that way…only not really because she didn't really want a boyfriend.

"I don't want a boyfriend," she finally said. "I just want a friend. Is that okay with you?"

He nodded his head quickly. "Thank goodness. Because I'm gay."

The O came back and she tapped two fingers on her closed lips before speaking. "Wow. I mean not that it's bad, it's just…Wow. I never would have guessed. I mean the guys around you treat you like you are really macho."

He chuckled wryly. "I am macho. I just like other machos."

"Does, like, everyone in school know but me?"

"No! Well, not exactly. I don't hide it but I don't sing a song about it from the top of my lungs either. Some people just assume I'm gay because I like musical theater and acting and dancing. Which is stupid because straight guys like it, too. But then there's girls like your friend, Jessa, who obviously don't know."

Akna never really knew a gay person before. At least she didn't think she did.

"Does it bother you?" Jorge asked. "Are you Catholic? My family is Catholic and my parents keep praying I'll change."

"I haven't decided what religion I am," Akna answered. "Nana was Catholic and Tata was not. He believed in the Tzuultaq'a" which are many gods who helped the K'iche' people."

"I've never heard that name," Jorge said. "I've never heard of the key-chay people or the zule-tak-a. I figured your people were Mexican."

Akna shook her head. "Tata, Nana, and Mama came from Guatemala. The K'iche' in Guatemala are kind of like the Native Americans here. They've lived there for thousands of years."

"Cool. Completely different from my family." Jorge leaned forward.

"Tata told me a story about the creation of the world and animals and humans. He said the creator gods were sometimes both male and female. They could choose to be one god or two gods and often switched back and forth. The Heart of Sky, Heart of Earth was one god and two gods at the same time. He said this means everyone has both male and female inside them. Some people are more one way than another. And some people can be both just like Heart of Sky, Heart of Earth."

"I like that," Jorge said. "Now if I could get you to convert my parents it would help."

"Your parents don't accept you?" Akna asked.

"No. They think being gay is a sin and I'll go to hell, or at the best get stuck in purgatory. They think I can be talked out of it if I find the right girl. They watch me like a hawk if I have any guy friends over, like their waiting for us to start kissing or something."

"Awkward," Akna agreed.

"Yeah, and if you ever come over to my house or they see us together, they'll immediately start telling me what a great girl you are and hope that I'll fall for you and give up the gay thing."

"Would it help if I told them I was gay?"

"But you're not." He said, then wrinkled his forehead. "Are you?"

"I don't think so. Honestly, I never thought about it. Maybe I could be."

"Careful what you wish for. It's not easy being green, you know."

She chuckled. "Everyone has problems."

On the way to their music class, they both sang *The Rainbow Connection* song as they almost danced through the hall. Most people smiled. A few called them dorks. But they didn't care. They were friends. They'd shared secrets and survived.

CHAPTER THIRTEEN

MAMA CALLS

kna checked her calendar. It had been two months since she and her sisters had come to Mariposa Lane. For the first time, Mama was scheduled to call and talk to them. She didn't know why Mama hadn't called them before. Mrs. Sleeper had said she would be allowed to call after the one month in the treatment center. You never knew with Mama if it was that she was truly busy or that she didn't feel well. Akna hoped she was well, so she wouldn't have to worry about her anymore.

If she was honest, the truth was she hadn't really worried very much about Mama in the past couple weeks. It was easy to live with the Bohn's and her foster sisters. Not that they never got angry or anything. But when they did it seemed to get resolved fairly quickly. At least so far.

Once Polly got upset when Hai borrowed a sweater without asking. Even though Polly was three years older, they were both the same size. Akna tried to explain that at home they shared everything. There wasn't a sense of this clothing only belongs to one person.

Hai apologized and said she would never do it again. Polly said, if Hai had asked, she probably would have let her wear it. But it was the principle of the thing, that she couldn't just take it without asking permission.

Then a week later, Polly gave her the sweater and said she could have it. The truth was she never wore it. So now the sweater belonged to Hai.

Akna found it confusing that the fight even happened. She could understand if Hai had borrowed something sentimental or special, like Nana's quilt. But a sweater Polly didn't even wear seemed…well like that saying making a mountain out of a molehill.

After breakfast dishes were done, Mrs. Bohn invited Akna outside to the swing in the backyard. They sat across from each other and gently pushed the boards to cause it to swing back and forth. It was soothing.

"You remember your mother's going to call today, right?" Mrs. Bohn asked.

Akna nodded. It was on her mind all morning.

"Have you thought about what you want to talk about? Do you have any questions for her?"

"Well…mostly I want to ask how she's doing. If she's okay. If she's getting well."

Mrs. Bohn nodded her head. "That's a good start."

"I guess, I figured she'd do most of the talking," Akna said. "I mean that's the way it's always been before. She talks. I react and try to fix whatever the problem is."

"Do you anticipate any particular problems?"

"Well, kind of. I mean what if things aren't going so well with rehab? She'll want to tell me why and stuff. But I don't think I can say anything to fix that. Right? I mean I'm not there. I can't do it for her."

Mrs. Bohn's eyes sparkled as she nodded her head and her lips formed a half smile. "That's a very good insight." The swing slowed to a stop and a comfortable silence fell between them for a couple of seconds. "She'll want to talk to all three of you. Have you considered in what order that should happen?"

"I think youngest to oldest," Akna responded. "I want to talk to her last because if there is a problem, I don't want Hai or Nakia to be stuck with it."

"Good thinking." Mrs. Bohn looked at her watch. "Looks like five minutes until the scheduled call. Let's head in and round up your sisters."

Inside Mrs. Bohn took Akna and her sisters into Mr. and Mrs. Bohn's bedroom. She set a mobile phone on the desk in the corner. "This is the most private room in the house. Your mother will call this number. Akna, you can answer it and let her know the order of who's talking. I'll close the door and keep everyone out of the hall so no one can hear. It's up to you if you want to share any of your conversation with anyone else. Okay?"

All three girls nodded.

When Mrs. Bohn closed the door, Akna's breath suddenly felt trapped inside her throat. She closed her eyes and forced herself to let it out. Then she took another deep breath in and let it out.

"I don't know what to say," Hai said as she rocked back and forth on the edge of the Bohn's bed. "It's been so long. I don't know what to say."

"You can talk about what you're learning in school," Akna suggested.

"I'm going to tell her how much I love it here," Nakia said. "I'm going to tell her that I want to stay here from now on."

Akna blanched. "Um…maybe, instead, you can talk about your school, too. I don't think Mama is ready to hear about you wanting to stay here yet."

"Pero es la verdad," Nakia said.

"Yes, but there are many true things to talk about. It is true to talk about how much you enjoy school. It is true to talk about how you get along with your foster sisters or what you like doing here. But I think telling Mama you want to stay here and not be with her, would hurt her. You don't want to hurt her feelings, do you?"

Nakia pressed her lips together hard. Akna could hear the air moving through Nakia's nose.

Finally, Nakia said, "Okay. I will not say I want to stay here. But is still the truth."

"I understand," Akna said. "Thank you."

"I'm just going to stick to talking about school," Hai said. "And maybe talking about how nice everyone is."

"That sounds good," Akna said.

"What are you going to talk about?" Hai asked.

"Well, I—"

Ring. Ring. Ring.

Akna tapped on the phone and held it to her ear. "Hello, this is Akna."

Her mother greeted her in Spanish saying how happy she was to get to call them, and how everything was so wonderful for her right now. She said she couldn't wait to see them all again.

"That's great Mama," Akna finally said when Mama finally stopped for a moment. "I'm going to let you talk to Nakia first and then Hai, and then I'll catch up with you at the end. Okay?"

She handed the phone to Nakia, hoping she would stick to their bargain.

Nakia spoke in Spanish, telling Mama almost to the word what they had discussed in advance. Then she was silent for a long time, with only the occasional single response. No. No. and then a Si. "Adiós, aquí está Hai." Nakia handed the phone to Hai and then flopped backward on the bed and stared at the ceiling.

"Hola, Mama," Hai began.

Akna followed Hai's end of the conversation. It seemed perfunctory, without much emotion. Hai talked about school and how much she enjoyed living with the Bohns. She also talked about getting that sweater from Polly and about making bread with the whole family. Hai ended with, "Bueno. Voy a darle el teléfono a Akna ahora. Solo un minuto." She pressed the mute button and said, "Can Nakia and I leave now?

Akna nodded. "If that's what you want."

Hai handed the phone to Akna and she and Nakia scurried out the door, closing it a bit loudly behind them.

"Estoy de vuelta, Mama," she began.

"Nakia and Hai seem happy there," Mama said.

"Yes, we are all very comfortable. The Bohns have been very kind to us and the other foster kids are like sisters already."

"That's…um…good," Mama responded as if she wasn't sure she liked everything being so good. Did she expect us to be begging to get out of here? After a short silence, Mama said, "Mrs. Sleeper told me this was one of the best foster homes. I'm glad…I'm glad you are doing well."

"Yes, there is nothing for you to worry about with us. How are *you* doing, Mama?"

"It's not easy. I've missed a couple of the rehab steps since I left the facility. But my counselor got me back on the plan pretty quickly."

"That's good. Are you okay by yourself at home? Is there anything I can do to help?"

"No. No. Nothing you can do. I wish you were here and I miss you…of course, I miss you."

Akna said nothing in the ensuing silence.

"I…I don't know if this is really going to all work out in the end," Mama hedged. "It's very hard. It's the hardest thing I've ever done and…well…maybe it's for the best that you are happy there."

Akna's heart raced. What did that mean?

"You're not giving up, are you?" she asked. "Things are good here, but Mrs. Bohn is *not* our Mama. You are our Mama. You can't give up so early. Please, Mama. We want to come home. We love you. We really do."

Silence.

"Mama?"

"No…I'm not giving…up. It's just I need a…um…a…vacation. Yes. I need a vacation. But, if I take a vacation, then I will…I mean…they will…put me in jail. They will put me in jail because the six months isn't up. So, I can't do that. And it's just…it's…hard. You understand, right?"

"Yes," Akna whispered, though she didn't really understand. She didn't understand why it was so hard, why Mama couldn't choose her children over alcohol or drugs.

"I *am* trying," Mama said again. "You can't imagine how hard it is."

"I know it's hard," Akna said slowly. "When Tata was with us, he told me I could use my SAD powers to be strong and it always helped. Can you use your SAD powers to be strong, Mama?"

"Sad powers? I don't know what you're talking about."

"S.A.D. Strength and determination. Tata said I had lots of strength and determination and it was like a super power. He said you had those powers, too, but they were buried deep inside you. Did you forget how to use them?"

Mama sighed loudly. "Oh, Akna. Tata was good at telling stories, but that's all they were…just stories to make you feel better. There are no super powers that the Sales family has. If anything, our family is cursed. Tata's stories are fantasy. Pretend. I'm sorry to tell you this. But it's the truth. Life is pain. That is the way it has always been and will always be."

Akna swallowed hard. She would not cry. She would not let Mama sully her memory of Tata and all he told her. She would not let her take this one good thing away from her. Tata taught her life was filled with beauty. Even when things were very bad, she should seek out the beauty to remind her that it could become better; but she had to reach for it. While living with the Bohns and her foster sisters, she'd learned life does not always have to be painful.

Her mother hadn't spoken for a while.

Akna gathered her own SAD powers before speaking again. "It's not that I think I'm Supergirl or anything," she said. "But it does help to remind myself to use my strength and determination to get me through something that is hard. That is what I'm saying to you. Sometimes thinking of it as a super power helps me. It helps Hai and Nakia, too." She paused and braced for Mama denial again. But nothing came. "So, I'm saying that you have strength and determination, too, Mama. That is what you need to get through this hard time, so we can come home again."

Silence.

Akna waited, even though she wanted very badly to keep talking to force Mama to say she could do it. But she knew Mama had to want to do it. Mama had to believe she could do it.

"You are right, Akna," Mama finally said, her voice sounded tired. "That is what I need. I'm just…not sure…I have the strength to last the whole six months."

"But you will try, right?" Akna asked.

Silence.

"Yes…I will try," Mama said slowly, as if her voice was caught on barbed wire. "I'm happy for you, Akna. You are a good girl. You've always been a good girl."

"I love you, Mama. I know you can do this."

"Yo también te amo. Adiós, mi cielo."

The line went dead.

Akna stared at the phone. What just happened? Did Mama really agree or did she give up? After a few minutes, she got up and left the bedroom.

As she made her way down the hall, laughter drifted from the kitchen. She'd forgotten it was bread-making day. Everyone had their mixers and bowls, and all the things they would need in front of them. Someone had placed her things at an empty spot on the table. They'd already chosen their coins.

Polly held the bag for Akna when she entered the room. "I hope you get an interesting one," she said.

Akna placed her hand in the bag and fingered several coins. Settling on one toward the bottom, she pulled out the wooden coin. "Brioche," she read aloud. She hadn't made this before, but she had tasted it. It was golden, soft, and pillowy. The taste was sweet, a cross between a pastry and bread. It was the favorite kind of bread to use for French toast in the morning. But she loved it best with scrambled eggs and bacon and a slice of brioche bare. It was sweet and savory at the same time.

She threw herself into the rhythm of baking with all her sisters. It still amazed her how four simple ingredients: flour, water, yeast and a little salt could combine into a messy, sticky substance that had the potential to transform into something beautiful and tasty. This recipe also added six eggs, plenty of butter, and a little sugar.

To make a really good loaf of bread required practice. Akna had been fooled into thinking her first bread baking experience meant it was easy and they would all turn out well. Unlike the couranne, when several people helped her at every step, the past few weeks she was left to do it on her own. She'd made even bigger mistakes than accidentally throwing the dough across the table. Once she didn't pay attention to the recipe and but in too much salt. That loaf wasn't edible. Another time she was impatient with the rising process and put it in the oven too soon. Though it was edible, the loaf was too dense.

Today, she eagerly joined the rest of the family. Her wire whip tapped a rhythm on the sides of her stainless-steel mixing bowl as she mixed six eggs with water for a brioche. She then added it to the dry ingredients in the bowl on the stand mixer. Akna savored the aroma of warm, growing yeast while imagining the bubbles vying for a spot atop a mysterious world of growth and change. She asked Mrs. Bohn to check that the dough was the right consistency.

This dough was different, instead of the punch or slap of kneading, it needed a light touch in shaping before the first proof. Akna turned the dough out onto a floured work surface and shaped it with only her lightly-floured fingers folding it over and over until she'd shaped it into a smooth round ball. As she worked the dough, her mind went back to her mother.

She'd been holding herself back, always waiting for the next punch down or the slap of circumstances dictated by Mama's decisions. What was she waiting for? For Mama to...what? To be different? To be like Nana? Like Tata?

After Akna had molded the dough into a soft round ball, she turned it upside down and placed the ball into a clean large bowl, covering it with plastic wrap. Today, Akna was the last to get her dough ready for proofing. She placed her bowl in a warm spot in the kitchen, near the ovens that were already baking the non-yeast breads. The recipe said it would take between one and two hours for the dough to proof. It should *at least* double in size.

Then it would be put in the fridge overnight to slow the proofing. The low temperature would develop the flavor of the dough, giving it time to rest. When she took it out tomorrow, the dough would be easier to handle. She could choose how to divide it and shape it. She could divide it into three long rolls of dough and braid it. She could cut it into eight pieces and fold each piece into its own round ball and then put the balls into the loaf pan to look like a casual braid. Whatever she decided, it would have to be covered and given a chance to rise again in the pan.

In the end, she had to trust that all the ingredients, the work of her hands and fingers, and the magic of the yeast and the baking would result in a beautiful brioche. There was no certainty it would turn out the way she hoped. She could not force the exact transformation she desired. She could only put in the best ingredients she had today, mix them and let them intermingle. Patience and a little time before baking would produce the best she could manage at this moment, with the knowledge available to her.

Perhaps she could learn something from Hai and Nakia. Instead of worrying and questioning and making exact plans that boxed her into a pan that was too small, she could allow herself to live in a slightly larger pan. What is the worst that could happen? Perhaps she would rise too much? She doubted that. She wasn't going to lift all the restrictions she put on herself. Perhaps her flavors wouldn't develop as robustly as she wanted? But then, like her bread, she could tweak the recipe.

CHAPTER FOURTEEN

RIGHTY TIGHTY, LEFTY LOOSEY

*A*kna stood at the calendar above her small desk and marked a big red X over yesterday. She'd marked off each day since they got here. Three months gone and three months to go before Mama came to get them and they would go home.

If she came to get them. Mama hadn't called again since that first conversation a month ago.

She knew Mama loved her and Hai and Nakia. But over the past three months she'd come to half-way accept that Mama might not be taking them home when she finished rehab.

The more she talked with Gianna, the more she learned that addictions were really hard to overcome and that it usually involved a lot of people for a long time. People like doctors and nurses and therapists. Gianna also said that it was very hard work and that backsliding was the norm. That meant that the person got tired of trying or stopped believing they could get well and then went back to drugs.

It sounded a lot like what happened to Mama when Akna lived with her.

Tata always said that SAD powers ran in the family, but sometimes those powers weren't as strong. When you didn't use them, they went into hiding. Then the only way to get them back was with a SAD wizard.

When they lived in Guatemala, they had this type of wizard in their community. They were called healers. And they had ceremonies to expel the demons that were stopping the powers from working. But in America they didn't have that. Also, neighbors didn't always become friends or supporters. The concept of community was very different.

In Guatemala, when someone lost their powers, they might go to a special friend or someone they trusted who understood how to activate SAD powers. But in America people went to a therapist.

A therapist was like a detective. They worked with you to tear back the layers to get to the powers still inside you, to help free them again. One time she'd asked Mama to make an appointment with one of these therapist wizards; but Mama said in America therapists didn't understand. She said Nana was her therapist.

But when Nana died, who did Mama have to help her find her powers?

Gianna flopped onto Akna's bed. "Another day marked off?"

Akna nodded.

"Well, after breakfast, today is your tire initiation day."

"What's that? I'm not tired."

"Not tired. Tire. T. I. R. E. like the tire on a car."

Akna raised her brows. Gianna must be pulling her leg. There was no such thing as tire initiation and she was much too young to drive a car or worry about tires.

Gianna jumped from the bed and pulled at Akna's arm. "Come on, you'll see. It's fun. Kind of."

After breakfast the whole family gathered in the driveway. Mr. Bohn was kneeling in front of the minivan. "How did this tire get flat?" he said loudly.

Everyone laughed except Akna, Hai, and Nakia.

"Did you poke a hole in it?" he asked, pointing to Akna.

"No. Of course not."

He turned to Mrs. Bohn. "Did you run over something in the grocery store parking lot that was sharp?"

"I don't think so, Virgil. Stop playing around and scaring the girls."

"Who's going to change this tire?" he asked. "Someone has to change this tire and I'm too tired to do it."

Everyone giggled, and then Sandra, Polly, and Gianna said, "Akna. Akna. Akna. Akna will change the tire."

Akna looked at each of them and shook her head. What was this? Some kind of crazy initiation?

Again, the girls repeated, "Akna. Akna. Akna. Akna will change the tire."

"Come on, Akna," Mr. Bohn gestured for her to come stand next to him.

"But I don't know anything about changing tires," she said.

"Then it's time you learned. What if you were in the car with Mama Bohn and the tire suddenly got a flat. Would you want her to be down on the ground trying to do this herself?"

"Well, no, but…"

"So, you need to learn how to help her."

"Couldn't you just call triple A or someone like that?"

"What if you were out in the middle of nowhere and triple A couldn't come?" Sandra said.

"What if you were in the snow and it would take five hours before they could come?" Polly said.

"What if you didn't have a phone with you to call?" Gianna said.

"Okay, okay. I get it." Akna knew there was no getting out of this.

Gianna continued, "Papa Bohn says there is no excuse for anyone, especially a girl, not to be able to change her own tire. You don't want to rely on a stranger happening by. Someone who might not have your best interests in their heart."

"Or worse," Sandra added. "Your ex-boyfriend who would really rub it in."

Akna ran her tongue around her lips, and stiffened her spine. "Let's go then."

"Do you know what these two things are?" Mr. Bohn asked

Akna pointed at the first one. "That's a jack. I've seen Tata use that on our car at home when he changed the oil." She pointed to something that was at a right angle with a hole at each end. "That's to hit someone over the head if they bother you."

"You go girl," Gianna said while everyone laughed except Mr. Bohn.

"Maybe," Mr. Bohn said. "If they are going to hurt you. But only then. That's a lug wrench. It helps remove these bolts that hold the tire to the axel." He pointed to the five bolts on the inside of the tire. "Is there anything missing?"

Akna shrugged. She didn't know all the tools you needed to change a tire.

"What are you going to put on here when you get this flat tire off?" he asked.

Akna blushed. "A tire. But where is it?"

"Good question," Mr. Bohn said. "In this car it's hidden underneath. Can you get down on your knees and look under there?"

Akna bent to the ground and scanned beneath the car in the direction he was pointing. "I see it, but I can't crawl under there and get it. Should I jack it up?"

"No. You should never use the jack to put the car up and then crawl under it. These jacks can collapse and you don't want to be under it if that happens."

Akna dusted off her jeans as she stood. "I don't want to be smashed. But Tata used to jack up our car to change the oil and he would get underneath."

"Perhaps he used a better jack than this one," Mr. Bohn suggested. "Now follow me to the back and I'll show you how to get that tire out."

Akna was surprised at all the other tools. He taught her to put together these three pieces to make a long stick with a square on the end and then put another thing across the top for turning. Then they went inside the car and had to open the console and another part and another part and then put the stick in there and turn it to drop the tire.

"What if I forget all this?" she asked.

"Whoever is driving this car will know all this part. Before you get your license, you will know all this part. But today what's most important is just changing the tire."

After following every instruction, including pulling the tire out from beneath the car with that same funny tool, they were finally ready to actually change the tire.

"Now, what do you think happens next?" Mr. Bohn asked.

"We jack up the car."

"No," everyone else answered together.

She could tell this really was a thing everyone went through. Evidently, everyone made the same mistakes too.

"You take off the tire?"

"You're close," Mr. Bohn said. "You want to loosen those lug nuts while the tire is on the ground. If you jack it up first it is really hard to loosen them because the tire will try to spin when you try to turn the wrench."

She put the three parts of the wrench together as he instructed and then put one end on the nut at the top. She pulled hard toward her and it didn't budge.

"Righty tighty, lefty loosey," Mr. Bohn said as he knelt next to her. He put his hand on a bolt and made a motion to the right with his hand. "If you turn to the right, it makes things tighter." Then he motioned with his hand to the left. "If you turn to the left, it makes it looser. This is the case with all things that screw into something— tires, wood, metal, all kinds of screws."

Akna stood over the lug wrench and used all her strength to push to the left this time. It still didn't budge. "I can't do it. I'm not strong enough."

"Yes, you can," Mr. Bohn said. "Sandra, Gianna, and Polly have all done this and they aren't any stronger than you."

Akna tried again and it still didn't dislodge. She sat on the ground and reached up and used all of her weight to pull it down and it moved a little! She tried it again and it revolved almost a quarter turn. Now she was able to loosen the whole thing.

"Whoa," Mr. Bohn said. "Don't take it completely off yet. Leave it on enough so the tire doesn't fall off."

"Okay."

She did the same thing with the second bolt on top. When she got to the ones on the bottom she couldn't use her weight to hang from the bolt and get it started, so she kicked at the wrench and that loosened it. Finally, all four bolts were loosened.

"Good job," Mr. Bohn said. "You are a quick thinker and problem solver. Now let's jack up the car just a little bit."

He had her get down on her knees again and look under the car as he pointed to a ridge where the jack had to be placed. "You want to place it there because that piece of metal is very strong. It's like a brace under the car and when the jack goes it will lift easier."

It took a couple of tries for her to get the jack in the right place. Then it took lots of turns to get it to start lifting. But once it did, she was surprised she could do it herself. She was lifting a car all by herself!

"Just a few inches," Mr. Bohn said.

When the tire was barely off the ground, Akna said, "I don't have a ruler. How high?"

"You can use your hand," he said. "If you can put your hand on the side and put it under the tire that is high enough."

A couple more cranks and Akna was able to get her hand, standing on edge, under the tire.

"Now I can take it off?" she asked.

"Take the bolts off and put them to one side. Then lift off the tire. But be careful. It's heavy."

She did as he instructed, slowly pulling the tire toward her until it fell to the ground and leaned against the empty wheel.

"Good job. Do you see now why we didn't want the tire high in the air?"

Akna nodded. "It would have been heavier and had a longer way to fall."

"Right. Now let's put the spare tire on."

Akna reversed everything she had just done. She lifted the spare onto the bolts and tightened them as much as she could with her fingers. Then she put the jack down so the tire was on the ground. Finally, she used the lug wrench to tighten the nuts. Righty tighty, she told herself. This time using her weight to tighten in the other direction.

When she was done, she stood with a big smile on her face.

"Let me check," Mr. Bohn said. He gave a small tug on the lug wrench for each nut. "Just right!" Then he gave her a big hug. "Congratulations! You pass."

Everyone gave her high fives all around. Mrs. Bohn told her she was so happy to know that if she ever got stuck with Akna and a flat tire, Akna could help and she wouldn't have to be crawling around on the ground.

Hai and Nakia said they wanted to learn too. Mr. Bohn said he would teach them, too, eventually.

Akna doubted she'd ever really have to change a tire, but she felt good knowing she could. She could count on herself instead of waiting for someone to stop and help. Sandra told her it was a requirement before being allowed to drive the car and get her license.

Later that night, as she studied the ceiling above her bed trying to get to sleep, she was still thinking about that accomplishment. For the first time she tried to imagine what it would feel like if she still lived in this house five years from now. What it would feel like to get her driver's license and be allowed to drive herself places.

She waited for the fear to take hold at the thought of still being here, but it didn't. She waited for the sadness to come, but it wasn't as bad as before. She would miss her Mama but if she left she would miss everyone here. Sometimes she really didn't want to go home. At least not home to how it was before.

If she didn't miss her Mama as much anymore, did that make her a bad person? What if her Mama gave her a choice of where to live? What would she choose?

CHAPTER FIFTEEN

THE UNFURLING

*A*kna and Jorge peeked between the curtains at the crowd assembled in the high school auditorium. They'd only practiced there a couple times. It was massive compared to the cafeteria at Margarita Elementary. It could seat six hundred and twenty people and Mrs. Cosgrave said it would be full for the show. It was a real auditorium with seats that rose like at the movie theater. It even had a balcony.

"It's packed," Jorge said. "Do you see anyone you know?"

Akna scanned everything to look for the Bohns, Sandra, Polly, and Gianna. But she couldn't find them in the seats. "Do you see your parents?" Akna asked.

"No, but they wouldn't sit at the front," Jorge said. "They tend to sit at the back. They are probably in the balcony. How about you?"

"They are probably in the middle somewhere," she said. "It's hard getting five seats together."

Jessa strode toward them. "Make way," she said in lower register. Then she mimicked playing the piano. "What do ya think?"

She wore a blue and white suit and a very long, oversized white wig with big rolled pieces of spray-painted paper to look like hair trailing down on her back and in a long train behind her. She was going to play Beethoven in the final choir piece. They picked her because she was the tallest person in school.

"Oscar material?" she asked as she twisted from side-to-side.

"Oscar something," Jorge said.

"You look good," Akna said. "It's going to crack everyone up."

The program was for all kids who participated in Music, which was pretty much everyone. It wasn't just the choir classes, but every grade had music they learned. In fourth and fifth grade you could pick band, orchestra, or choir.

The show would go back and forth between choirs and instrumentalists. Each grade got to pick what they were going to do for their one song, and there was a finale song that everyone would participate in where Jessa would be Beethoven.

"No peeking," Mrs. Cosgrave said from behind them. "You'll find your parents quick enough after the show. It's time to line up the kindergartners and first graders. Jessa, you get off stage too before someone trips over that thing." She gave them a nudge away from the curtain.

Akna and Jorge got in line with their class in the wings.

Nakia walked on stage with the kindergarten and first grade classes. She turned and waved to Akna in the wings. Akna gave her two thumbs up.

The curtains opened and the lights came up, blinding them from seeing the audience at all. But Akna heard the applause. It was louder than she expected and she bounced back and forth between pride and sheer terror that she'd mess up when their song came.

Mrs. Cosgrave queued Mr. Sanderson at the piano and the first group sang *I Am Here*. It was a morning song used in the kindergarten and first grade classes but it was fun because you got to clap your hands, stomp your feet, and walk like a chicken. Even though it was silly, Akna loved singing it and often did at home with Nakia.

Hai sang with all the third graders. They'd chosen *The Bull Frog* song because they liked all the silly words like *sing song polly wolly won't you kai mee o*.

Finally, the fifth graders got to sing. They'd voted between three songs and chose *Hall of Fame*. It was a good song for leaving Margarita Elementary school and going to middle school next year. It talked about not letting fear get to you and keep going. No matter what you choose to be, be your best and you could be in the hall of fame. Akna loved the line, *do it for your people do it for your pride. How you ever gonna know if you never even try?* Maybe Will. I. Am had SAD powers too when he wrote that song.

She sang with all her heart and it felt soooo good. Whenever she sang this song it gave her courage that no matter what happened, she could get through it. She still didn't know if she was going to be going home or staying here and going to Serrano middle school in the fall.

Then all the children from all the grades came back on the stage for *Beethoven's Wig*. It was a funny song with silly lines. But it sounded serious because they sang to the melody of Beethoven's 5th Symphony. The younger kids mostly sang *Beethoven's Wig is big. It's very big*. It happened many times during the song. The fourth and fifth graders sang the rest of the lyrics. Jessa did a great job parading across the stage with her very long wig and the audience laughed a lot.

When it ended the audience stood up and applauded. Some whistled. Akna's entire body buzzed with confidence and excitement. It was amazing! Akna had never been in anything like this—all the music, all the attention, everyone feeling happy.

She hugged Jorge before going to look for her sisters. "I'm so glad you suggested music as my elective. See you next week."

She found Nakia first because the younger kids were kept in one place by the teachers so they wouldn't get lost. Then a familiar voice yelled, "Akna over here," and she spotted Gianna jumping up and down and waving. Hai was already with them.

Soon her family was all crowded around and talking about what a great job everyone did and how fun the songs were. Polly suggested they should have a family music group so they could sing all summer and maybe put on their own show.

"Jorge!" Hai waved at him just a few feet away. "Come meet our family."

Akna turned quickly. She saw Jorge with a middle-aged man and woman. They were smiling but looked very uncomfortable. She wasn't sure what to do. Would they want to meet?

"Hey everyone," she said. "I want you to meet my best friend at school. The one who talked me into music class." She started walking in Jorge's direction and everyone followed. Soon they were face-to-face with Jorge and his parents.

Akna stuck out a hand and the woman took it and shook. "Hi, I'm Akna. Jorge was the one who talked me into music and he's been really nice to me and my sisters." She put an arm around each sister. "I wanted to meet you because Jorge is so talented. Wasn't his solo great in Beethoven's Wig?"

"We are very proud of him," she said with a heavy accent.

Then Mrs. Bohn introduced herself and said, "We are having a celebration at our house for the girls. We'd love to have you and Jorge come if you have time. It's just a light meal. We'll be talking about all the lovely music we heard today."

Jorge's parents stiffened. "I don't know," his mother started. "We have nothing to bring. Jorge if you want to go without us that's fine."

"Please, Mrs. Rodrigues," Akna said. "I know we are kind of a big family but we aren't scary."

"Only a little scary," Gianna added. "But we don't bite. We never bite."

Sandra grabbed Gianna's shirt and pulled her away. "Don't listen to her. She clowns around a lot."

"If you have the time," Mrs. Bohn said. "Jorge has been such a good friend to Akna, making her transition to live here so much easier. As they will be graduating in a month, and people may disappear for the summer, it would be great to get to know the parents who have raised such a fine young man."

"We will come," Jorge's father said. "Please write down the address."

As they drove home, Akna basked in what a wonderful day this had been. Maybe the most perfect day ever.

When Jorge and his parents arrived, Akna took Jorge by the hand and rushed him through the buffet of salads and baked chicken, mashed potatoes and fresh fruit. She gestured him out into the backyard. "Let's give the adults time to chat while we disappear."

"Okay," he followed her out the door.

"Isn't this beautiful?" she asked as he followed her toward a very large glider swing.

She sat on one side and he sat across. There was plenty of room for four more people the swing was so big.

"I've never seen such a big one of these," Jorge said. "I've only seen ones on a porch like for two people. And I've only seen that on a TV show."

"Mr. Bohn built it. He used to be a carpenter. In fact, he built the second story to the house. That's where our bedrooms are. All of us girls sleep up there," Akna said.

"Wow, all of you in one room. I don't know if I'd like that. I'm used to being alone in my room."

"It's not too bad. At least I have my own bed. Back home I shared a bed with Hai and Nakia."

"You always talk about back home," Jorge said. "Do you think you'll ever consider this home?"

Akna pursed her lips and looked down. "I do think of this as home. I mean the Bohns are good parents and I've had a pretty good time here."

"And your foster sisters seem to really support you. They were all over you after the show."

Akna smiled. "Yeah, they're good pretend sisters to have."

"I'd love to have a sister or brother," Jorge said. "You know, someone to talk to who's not your parents."

Akna nodded. "Yeah, that's nice."

An uncomfortable silence fell between them for a bit.

"Do you have plans for the summer?" Akna asked.

"I don't know. Usually, I try to make some money like mowing lawns or pulling weeds or something like that. Though it's getting harder with all the laws about child work and stuff. Rich people who make the laws don't understand that kids need money too. It's not like

I can ask my parents for new shoes or maybe a phone or something. They can't afford that. So, I have to make money."

Akna never thought about that. Probably because she knew she wasn't old enough to work. But if she'd stayed home and had to take care of Hai and Nakia without Mama, she may have had to find work —lie about her age to get it.

"I'd ask the Bohns but I already know the answer. All of us pitch in on the yard work."

"Was the rose garden here when you came?" He gestured to the other side of the yard where there were at least thirty roses planted.

"Yeah, cool isn't it? Mrs. Bohn loves roses. I think Mr. Bohn planted them all, but she is the one who tends them. Wanna see closer?"

"Sure." He put his plate down on the seat.

Akna led him up and down the rows as they smelled each one. "This is my favorite." She pointed to a deep orange rose with a red lining on the edges of the petals. "It's called Independence."

He smelled. "It doesn't have as strong a smell as some of the others." He ambled down a few rows, smelling each one. Then stopped at a deep red one. "This one smells the most like rose."

"Mrs. Bohn says the red and pink ones are the most fragrant. I guess because they've been around forever. They haven't been crossed or mated, or whatever you call it to make a new rose."

Jorge chuckled. "I don't think roses mate."

"I know. You know what I mean. Hybrid something."

The rest of the girls appeared in the yard.

Nakia started chanting, "Akna and Jorge sitting in the tree K-I-S-S-I-N-G! First comes love. Then comes marriage. Then comes baby in the baby carriage, sucking his thumb, wetting his pants, doing the hula, hula dance!"

Jorge snorted.

Akna shouted, "We're not in a tree and we're not kissing." One thing about kindergarten was that Nakia had learned lots of taunts.

"Akna and Jorge sitting in the garden" Nakia started again. "They liked each other until he…" She paused. "Oh, I know. Farted." Then she cracked up and ran in circles.

Akna couldn't help but laugh this time.

"Pretty clever," Jorge said.

"I think she's turning into a boy," Akna suggested. "I thought only boys made fart jokes."

Polly appeared at the edge of the rose garden. "I think your parents are ready to leave, Jorge."

"Oh. Okay." He started back toward the swing. "I better clean up my plate."

"I think Gianna already got both of them and took them in."

Jorge awkwardly shook Akna's hand. "Well thanks. It was fun."

She threw her arms around him and hugged him tight. "Thanks. You're like the best brother a girl could ever ask for."

He beamed back at her. "Maybe I could be like a brother from another mother. Wait, that doesn't sound right."

"You could be my heart brother," Akna offered. "Mrs. Bohn says all of us fosters are like heart sisters. We care for each other like sisters even though we aren't biologically related."

"I like that," he said.

"Jorge," Mr. Rodrigues' voice called into the yard before he stepped through door. "We're leaving. Get your things."

Jorge gave Akna a quick hug. "Thank's, heart sister." Then he turned and ran toward his father.

Everyone gathered in the driveway to wave goodbye to the Rodrigues family.

"That is a nice family," Mrs. Bohn said.

"You think so?"

"I know so."

Akna wondered what Mrs. Bohn would say if she knew Jorge was gay and his parents didn't like it or want to talk about it? Would she still think they were nice? She wasn't going to bring it up now, not with so many other ears around.

CHAPTER SIXTEEN

LANGUAGE ARTS

Today was presentation day. Akna sat at her desk and kept pushing at the back of her seat. It bent just enough that her whole torso could move back and forth. She didn't want to make any noise, but she couldn't sit still. She'd have to sit through all of Katrina's presentation and then it would be her turn.

"Katrina, are you ready to share your presentation with the class?" Mr. Serna asked.

"Yes," she said and she came to the front of the room with an instrument case. "Hi, I'm Katrina but I go by Kat."

"We know that," a boy in the back of the class said and everyone laughed.

"Right. But you may not know I play the clarinet."

"I do. I'm in band with you," another person said.

Akna felt bad for her. She wished people wouldn't say anything until the end of the presentation. But Kat seemed fine with it.

Kat opened her case and showed it to the class. It didn't look like a clarinet because it was all taken apart. But the block wood was pretty and the shiny silver parts caught the light just right.

"It comes with five separate pieces," Kat said. "You have to put them together each time before you play and then take them apart and clean them after you play."

No one said anything this time.

Kat explained what each part was and how to put it together as she assembled it. You start from the bottom, the bell, and work your way up. When she got to the reed part and explained why you had to lick it a few people said. "Yuck." But Kat just laughed. Once it was all together, she played a couple of scales and tuned it. Then she played the *Happy Birthday* song. It sounded really good.

"Anyone can play that," the same boy from the back said.

"Why don't you come up and show us," Mr. Serna suggested.

"Ooooo. She already put her spit on it."

"Good point. Then just tell me the notes she was playing," Mr. Serna said.

"The Happy Birthday notes."

"Come on Don, you don't know how to play the clarinet," another boy shouted. "Just shut up and let Kat speak."

After that, Don didn't interrupt anymore. Akna looked at the boy who had spoken up. It wasn't someone she really knew, but she was definitely going to thank him after class for speaking up.

"Perhaps you can play something a little more difficult," Mr. Serna suggested.

"A popular song," one of the girls said.

Kat smiled. "I know *Love Yourself* by Justin Bieber."

A number of people seemed impressed by that. Then she played it and Akna recognized the melody. She was good. She didn't think that in two years anyone could learn to play a popular song.

Everyone clapped.

Kat bowed and began to disassemble her clarinet, but she still had lots of time left in her presentation. She talked about why she chose to learn an instrument, even though music was not a regular part of her family. They didn't sing around the house. Her parents and her brother didn't play any instruments. In fact, they didn't even listen to music on the radio in the car when they traveled. But in fourth grade, when the school brought in an orchestra to perform *Peter and the Wolf*,

Kat fell in love with the sound of the clarinet because it portrayed the sneaky cat in the story. When she heard it, she believed it because she could see her pet cat acting like that.

Kat convinced her parents to let her be in the Margarita School band program. The school provided band and orchestra instruments for free to any child who wanted to participate. The only requirement was that they could stay after school for an hour of practice together, and that they would practice at home. Kat explained how when the band started in fourth grade, the whole band sounded really horrible. She was no exception. When she practiced at home she squeaked out the high notes so many times that her mother threatened to make her stop. So she started practicing in her closet where the clothes would dampen the sound. She also practiced when her mom went to the grocery store.

After a couple of months, she got better and stopped squeaking so much. She said the clarinet was very good at playing sneaky characters in music. That made everyone laugh. She ended her presentation saying she was going to learn how to play cats, and clowns, and maybe in middle school she would learn how to play witches and scare everyone trick or treating on Halloween.

Mr. Serna gave everyone a five-minute break, so that Akna could set up her PowerPoint presentation. Mr. Serna pulled down the screen at the front of the classroom and made sure she knew how to use the remote to move the slides forward or backward. She was so busy getting ready that she didn't have time to get nervous except for the minute Mr. Serna instructed everyone to sit down.

"Your turn, Akna," he said.

Akna took a deep breath and smiled. She was prepared. She'd practiced this in front of her family last night and they all assured her it was a great presentation.

"Nub'i'Akna," She began. "That means, my name is Akna in K'iche'. How many of you speak K'iche'?" she asked.

No one raised their hand.

"Yo también hablo español. ¿Cuántos de ustedes hablan español?"

Eight people in the class raised their hand.

"Hablo español, pero nunca había oído hablar de K'iche' antes de que me hablaras de tu Proyecto," Mr. Serna said.

Akna smiled at him. She silently thanked him for participating.

"For those who don't speak Spanish, do you know what Mr. Serna said?"

One girl raised her hand. "Kind of. I know he said he speaks Spanish. Obviously." She rolled her eyes. "But after that the only thing I recognized was the word key-chay because you already said that and I think proyecto might mean project."

"That's pretty good," Akna said. "The last part Mr. Serna said was that he'd never heard of K'iche' before I told him about my project. For those who don't speak Spanish, tell me if you felt left out knowing that several people in the classroom understood exactly what was said but you didn't."

Several people nodded their head.

Let me say a few K'iche' phrases and see if you can guess any of it.

"Saqarik! La utz awach." She looked around the room. "Any guesses?" Everyone shook their head, including Mr. Serna. "It means, good morning. How are you?"

"It doesn't sound like any language I've ever heard," said a girl in the front row.

"Let's try this," Akna suggested. "It's only one word. Maltyox."

"Is it like Maalox," a boy asked. "My dad takes that for his stomach."

A few people laughed.

"No. Maltyox means thank you or thanks. It's nothing like gracias is it?"

Everyone shook their head.

"The language is very different from most languages spoken today. The closest in sound would probably be some of the languages of Native Americans. But they are not the same."

Akna checked for boredom. No one was fidgeting yet. "Even if you don't speak Spanish, when you live in a community where you hear it all the time, you pick up words or phrases. But what if the language you learned growing up was never spoken where you lived? What if that language was dangerous to speak? So dangerous it could get you killed?"

It seemed that the entire class leaned forward, their eyes wide.

"K'iche' is a language that has been around for thousands of years. It is the language of many of the native people of Guatemala, where mi abuelos y mi madre, my grandparents and my mother came from. K'iche' is one of many languages of the Maya. It is the most prevalent language, spoken by nearly two million people today."

Akna pressed a button and her first chart showed on the screen. "Unfortunately, the Maya and their languages, including K'iche' have been under attack for hundreds of years. First, the Spanish came and conquered Mexico and then moved into central America. The K'iche' fought back, some for many generations. But a combination of disease and technology overtook them.

K'iche' were considered less than human and they were forced into slavery to work the plantations of the conquerors. According to the Encyclopedia Britannica, it is estimated that in 1520 there were more than nine hundred thousand K'iche. That population declined to probably fewer than one hundred thousand over the next one hundred and fifty years.

"The K'iche were also forced to speak the language of the conquerors and to abandon their spiritual beliefs and accept Catholicism. Though they are not physically enslaved today, most K'iche' are still very poor and there have been many dictators and military groups who continue to kill them or make them work for nothing."

Akna pressed a button again to show the next slide. It was a picture of the highlands of Guatemala. She imagined that was near where Tata and Nana and Mama used to live. "This is where my family is from. I don't have pictures of them, but my grandfather told me they lived in a small adobe home, roofed with corrugated aluminum. They were fortunate to have two rooms. Many K'iche' only had one big room. In my grandparents' house they had a small bedroom barely large enough to fit a double bed. The other room was large with a hearth for the fire. It was where they ate and the children slept. My grandfather built a table and stools for eating, a wooden chest for clothes and valuables, and a cabinet that sat on the floor for dishes and utensils.

"The children—my mother and two brothers—slept on petates. Those are reed mats placed on the floor. The mats were rolled up when not in use. They did not have running water in their home. Every day they would go to get water from the community pump and put it in a large ceramic water jug. They also had other ceramic storage jars for dried food and spices. They did have some electricity for a refrigerator. "

"How old are your grandparents," someone asked. "They must be over a hundred because nobody here lives without water in their house."

"Is that true?" Mr. Serna asked the class. "Do you think no one in America lives like this?"

The girl at the front raised her hand and Mr. Serna called on her.

"I've seen pictures of poor places like that on some Native American reservations."

Another girl said, "Homeless people live in tents and they don't have any of those things."

"None of those count," the boy said. "I mean people like us."

"Do you think I am like you?" Akna asked.

"Sure. I guess," the boy answered.

"But I am telling you the truth about my grandparents. They left Guatemala in 1980. That wasn't very long ago. And that was how they were living."

"Oh." The boy wiggled in his seat. "I guess I didn't know."

Akna showed the next slide. It had a picture of people on a raft crossing the river. "K'iche' people have come to America at different times because there have been so many times when they were being killed for no reason other than being K'iche' or suspected of being the enemy. My grandparents came in 1980. This was during a time now called the genocide of the K'iche'. Some people call it a civil war, but the K'iche' were the ones hurt the most. Many people saw their families murdered by the military and other bad things. That is why my grandparents left. My grandfather saw his son killed by soldiers.

"Refugees walked for hundreds of miles to get to America. When they got to the border with Mexico they were met with resistance from the Mexican government. Many people had to pay for rafts like these." She pointed to the picture on the screen. "They paid coyotes—those are people who take money from immigrants to get them across the river between Mexico and Guatemala. There was a bridge, but it was closed."

She clicked to the next slide which showed people crowded together in a refugee camp in Nogales.

"Even if they got across the river there was still no guarantee they could come to America. Many K'iche waited years in refugee camps. I know my grandparents came through Nogales. I don't know exactly how long they were there before they could cross to America. Once they got across I don't know how long it took to come to Oregon. It is something they don't talk about, except to say the trip was horrible. They all became American citizens. My grandfather worked at a vineyard in Yamhill county. My grandparents died two years ago, so I can't ask them about their journey. But I'm glad they made it."

She clicked to the next slide. It showed the picture she had brought from home to Mariposa Lane—the picture of her grandparents, her mother, and Akna with her sisters. "This was taken two years ago at a church where I used to live. Before my grandfather died, he asked me to always speak K'iche' and Spanish and English. He asked me to tell the story of our people so that it would never be forgotten. Now I have told you and I hope you will remember it. The K'iche' are a strong people to survive so much sorrow. I am proud to be K'iche' and American."

Akna clicked to the last slide. It was titled the Declaration of Human Rights. "To understand the K'iche' of today, you must understand the K'iche' of the past. I will say this declaration of human rights in K'iche' first. Nab'e taqanik 1. Konojel ri winaq are taq ke'alaxik pa junaman ya'tal chkech kakechab'ej ronojel ri utzil; utz kakib'ano, kakichomaj, kakib'ij jasa je' ri k'o pa kanima, rumal che ri junam kib'antajik. Rajawaxik xuqe' kakimulij kib' che utzukuxuk ri loq'ob'al pa we uwachulew.

"As you see written on the slide it says: Article 1. All human beings are born free and equal in dignity and rights. They are endowed with reason and conscience and should act toward one another in a spirit of brotherhood."

She turned to face the class. "I believe this with all my heart. I wish that all people would believe this, too, and then act on it." Then she bowed with her hands pressed together in front of her and said, "Utzil. Maltyox. Peace. Thank you."

Everyone clapped and the bell rang.

"That was a wonderful presentation," Mr. Serna said as Akna turned to leave. "I learned a great deal."

"Thank you. It meant a lot to me. More than you'll ever know."

Don, the boy from the back of the classroom met Akna at the door. "That was dope," he said. "A lot of stuff I'd never heard of."

"Uh…thanks."

"How do you say see ya later in key-chay?"

"I'm not sure exactly," Akna said. "There's lots of different good-byes. It depends on what you really mean, like Ch'abej chik means goodbye, we will talk again. Chue'q chik also means goodbye, but more like another tomorrow or I'll see you tomorrow. Then there is matzaqik which also means goodbye but don't fall down."

"Goodbye, don't fall down? That's crazy."

"It's more like stay well, don't get hurt," Akna said. "The one my grandfather said the most was Ch'abej chik, we will talk again."

"Cha-bidge-a-cheek?" Don asked

Akna chuckled. "Close enough."

"Cha-bidge-a-cheek," Don said again then strode down the hall in the opposite direction to where she was heading.

"Hey, Akna." Kat grabbed her arm. "I loved your talk. I'd love to learn key-chay. Maybe you could start a club and teach us. I bet a lot of people would like to learn a language they've never heard of before. It would be something our parents would never figure out."

"I don't know if I could teach enough of it with only one month of classes left," Akna hedged.

Kat scrunched her mouth to one side, then said "Yeah, that's true.

It's almost time for graduation. Think about it for Serrano next year. They have a lot more clubs. It would be super lit, ya know."

Akna smiled. Maybe, if she was still living here in the fall, she would look into that. It would be great to have other people learning K'iche'. Maybe she could even find an official class online somewhere and she could learn even more herself.

Kat held her closed hand up for a fist bump. Akna bumped her fist and Kat said, "Think about it. Really." Then she headed toward the lockers with her clarinet case, her hand waving goodbye over her shoulder.

CHAPTER SEVENTEEN

GRADUATION

Akna stood for every picture Mrs. Bohn wanted to take. First it was in the living room in front of the fireplace. Then it was one foot on the stairs. They went outside in the garden and she stood among the roses, then under the large oak tree. She turned this way and that. A full smile, then a half smile, then not smiling.

She fingered the simple cotton dress they'd bought for her. At first, she didn't think she'd want a dress. Ninety-nine percent of the time she wore pants or shorts everywhere. But when she saw this one in the store, she loved it immediately.

The background teal was the color of peacock feathers and some butterfly wings she'd seen among the roses. The patterns of greens, blues, greys and orange mandalas reminded her of symbols Tata had shared with her from his home in Guatemala. Mrs. Bohn explained that many people think of these symbols as meditation wheels or prayer wheels.

The cap sleeves were just right. She didn't like sleeveless tops because they exposed too much skin. But she didn't like anything binding her arms either. The best part about the dress was that it had pockets. She always needed a place to put her hands or to hold something she might need to carry with her like a notepad or a hankie. She never had a purse. That seemed way too girly-girl and she was likely to leave it somewhere and forget it.

"Last one," Mrs. Bohn said. "I don't want us to be late." Then she tapped the phone again.

Hai and Nakia ran forward and gave her a big hug.

"You look so pretty," Hai said. "I can't wait until I get to graduate and go to middle school, too."

"Everyone in the car," Mr. Bohn called up the stairs.

Sandra, Polly, and Gianna practically chased each other down the stairs. Sandra was dressed like she was going to church. The other two girls looked normal—Polly in jeans, tennis shoes, and t-shirt knotted in the front and Gianna in her usual black pants, boots, and a black t-shirt covered by a black jean jacket.

"Like your hair," Akna said to Gianna. "The braid down the back is cool."

"Exactly," Gianna responded then tossed her head side to side to swing the braid wildly. "Like a horse's tail, it will keep the flies off me."

Akna bit off a chuckle. "I won't stand behind you then."

Gianna swatted her arm.

"Let's get moving," Mr. Bohn said again. "You can tease each other in the car."

Within two minutes everyone was strapped into the seats and they were heading to the high school auditorium again. The high school was the only place in town for events. All important events for more than a couple hundred people were there—theater, music, dancing, and graduations for every elementary school, the middle school, and the high school.

Starting the second week in June, every Saturday was booked. Sometimes, like today, they did three fifth grade graduations back-to-back. Margarita School was at 10am. Then Garfield at 1pm, and finally Mountain View was at 4pm. Akna was glad hers was first, then she could relax the rest of the day.

"See you later," Mrs. Bohn said, giving Akna a quick hug. "Look for us to be seated closer to the front this time."

Akna was sure they'd get in the front. They were almost forty-five minutes early.

She took her time walking to the stage door on the other side of the building.

"Hey," Jorge said. He was standing next to the door. "I like your dress. I've never seen you in a dress before."

Akna felt her cheeks warm. "It's a special occasion. I mean we're celebrating, right?"

"Right," he agreed. "Anyway, you look good, not too fancy and not too casual."

"Thanks. You do too. I've never seen you wear a suit jacket before."

"No tie, though. Don't believe in ties."

Jorge stood tall against the closed door. He turned to one side, in profile, then canted his head toward her dramatically. "What do you think? Javier Muñoz or Robin De Jesús?"

Akna laughed. "They are way too old for you. No, I think your voice is like Neto Bernal."

"Neto?" Jorge stepped away from the door. "My voice is nowhere near as good. Besides I sing mostly in English. He sings only in Spanish."

"Your voice *is* that good. And he started singing very young, like you."

Hmph. Jorge shrugged. "I don't want to be a singer like that. I want to be on Broadway."

"You will be if you want it that bad. Tata always said I could be anything I wanted if I put my mind to it. Even without money, America gives opportunities."

"I don't know. Mi padre says education, education, education. He doesn't want me to be a janitor like him. He thinks acting and singing is a hobby, not a profession. A profession is like doctor or lawyer or scientist."

"Maybe he'll change his mind when he sees you being the star in middle school or high school."

"Maybe...I doubt it."

Akna glared at the door. "We got here way too early."

"Yeah, my parents decided they wanted to be as close to the front as they could."

"Then they'll probably be sitting next to my rowdy family."

"Good! You know, since we came to your house after the spring show it's like a weight lifted off them. They're no longer so scared about mixing with people on the other side of the tracks."

"Really?"

"Well, at least not with your family. I think your family has a special power for making people feel good about themselves."

Akna nodded and smiled. "I'm pretty sure it's because we all come from different backgrounds and to get along, we have to make some magic. The Bohns taking in kids after they already raised their own family is awesome. I mean they're not perfect, but they try so hard and care so much that they get a pass from all us girls when they mess up."

"Hmm. You'll have to tell me about those mess ups someday," he said.

"Not my story to tell," she said. "But if you hang out at our place at all this summer, you'll probably meet some of their kids and grand-kids and then the stories fly."

"So…do you know yet if you're staying here?"

Akna shook her head. "The social worker called to say Mama was coming for a visit in two weeks."

"Then she's out of rehab?"

"Obviously."

"Then she's coming to take you home," Jorge said quietly.

"I'm not sure. You'd think if she was coming to take us home, Mrs. Sleeper would have said that. But she didn't. When I asked her, she said Mama would explain when she came to visit."

"That doesn't sound good."

Akna sighed. "Maybe it's good. I mean at least she's out of rehab, right? Maybe she just needs more time. You know, maybe she has to stay clean for a bit longer before she's allowed to take us." She stubbed her toe into the ground and let out a breath again. "I don't know. I'll just wait and see."

"If you do leave, will you write me?" Jorge asked. "I'd miss you like crazy and if we wrote each other it would help."

"Sure, I'll write. But if you don't write me back, I'm going to come after you."

"I'll write. I'll write every day if you want. And maybe I'll even come visit. I mean, if you want."

"We'll see." Akna wasn't sure what things would be like. She wasn't even sure if they had a place to live or if someone else lived there now. She wasn't sure how long her Mama could go without her drinks and medicine. She couldn't remember a time when she lasted for longer than a couple weeks.

The door behind them creaked. They both turned and Mr. Serna smiled at them. "Hello Akna. Jorge. You are a little early but that's better than being late. Come in. Come in." He opened the door wide and put the kickstand down to keep it open. "Mrs. Cosgrave will be happy to see you. Go on. I'm the door monitor until everyone gets here."

Mrs. Cosgrave was playing the piano on the stage. The melody was the song they'd sing before the ceremony. Akna couldn't help singing the lyrics in her mind.

When Jorge and Akna climbed the steps, Mrs. Cosgrave stopped playing. "Jorge, so glad you're here early. Do you feel confident in your solo part at the beginning?"

Jorge nodded.

Akna knew he would do great. He was the best singer in the whole choir. He could do the whole song by himself if he wanted.

"Of course you're ready," Mrs. Cosgrave continued. "You are always ready." Then she smiled at Akna. "Good thing you're here. Until the rest of the choir gets here, will you sing your part with Jorge where you and the rest of the choir joins?"

Akna nodded, even though she was a bit scared. She didn't have a bad voice but she didn't have a great voice either. Except when practicing at home, she never sang alone in front of anyone.

Jorge began:

525,600 minutes,

525,000 moments so dear.
525,600 minutes -How do you measure,
Measure a year?

Akna joined him on the next phrase and the next. When they got to the chorus, seven or eight other students joined in. By the time they got to the final chorus, the entire choir was there and the sound overwhelmed her—everyone singing together, many with different notes but those differences made the song even better.

She wiped a hand across her eyes and swallowed. She wanted to hold this memory in her heart forever. She wanted to stop time and make this day last forever. Singing, her friends, Jorge, the Bohns, her foster sisters.

Things were going to change again. Whenever Mama was involved, things always changed. Usually not for the better.

Mr. Sanderson came in and relieved Mrs. Cosgrave as he took over at the piano and all the choir kids started talking all at once.

"Hey." Jorge put his arm around Akna's shoulder. "Was I that bad?"

She gurgled. "Yeah, a real stinko. Brought tears to my eyes."

"It was because you were singing with me," he countered. "I was in such awe I could barely remember the lyrics."

"525,600 minutes," she sang and then stopped as tears welled again.

He snapped his fingers. "Oh, that's the first line."

She bumped him with her shoulder. "You're welcome."

He bumped her back. "You're welcome, too."

Mrs. Cosgrave tapped on the music stand at the front of the stage. "Alright everyone," she said. "Get in your places. Let's go through it one more time now that everyone is here. Don't forget to pay attention to the dynamics. Remember, when I go like this"—she lowered her hands from head height to the stand—"that means we are getting softer. When I do this—" She raised her hands slowly.

"We get louder," someone shouted and everyone giggled.

"That's right," Mrs. Cosgrave said.

She pointed her baton at Mr. Sanderson and he played the intro. Jorge came in with his solo at the exact right time. Then Mrs.

Cosgrave pointed to one section of the choir to join on a few lines, and then another section. By the first chorus, the entire choir was singing together in harmony.

Though Akna was filled with emotion, she had to concentrate and pay close attention as all those harmonies joined together and the entire choir rose and fell with the baton's movement. She managed to get through the whole song without more tears.

The choir waited in silent anticipation as Mrs. Cosgrave smiled and made eye contact with each of them.

"That was good. Very good," she said, and a whoosh of air expelled from every singer in concert. Then she looked at her music on the stand and turned pages back.

No one spoke. Akna was worried. Usually they messed up something, and Mrs. Cosgrave always said that was good because they wouldn't do it in performance. But now…

"One little mistake," Mrs. Cosgrave said as she tapped the music stand again.

Akna smiled broadly.

"In this middle part where you sing, how about love." She sang the phrase for them. "Remember the word love starts soft, gets louder in the middle, and then comes back to medium. You need to all be looking at me during that part so everyone does it together and all the harmonies match perfectly. Let's practice that a couple of times."

After she was satisfied, she said, "We're ready and I know you will all do very well."

Mrs. Cosgrave had a rule to never do the whole song again after a section practice. She said that was because she wanted them to not over practice and get tired with it. She wanted everyone to bring all their energy and emotion during performance. She called it being open to the magic that happens.

Mrs. Cosgrave tapped at her watch. "Take ten, then get back here in your places. The principal will begin welcoming everyone at 11:00am sharp. That's in fifteen minutes. If you have to use the restroom, now is the time. No dawdling!"

Akna scanned the seats in the auditorium. All the other fifth graders had arrived now and were walking to their assigned seats in the front row. Last week, Akna had counted them up, and there were eighty-three graduating fifth grade students. Forty-two of them were in the choir. After they did their song, they had to all file down to the front row and join their home room class in alphabetical order.

She watched as Jessa found her seat. Fortunately, Akna's spot was right next to her. Sales then Smythe. Once again, Akna was happy that Jessa was tall and easy to spot. Then they opened the doors for all the parents and families. Sure enough, Jorge's family and her foster family entered together. They found a spot right in the center, just three rows back from the front.

Ten minutes later, everyone was seated and Mrs. Cosgrave signaled for the choir to follow her and Mr. Sanderson and line up on the risers. She peeled off to share the piano bench with Mr. Sanderson. The choir would have to stand until time for their performance.

The principal, Mrs. Barker, stepped to the lectern and clicked the switch on the microphone. "Today we are celebrating the graduation of our fifth-grade students as they leave Margarita School for middle school. We are very proud of all the hard work they've done."

Then she talked about the school, and the kinds of classes they've taken and the great work of all the teachers. It wasn't that it was boring. It was just kind of long and they were standing on risers and had to at least look like they were paying attention because everyone could see them. Akna wanted to get the show on the road and get that piece of paper in her hand.

"Before we start the ceremony," Mrs. Baker said. "Our fifth-grade choir has an important song to share with you."

Then Mrs. Cosgrave took the microphone. "Thank you, Mrs. Barker. The choir had a choice of several songs suggested for graduation. By a majority vote, they picked this *Seasons of Love* from the musical, *Rent*. It talks about everything that can happen in a year— good things and bad things—and how we can get through it together because we care for each other. Enjoy."

She tapped her music stand, pointed her baton at Mr. Sanderson and they began.

Akna listened extra close and followed easily. When they got to the part they had missed before, they all did it exactly right. The rest of the song she felt like she was outside her body, but not alone. Everyone was with her. They were singing together and moving and every word was true.

When they sang the last line, there was a moment of complete silence, then the applause rang out all at once. Then everyone started standing up and clapping louder and louder. She could see Mrs. Bohn with her handkerchief rubbing at her eyes. Mr. Bohn had his arm around her, holding her tight. All the girls were cheering loudly and clapping. Jorge's family was next to them and smiling more than she'd ever seen them smile.

The principal stepped to the microphone again and the moment ended. "That was beautiful everyone. It has been an amazing 525,600 minutes of a year seeing all of you, thinking about you, being so proud of everything you've accomplished here. Choir, please take your places with their home room teachers."

The choir filed out in silence, walking down the steps and into the rows. When Akna got to her seat, Jessa leaned over and squeezed her hand. She whispered, "You all were amazing. And Jorge, OMG what a voice. I dug crescents into my palms so I wouldn't cry." She showed Akna her other hand but evidently the marks had already disappeared.

Akna squeezed back. "Thanks. I had my cry in rehearsal."

Mrs. Barker took to the lectern again. "Now it's time to say thank you for making Margarita School a better place. Know that every one of us will be thinking of you as we say our final good-byes today. We will miss you, but we also want to see you do even more amazing things in middle school. There is so much more to learn. So many more experiences to have as you grow into teens and adults. We will be watching from the sidelines and cheering you on."

She turned toward a stack of papers, explained how everyone was going to line up and be called by homeroom. They went in alphabetical order by home room teacher last name.

Akna was glad she wasn't first, because she watched the others and knew exactly what to do. Mr. Serna's class was second to last.

Finally, Mrs. Barker said, "Mr. Serna, please present your class for graduation." They followed Mr. Serna up the stairs and across the stage then stopped until he stood on the other end of the stage behind Mrs. Barker.

Akna shifted from one foot to the other as Mr. Serna worked his way through the alphabet, calling each student by name. Then she heard it. "Akna Sales."

She froze for just a moment, but Jessa nudged her and she walked forward carefully, half in a daze. Mrs. Barker shook her hand and said, "Congratulations, Akna. We enjoyed having you at Margarita School. You are a talented young woman and I know you will do well in middle school." Then she handed her the diploma and pointed her toward Mr. Serna.

Mr. Serna stood with his card ready. Akna took the card and then suddenly gave him a spontaneous hug. He'd been such a good teacher, helping her find research for her big heritage project and buoying her up when she was down. Between him, Mr. Bohn, and Jorge, Akna had decided that maybe not all men were doomed to be like the ones her mother had chosen.

"Congratulations, Akna," he said when she let go of him. "I know you came in late, but you more than made up for it. You are an amazing young woman who will go far in life. Don't forget that. Middle school will be wonderful for you. You love learning and I'm confident you'll find many new opportunities." Then he gave her the card in the envelope and directed her to the other side of the stage where she would return to her seat.

She descended the stairs looking at her foster family. All the girls had big silly smiles on their faces, and Mr. and Mrs. Bohn were watching her every step as she returned to her seat.

When the last student finally passed through the line, the speakers blared out the song, *Celebration*. And all the graduates joined in for the "Celebrate good times, come on!" as they left their seats to join family."

Her foster family and Jorge's parents were right next to each other. They all hugged both of them and then headed out the door together. Nakia peppered Akna with questions about what the diploma said and what was in the envelope. Akna didn't even know. She hadn't had a chance to look yet.

Outside the two families took lots of pictures. Mr. Bohn took pictures of Jorge with his parents. Mr. Rodrigues took pictures of Akna with her foster family. Then they both took pictures of Jorge and Akna together and each of them alone. When Jessa dragged her parents over to meet Akna, they took pictures of Jessa and Akna together too, and then of Jessa and Akna and Jorge.

She wasn't sure how long they were there talking, hugging, taking pictures. A number of people from choir wanted their picture with Jorge, so his parents were taking lots of pictures with their phone. Finally, almost everyone had left and it was time to head home.

"See you soon," Jorge said as he waved goodbye.

This time Jorge and his parents had planned to come to Mariposa Lane to celebrate with Akna and her family. But they had to go home to get food first. Jorge had told her that his mom and dad had been making tamales for two days. She also knew that Mrs. Bohn had asked for a rice and beans recipe from Mrs. Rodrigues so she could make something to go with it.

Soon after they arrived home and changed into casual clothes, Jorge and his parents arrived. Jorge and his father each carried a very large pot. It was similar to the big pot Mrs. Bohn would use to make soup for everyone to last for many days. Jorge said his pot was cheese tamales and Mr. Rodrigues' pot was pork tamales. Mrs. Rodrigues followed them with a big bowl of salsa she'd made.

Jorge and Akna helped get the tamales on the table and she placed a little piece of paper next to each large bowl indicating if it was pork or cheese.

Finally, Gianna brought out a bowl of powder-coated round cookies.

Mrs. Rodrigues looked at the bowl. "Wedding cookies! Who made this?"

"It was Gianna's idea," Mrs. Bohn said.

"When did you make these?" Akna said. "There wasn't time for bread baking today."

"We're a sneaky bunch," Gianna said. "I searched Google for what kind of dessert to have with tamales and this came up. Mrs. Bohn asked a neighbor to let me make them at their house yesterday after school so it would be a surprise."

"They look beautiful," Mrs. Rodrigues said. "You are a good baker."

Akna gave Gianna a hug. "A good, sneaky baker."

"Hold praise until you actually taste them," Gianna said. "It's the first time I've made them."

The tamales brought back so many memories of better times, when Nana and Tata lived with them. It made Akna realize that she had missed those kinds of foods. She missed the stories and knowing that, even when Mama wasn't doing well, she at least shared the same background, the same ancestry with Akna.

As wonderful as her foster family had been, they did not share that background. Jorge and his family had brought a little of it back today. Because Akna knew she'd be leaving soon, she'd never wanted to impose on the Bohns or her foster sisters to make this kind of food.

Akna held on to Jorge a little extra long before he went out the door. "Let's get together before you go on vacation," she said. "Just in case."

He nodded. "Don't worry. I'll give you a call before next Saturday. Whatever happens, we will stay in touch."

Then they were gone.

Akna was excused from all chores that evening because of her graduation. She went upstairs to open the envelope she'd received from Mr. Serna. It was the size of a standard greeting card. Probably every student received one. She opened the envelope and pulled out the card. The front had a picture of a wooden sign that said 5th Grade and beneath it were three rocks with hands and legs and a smile. She opened it and a folded sheet of paper fell into her lap. The inscription read: *You rocked it. Congratulations for graduating 5th Grade.* It was signed *Mr. Serna.*

She examined the folded sheet of paper before opening it. It was white paper with blue lines, just like the ones they used for writing essays in class. She slowly unfolded it.

Dear Akna,

I wanted to take a moment to personally congratulate you and tell you some things I've noticed that may help you as you enter middle school.

First, you are a very good student. Even though you came in late and were behind in your studies, you worked hard to catch up. This isn't only my opinion; it is also the opinion of every teacher you had this year. You earned those good grades.

Second, you are a kind person. I've seen you help others in language arts with their reading and writing. I've seen you work with a student who was challenged by spelling, teaching them some of your tricks for remembering the rules of spelling. You are a good teacher. Kindness is something to always keep with you. It is more important than money or fame. Kind people will always have friends.

Finally, you are a person who takes the world on your shoulders. This probably comes from your kindness. The world is very heavy to carry by yourself. If you must carry it, you need to share the burden. Just like a hiker will take a donkey to carry some of the weight of her camping gear on a long trip, each of us needs a friend to help carry the weight in our life.

You have many people who love you, and many others who will be your friends. I hope you find a way to share your burdens with one or more of them. Together you can accomplish more than you can alone.

I wish you the best in life. I know you will go far and do amazing things.

Sincerely,

Mr. Serna

She stared at the sheet of paper and read it one more time. The card was cute and probably every student got the same card. Did he also write a personal letter to every student? She could tell this letter was just for her. Not just because her name was on it, but because of what it said.

She knew not every student got good grades. She'd been lucky because she loved to read, and Tata had taught her to love nature and figuring things out. Nana had taught her to be kind and to always help others. That's why she helped Mama all the time and her sisters. That's why she didn't mind going to the food bank every month with the Bohns and preparing bags for those who couldn't afford to buy groceries.

She was surprised Mr. Serna noticed her helping others. She never told anyone. She never made a big deal about it.

How did he know about her burdens? Did she say something in the essays she wrote in language arts? In her essays, she'd always been careful to never talk about Mama or the troubles they'd had. Did she accidentally reveal something about her thoughts in her pretend stories?

He wasn't the first person to say that she needed to share her burden with others. She just wasn't sure how to do it. Whenever things became too hard, Mrs. Bohn was there or Gianna was there. She knew this foster family would always be there if she asked. She just didn't know how to ask. It wasn't in her nature to ask for help.

She folded the paper back up and put it in the card. Then she added it to her special locked box where she had Tata's letter and her diary.

Soon after, Hai and Nakia came up stairs and got ready for bed. Hai sat on Nakia's bed with a book.

"I want Akna to read it," Nakia said loudly.

She looked up and Hai worked her lower lip. "Akna, you don't have to if you're busy."

Akna stood, "Of course I'll read. Can we all three still fit on that bed?"

"I'll sit on your lap," Nakia offered.

They squished together with Akna and Hai leaning up against the wall and Nakia on Akna's lap holding the book in front of her. Nakia had a new favorite called, *Giraffe's Can't Dance* by Giles Andrae.

As Akna read, Nakia pointed to the pictures and told her what was happening. For a moment Akna was taken aback at how much her English had improved in the last six months. The antics of the giraffe trying so hard to learn to dance were funny. The last line finished the story very well. It said the key to learning to dance was finding the right music.

Akna closed the book. "What kind of music makes you dance, Nakia?"

"Any music," she said. "In school my teacher said we make music all the time. Our feet make music. Our hands make music. Our voices make music. Everything makes music. We just have to listen and keep trying."

"That's right. Your teacher is very smart." She wiggled and Nakia climbed off her lap. Hai headed to her own bed and snuggled under the covers.

Akna gave Hai a kiss like she'd always done.

Then she turned to Nakia's bed and tucked her in and gave her a kiss as well.

"A magical kiss," Nakia said.

"That's right."

Akna began to walk away when Nakia called her back.

"Akna?"

She turned. "Yes."

"I don't want to go back and live with Mama."

Akna's breath caught in her throat as her heart plopped into her stomach.

She slowly returned and sat back on Nakia's bed. "Why is that?"

"I like it here better."

"I like it here, too," Akna said slowly. "But I love Mama, too, and she loves us and we love her."

"I don't love her anymore," Nakia said.

Akna's mouth seemed suddenly dry. She swallowed and ran her tongue over her lips. "You don't mean that," she said.

"Yes, I do. Mama is always sad and she makes you do all the work. Here, everyone is glad and everyone shares the work."

Akna's brain went into full denial. Mama wasn't *always* sad. She just had a lot of problems, and maybe the medicine...no, the drugs... Gianna was probably right about that. The drugs made it worse. "I know that things were difficult with Mama," she started. "But she might be better now. It might be…" She couldn't finish what she was going to say because Nakia was right. Things were pretty good here and Akna couldn't guarantee anything with Mama.

She turned to Hai. "Do you feel the same way?"

"I love Mama," Hai said slowly. "But…"

Akna waited for her to finish the sentence. "But what? You can tell me. I won't get mad."

"But you are more of a real Mama to me…and Mama Lois is more of a real Mama."

"Mama is our real mother," Akna countered. "She is our flesh and blood. She gave birth to us."

"But she doesn't act like it," Hai said. "When's the last time you remember her helping you instead of you helping her?"

"Well, I…" She couldn't really remember a time. "It had been always Tata or Nana that made life bearable."

"Exactly," Hai said.

"You can live with Mama." Nakia said. "But I want to stay here. Then you can come visit me. Okay?"

Akna couldn't imagine leaving her sisters alone here. That was not an option. She'd have to find a way to change Nakia's mind. What she said was true, but there were reasons. Good reasons. When Mama came to get them, she would be well and it would be different. Wouldn't it?

"Okay, Akna?" Nakia asked again.

"I'll have to think about it," she said. "How about you go to sleep and then we'll think about it when we have more information. Okay?"

"Okay."

Akna once again kissed Nakia on the forehead. "Magical dreams."

She pivoted and saw Gianna sitting on her bed. When had she come into the room? Had she heard all of that?

CHAPTER EIGHTEEN

THE THINKING TREE

"I need a run," Gianna said. "It's dark. Wanna come?"

Akna gestured for them to go downstairs.

When they got to the bottom of the stairs, she said. "What's wrong?"

"I need some exercise after all that food we had this afternoon." Then she popped her head into the family room where Mr. and Mrs. Bohn were watching a movie with Sandra and Polly. "Akna and I are going for a walk. We'll be back in a bit."

Mr. Bohn looked at the clock. "Got your phone?"

Gianna nodded.

"Okay. Have fun," he said.

They scooted out the door and Gianna started walking at a pretty good clip.

"You in a hurry to get somewhere?" Akna asked.

"No, just felt like making a little run. Are you up for it?"

"Sure. I guess."

"Nothing too rigorous. It's not a race or anything. Just keep up, okay"

"Sure," Akna said again. She'd never known Gianna to head out at night for a run. But she did know that Gianna was like her. When something bothered her enough, she had to run. Gianna had always been there for Akna through lots of complications. So, if she needed a run, Akna would go without questions.

After a few blocks, Gianna said between breaths, "Gnarly stuff I overhead with you and Nakia."

Akna concentrated on her pace. "I was surprised. I mean not completely surprised she feels that way. More surprised she said it."

"Five-year-olds don't really have any filters," Gianna said. "They're not like us, always thinking about other people's feelings. They just know what makes them happy at that moment and they will tell you."

"I guess," Akna responded, not really believing it. Nakia had never said anything like that before. Never.

They ran for a few more blocks in silence.

"I sometimes feel like saying that, too," Akna admitted. "But I never would. I love Mama and I kind of understand why it's so hard for her."

"I get that." Gianna turned another corner and they were at the park. The same park Gianna had followed Akna to months ago.

"You been to this park a lot?" Akna asked.

"Oh yeah. Long before you came. In fact, that tree…" She pointed to the one where Akna had hidden. "That's my favorite tree to hide in. I still go there when I can't deal."

No wonder Gianna had found her so easily.

"You can't deal?" Akna questioned. "You seem so confident. So put together."

"Fake it 'til you make it, my therapist used to say." Gianna continued toward the tree. "But sometimes it just all gets to me and I gotta let it out." She held up a long, droopy branch. "Come into my lair."

Once inside Gianna reached high above her head and part of her hand disappeared from sight until she pulled down a box.

Akna stepped back and stood on her tip toes to see if she could see a hiding place. "Is there a hole up there?"

Gianna nodded. "It was probably a bird nest at one time. But it's pretty low for birds, so I don't think it is anymore. I carved it out a little more to make it so this box would fit securely in there. And I keep a bit of old bark over the front so it's not easily seen."

She opened the lid. Inside were seven candles in little jars. She arranged them in a large circle, lighting each one with a lighter before she put it on the ground. Then she sat in the center, cross legged. "Want to join me?"

Akna wasn't sure. She wondered if maybe this was a witch thing or something.

"No spells or demons or anything," Gianna said. "I'm not a witch. Though some people may think I am. I don't really know anything about that stuff. The candlelight soothes my mind."

"Where'd you get the lighter?" Akna asked. "I don't even know how to make one of those work."

"Brought it from my previous foster home," Gianna said. "Actually, I took a bunch of them—every single one I could find—but I only have three left."

Akna was a bit worried that Gianna was a thief, or worse a fire-starter, but she didn't say anything. She just listened.

"The foster dad smoked the most foul-smelling cigarettes ever. He wasn't a nice man—far from it. I was the only foster child and if I didn't do something he asked me to do immediately, he would hold the cigarette to my arm until it burned me. I told the foster mom, but she didn't believe me because he always lied about it. He said I was hanging with bad kids and that's how it happened.

"I was only ten the first time. So, I ran away. When the police found me, I told them and then the social worker went to talk to the lady and she would repeat the lies he'd told. And they sent me back. A couple months later, the same thing happened and I ran away again. Back I went. No one would believe me, even with the burns. It was always just one burn.

"The last time it happened he burned my thigh in several places. It was much worse than any other time. He and the wife got in a big fight that night and they got really drunk. I waited until they were dead asleep in the middle of the night. I took every lighter I could find in the house and swore to myself if they sent me back, I'd light the house on fire.

"It was about 2am when a cop spotted me walking the streets without shoes and stopped me. When I explained what happened, the policeman took me to a hospital. The burns were pretty bad. My social worker wasn't available to come to the hospital, but Mrs. Sleeper was. She took over my case and brought me to Mariposa Lane."

Akna didn't know what to say. She knew some foster homes weren't great. Tonio had told her about his experience, but it was nothing compared to what Gianna just said. Akna suspected it might be even worse than getting burns. Her Mama had told her about evil things some men did to children.

Akna stared at the candlelight for a long time looking for the right words.

"The Bohns are the best thing that ever happened to me," Gianna said. "I know you love your mama, but you'll never find a better family in foster care. You and your sisters were very lucky this was your first stop."

"Are the Bohns the only good foster parents?" Akna asked. It needed to be part of her plan. If things didn't work out with Mama, they would put her in a foster home again and it might be bad like the one Gianna was in. She couldn't let that happen to her sisters.

"There are other good people," Gianna said. "I've met other kids who had good homes. Mrs. Sleeper says there are more good ones than bad ones. The problem is it's really hard to find enough foster parents for all the kids who need them. Because of that, at least here in Oregon, they now try to get kids adopted instead. But even that's not a sure deal. Look what happened to Polly. They sent her back like she was a bad dog or something."

Akna shook her head. She couldn't imagine that kind of devastation. Thinking you found a forever family and then they say: We made a mistake. You're not good enough to be our kid.

"We don't want to be adopted," she said. "We want Mama to get better and have a nice, normal family. That's all."

"Yeah well, sorry to break it to you. There are no nice, normal families," Gianna said. "That's pretend. That's like the old *Leave it to Beaver* and *Father Knows Best* shows you can watch on reruns. Those are pretend families, not real ones."

"The Bohns seem normal," Akna said.

"They are, I guess. But look at us as a family. Six kids without bio parents living under one roof. No two look alike. I take that back. You and your sisters kind of look alike. We all have problems. That's not normal. I mean I'm glad I'm there, but it's still not normal. I don't think there is such a thing as a *normal* family."

Akna nodded. Gianna was probably right. Normal was pretend. Maybe she needed to stop pretending and be more realistic like her sisters. She shook her head from side to side as if she could clear out the doubts. She'd been working on her plan for so long, if she let it go now then she'd have nothing. All that work...all those tries to get Mama well...everything they survived was all for nothing.

There was no way she could make everybody happy. Someone had to lose.

Whenever Akna thought of the past couple years, it felt like someone ran over her chest and then backed up and ran over it again and again. Every time she got up and tried to repair it, someone ran over it again. Every time Mama apologized, but then...

Nakia and Hai were right. Mama was the problem that Akna could never fix.

Gianna closed her eyes and took in a deep breath. "When I'm really stuck, I close my eyes and try to block everything out."

Akna closed her eyes, too.

"I listen to the breeze and just be quiet."

Akna tried to just listen, but a car drove by slowly with loud rap music booming into the park. She tried to think back to home and living with Mama and what she'd heard when she'd walked or ran around the mobile park loop. It was similar, except she could also hear inside the mobile homes more. She could hear what they were watching on TV. She could hear if people were fighting inside, screaming at each other. Their lives were on display if anyone was around to listen.

On Mariposa Lane, the houses were far back from the sidewalk and most of them were brick or stone. She couldn't hear inside the houses when she walked around the block or to school. She didn't know if they were happy or sad, fighting or having a party. It was hard to trust people who kept everything inside for no one to see.

"Then I open my eyes," Gianna said after silent listening, "and look into the candlelight. They are so beautiful, and all I can see is the candlelight."

Akna did as she said. It was beautiful but she could see much more than the candlelight. She could see the grass beneath it, the drooping fir branches beyond it, and the light from lamps around the park filtering through the needles in places where the branches were not as thick.

"Then I can ask questions and think more clearly," Gianna said.

Nothing was clear to Akna. Maybe Mr. Serna was right. Maybe she had to share the burden with someone else. But not today. She wasn't ready. She didn't know enough.

"Does this always work for you?" Akna asked. "Do you always find the answers you need?"

Gianna shrugged. "No, not always. But when it works it's good."

"Is this a pagan religion thing—the candles and the closed eyes and all that stuff?"

Gianna stood and held her hands in front of her, pressed together like a prayer and then bowed and said, "I walk back into the world with love and light." She then picked up each candle one-by-one and blew it out.

After she'd replaced the box back into the tree, she stood cocking one hip and stared at Akna. Then she took in a big breath and pushed it out. "The answer is yes."

"Yes?"

"Yes, it's a pagan thing in that the natural world helps to calm me. I bet your ancestors did that too. The Native Americans here have lots of rituals for getting rid of demons. It doesn't have to be real demons, just bad thoughts. I read about making the circle and using the candles and stuff online, so I started trying it and it does help...sometimes."

"Running helps me," Akna admitted. "But this candle thing didn't really help me get any answers."

"Sorry. I was hoping."

"Is that why you wanted to go running? To help me?" Akna asked. "Because I came to help you."

"I know it sounds crazy, but helping you helps me too," Gianna said.

Akna rolled her eyes.

"Really. I don't want you to make the same mistakes I made. I kept hoping my mom would become the mom I needed. But she never could. That made me a very angry person. I don't want to see that happen to you."

"I know there's a chance she won't be able to take us home," Akna admitted. "In some ways that would be a relief. But I can't think about that. Whatever happens, it won't be our choice. It will be hers."

Akna opened her mouth, then closed it again. She drew in her bottom lip, then put a thumb there to hold her mouth closed. She didn't really want to think about this right now. She didn't want to talk anymore.

Today was supposed to be a happy day. A celebration day. She wasn't going to let all her worries ruin the memories of today. She wanted to spend the next two weeks being with her foster sisters. She wanted to see Jorge again.

She wouldn't let Mama ruin the next two weeks for her. Not this time.

CHAPTER NINETEEN

MAMA VISITS

"Yes, I understand," Mrs. Bohn said into the phone as Akna stood waiting.

She knew Mama was on her way. She was coming with Mrs. Sleeper. The social worker said she would call when they were fifteen minutes away.

"Okay, I'll ask her," Mrs. Bohn said. "We'll all be ready."

She hung up.

Akna raised her eyes to Mrs. Bohn's face waiting.

Mrs. Bohn took a deep breath. "She'll be here in fifteen minutes. Mrs. Sleeper said she will be in the room while you and your sisters visit with your mother. She won't leave you alone with her."

Akna nodded. She was actually happy about that. She wasn't sure if she wanted to be alone with her. She didn't know what Nakia or Hai might say or do. She'd talked to them yesterday to try to explain what might happen. She asked them to please listen to what Mama had to say before getting upset. They promised they would be good.

"Mrs. Sleeper said I could be there with you, if you want me."

Akna cast her eyes to the floor. She did want her there. But would her Mama want her there? She didn't want to upset her Mama.

"What do you think, Akna? It's up to you."

"I don't want to upset Mama."

"That's very kind of you. But this is also about you. What do *you* want?"

"I want everyone to be happy."

"We would all like that," Mrs. Bohn said. "That would be the perfect solution. Do you think that is possible here? No matter which way it goes, is there one way that will make everyone happy?"

Akna shook her head.

"I agree. So, if everyone can't be happy who should make the decision?"

Akna pointed to herself. As much as she hated to admit it, she had to make the decision.

"It's your decision, Akna. I will be happy either way. So do you want me to stay with you and your Mama and Mrs. Sleeper or do you want me not to be there?"

"Stay," Akna said in a whisper. "Please," she said a little louder.

Mrs. Bohn gave her hug and Akna held tight. This was the scariest thing she'd ever done.

"I will stay." Mrs. Bohn didn't let go. "I will support you no matter what happens."

After a few minutes, Akna loosened her grip. "I better go get Hai and Nakia."

"That's a good idea," Mrs. Bohn said. "I'll bring out some coffee and tea, and milk for you and your sisters. And the girls made a nice coffee cake for everyone to share while you're talking."

Akna started for the stairs. She turned and looked back at Mrs. Bohn. "Thank you," she said and then fled up the stairs.

Hai and Nakia were both sitting on Nakia's bed. Hai was reading the giraffe book again. But neither one was laughing. Hai was trying hard to get Nakia to talk about the book, but she would just turn the page for Hai to read the next one.

"It's time to come down," Akna said.

They both stood and held hands, their heads bent looking at their feet.

Akna bent on one knee in front of Nakia. She wanted to just hug her and cry with both of them. But she knew that wouldn't help right now.

"Where are your SAD powers, Nakia? You need to find them. We all need to find them right now."

"They got lost," Nakia said.

Akna stood and put her arm around Hai. "Do you have your SAD powers?"

Hai's bottom lip quivered and her eyes watered. "They're here," she said with a quaver in her voice. "They're hiding right now. Let me see." She looked up to the ceiling. "Wait, I see them." She pointed to the sunshine just on the edge of the skylight. "Do you see it, Akna? It's outside trying to get in."

Akna looked up. "I see it she said. I see it." Her voice caught in her throat. "Look up Nakia. Do you see it?"

Nakia looked up, too. "Where? Where is it?"

"It's trapped in the sunshine. It can't get in. What should we do?"

"Open the skylight," Nakia said. "Hurry. Hurry before Mama gets here."

Akna found the automatic button. She took Nakia's hand and Hai took the other hand and they positioned themselves under the skylight. They all looked up.

"Close your eyes so it doesn't blind you," Akna said as she pressed the button.

The three of them stood there. Akna felt the warming of the sun on her face and she basked in it. "I feel it. Do you feel it?"

"I feel it," Nakia said and she really meant it. "My SAD powers are coming back."

"Yes, I feel it too," Hai said. "I'm getting stronger."

Akna hugged both of them to her, unable to say anything as the tears coursed down her face.

She gathered every ounce of sunshine she could. She'd never needed her SAD powers as much as she did today. Finally, she said with a strong voice, "I feel it too. I'm ready."

Just then she heard the doorbell ring. They still stood there under the skylight soaking in the sun as Mrs. Bohn greeted Mrs. Sleeper and

Mama. She didn't hear Mama say anything. But then Mrs. Bohn invited them to sit in the living room where she'd already set out the coffee and cakes to enjoy.

Then the familiar clopping of Mrs. Bohn's shoes came up the stairs.

She looked at the three of them square in the eye. "Good," she said. "I can see you all have your SAD powers very strong. I have a special power to add too. It's very important."

"What?" Hai asked. "What is better than SAD power?"

"It's not better," Mrs. Bohn said. "It's equal. When you add this power to SAD, no one can stop you." She looked directly at Akna. "It's something the three of you have had even before you came here. But now it's been multiplied fivefold."

Akna looked into Mrs. Bohn's eyes. They appeared filled with all the empathy and compassion that she'd always offered them. A misty film covered the speckled blue of her eye and tears pooled in the bottom. But not one fell. How did Mrs. Bohn manage that?

"It's love," Akna said quietly and then hugged Mrs. Bohn hard.

"Yes!" Hai said, as she and Nakia joined in. "We love each other. We love this whole family and they love us back."

Mrs. Bohn nodded without saying anything for a few moments. Then she lightly pushed them away. "I think we are all ready now. Let's go greet your mother."

Akna straightened her spine and held tight to her sister's hands as they descended the stairs together. They walked into the living room where Mrs. Bohn had set chairs on the other side of the coffee table. "Sit wherever you like girls."

Mama stood and spread her arms wide. "Mis hermosos hijos. Te extrañé mucho. Ven a darle un beso a Mama."

Nakia went first, straight as a rod she approached Mama. Mama bent down to hug her and Nakia stiffened. She placed a quick kiss on Mama's cheeks and then wiggled out of her embrace and ran to Akna's side.

Hai stepped into her embrace and gave her a soft hug. "Hola

Mama." She kissed her on the lips as Mama used to do. "¿Estás bien ahora?"

"Si. Si," Mama answered. "¿Y tu?"

"Depende de lo que digas si estoy feliz o no hoy," Hai responded.

Mama's eyes opened wide. She turned to Mrs. Sleeper. "What is this? What have you told them? Why are they acting this way?"

"I have not said anything," Mrs. Sleeper said. "It is for you to tell them what will happen next."

"Akna?" Mama asked. "Mi querida niña. El que entiende mis problemas mejor que nadie. Ven aquí, mi tesoro."

Akna stepped into her mother's embrace and held on to her as if she would never see her again. She wanted to remember her as a loving mother, not as an alcoholic or an addict. No matter what happened, she would always love her. "Te quiero Mama. Siempre te he amado. Te amaré pase lo que pase."

Mama didn't let go. "Lo siento. Siento no haber sido una buena madre. Lamento haberte decepcionado. Te amo, Akna. Los amo a todos ustedes."

Akna took in a big breath. She was apologizing already. She was going to tell them a story now of why it was not her fault. Akna wished that, for once, Mama would take responsibility. Perhaps, if she could do that, she could get better. She wanted to be angry. She wanted to shout and scream at her and call out all her lies. But it would do no good. It would change nothing.

She hugged her tight again. "Te perdono, Mama. Te perdono todo. I forgive you. You may go in peace."

Her mother started to cry, just as she had so many times before. Her Spanish became rapid and broken. Akna simply let her talk and held on.

Mama said she couldn't stay in rehab. She'd tried again and again but it was too hard. Her counselor kept giving her another chance and she'd be okay for a while but then backslide. She said one person kept her sane, a man she'd met in rehab and they fell in love. He was nothing like Ruiz. He tried to keep her clean. He was better at keeping the ghosts at bay. Three weeks ago, she convinced him to run away with her. She'd wanted to be on her own, without supervision. She'd wanted to feel that glorious high of love and freedom. She'd hoped the police would give up on looking for them, but they didn't. And now she must go to jail. She knew it would be five years because she had helped bring in drugs from Mexico with that low-down, no good Ruiz. She went many times for him and he ratted her out, making some kind of deal with the court so he wouldn't get as long of a jail sentence. He got ten years.

But there were other bad things she did, too, things she refused to talk about. If she is convicted on those, she might be in jail longer. Her lawyer said maybe ten years, maybe more. But maybe she could get out if she became a snitch like Ruiz and talked about other people who were part of this group of drug mules. Maybe.

Akna cried with her. She cried for whatever had made her mother need drugs and drink. She cried for herself, for all the times she tried to help but couldn't. She cried for Nana and Tata who had their dreams dashed of a daughter who would thrive in America but never had. So many dreams. So many years.

Hai and Nakia came forward and embraced Akna. Everyone was crying. Even Mrs. Sleeper and Mrs. Bohn wiped away tears even though they certainly had no idea what Mama had said in all of her rambling Spanish.

"Tengo que ir ahora. No puedo quedarme más tiempo. Te amo, Akna. Te amo, Hai. Te amo, Nakia. Te libero a la oportunidad de una vida feliz." Mama loosened herself from Akna and turned to Mrs. Bohn. "Everyone has told me this is the very best home for my girls. I thank you for taking all three of them. They are all good girls. They are the best of girls."

"They are," Mrs. Bohn agreed as she encircled them with her arms, bringing them all to her side.

"May God Bless you," Mama said to Mrs. Bohn. "May God shine his love and light forever upon this home. May His glory reign hope and peace upon you all ever more."

"Amen," Mrs. Bohn said.

Mama hugged Mrs. Bohn. "Thank you. Gracias. Gracias."

Then she turned and fled out the door to the car.

Mrs. Sleeper pointed to a box she'd placed by the door. "Your mother wanted you girls to have this. She says it is pictures of your family in happier times. There are also pictures of her and her parents and her brothers when she lived in Guatemala. She said it is your heritage and you can be proud."

Then Mrs. Sleeper left, closing the door behind her.

CHAPTER TWENTY

THE SALES STORY

Akna couldn't look at the box of scrapbooks for a week. Without Mama or Nana or Tata to look with her, how would she know what they meant? If she wasn't born yet, how would she know the stories attached to the pictures? Eventually, she asked Mrs. Bohn to go through them with her.

In the end, the pictures were joyful. Nana had written brief captions in Spanish beneath each one. Some were pictures that journalists had taken and shared with them. Others were drawings Tata had created to detail their community. One had their garden and he'd labeled every plant, as if he needed to track what was being planted. She trailed her fingers across the writing and the hand drawn pictures as if she could transfer it from the page directly into her heart and hear Nana's and Tata's voices once again.

The pictures depicted a life that Tata had described—not one of material wealth but one of family and spiritual richness. The land was beautiful. Their love of the land was palpable. She was glad her mother had the presence of mind to keep these and to bring them. It seemed there had been times since her birth when her mother had been clean and thought clearly, times when she remembered her children and wanted them to be happy and loved. Except for brief snatches of single day happy memories, Akna had a difficult time remembering when Mama had been well for more than a few days.

The last few pages of the scrapbook contained pictures of Akna and Hai and Nakia. They were pictures she had never seen before. Pictures taken when they were babies. There was always one with Mama and a newborn, but the rest were with Tata or Nana. Akna learning to walk. Hai and Akna with Easter baskets. Akna carefully cradling Nakia with Nana sitting close. Tata in the garden with her sisters helping to plant seeds. Where was Mama? Is it possible she was taking the pictures?

She shook her head. Akna knew the truth. She'd always known the truth but couldn't let it settle until now. Her Mama wasn't there. She was somewhere else, seeking escape, or looking for someone else to magically make her world happy again.

The final picture was one Akna did remember. It was when Tata was very close to dying. He held Nakia on his lap with Akna and Hai clinging to him on either side. Nana had taken the picture.

She turned the page to a blank one—a page waiting for another memory to be placed there. It was for her to continue the story now. It was time for her life and her sisters lives to become the story, to tell the truth of the past and the present.

She opened the drawer near her bed and drew out the picture Jorge's parents had taken at graduation. They'd had it printed at Walgreens. It showed Akna and her sisters with Mr. and Mrs. Bohn and three foster sisters. They all looked so vibrant and happy. "Would it be okay if I put this in our book? This is where the Sales family continues. This is where a new story begins."

Mrs. Bohn swallowed and nodded.

Akna pulled back the clear film that kept pictures in place on the page. She carefully placed the photo in the center. Then, just as Nana had done, she added a caption. She began by naming each person in the picture: *Mama Lois, Papa Virgil, Akna, Hai, Nakia, Gianna, Polly, Sandra.* Then she added a brief description: *Akna graduates from elementary school and will be attending Serrano middle school in the fall.*

She carefully placed the clear film over it to seal it onto the page.

She looked up to Mama Lois and noticed her eyes were misty. "Is it okay?"

Mama Lois swallowed again and hugged Akna tight against her. "It is perfect. Absolutely perfect."

———

THE END

TATA'S LETTER

Dear Reader,

The letter below is from Akna's grandfather (Tata). It is a difficult letter that talks about his home in Guatemala and their journey to America. The difficulties they faced and the horrible things that happened to Akna's mother in the journey. It is those things that shaped her life and continued to break her heart. It is difficult to read and understand.

There is a reason Tata and Nana told Akna not to read this until she is fourteen years old. It is for that reason that I warn you, too, that you may not want to read it until you are thirteen or fourteen. Or you may want to ask someone you trust who is older than you to read it first and help you decide.

After dinner, Akna excused herself from watching a movie with the family. She had one more thing she had to do. She had to do this alone.

She opened the trunk at the end of her bed and removed several layers until she got to the wooden puzzle box at the bottom. She pushed on one side and then pulled on another to reveal a hidden compartment. She drew out a letter-sized envelope.

It was the envelope she'd been saving since Nana died. She didn't know how it ended up in her money box. It wasn't there one day. Then, when her mother had once more disappeared for several days, she checked her puzzle box for the grocery money she'd stashed there and next to the money was this envelope.

She thought no one knew about her puzzle box. When she told Nana she'd found it, Nana simply nodded her head and said, "It's from Tata. I promised him I would make sure you had it if I ever got sick. But you must keep your promise. Don't read it until you are at least thirteen years old. Even fourteen would be better."

No one had known Nana was sick, not even Mama. She didn't look sick. She didn't sound sick. But then a week later she was gone.

There had been so many times she'd wanted to read it after Nana died. But she'd promised. She still wasn't thirteen, but her twelfth birthday was only a month away. She knew she was breaking the promise, but she just had to know. Tata couldn't have known Nana was going to die so soon after him. He couldn't have known how awful the last two years with Mama were going to be. She was sure if he knew how hard Akna had tried to fix her Mama's broken heart, he would want her to know the story. He'd said that once she read it, she would understand why Mama was sad all the time. She would understand why Mama's SAD powers were failing instead of making her stronger.

She sat on her bed, her back against a pillow, her knees drawn close to her chest. She ran her finger across the front where Tata had written in K'iche': *For Akna Sales, who has the best SAD powers of all Supergirls. Love, Tata.*

Her finger hovered a moment as she asked herself one more time if she should wait another year and keep her promise. Then she put her finger in the corner and quickly ran it across the flap to tear it open.

She let out a breath. That wasn't so bad. She'd kind of expected the envelope to spew smoke and fire because she was breaking her promise. She peered inside and carefully extracted a single folded page from the envelope. It was folded in thirds. She could feel something heavier inside. Something small and flat, not even as thick as a key.

Holding the paper over her lap to catch anything, she slowly unfolded it. A small, rectangular object, barely more than an inch long, and not much wider than a fingernail, lay nestled in the fold. It looked like a jump drive that fits in a computer or a tablet like they had at school. She carefully put it into her front pants pocket as deep as she could.

The single page contained a handwritten letter in English instead of K'iche'.

Dear mi amorcita, Akna,

I am writing in English because it is easier for me than K'iche'. As children we were not taught to read and write in K'iche' and the story of your Mama is much too important to leave to misinterpretation. This tiny object contains my voice and my image. Attempting to write the story would rob it of its power.

The power of our stories are in the telling. They are in the lived experience shared from one person to another with all the memories and drama that can be brought to bear. I had to tell it to you myself, as if we were sitting in the backyard together. I had to tell it in the way of our ancestors.

I pray that your SAD powers have grown stronger since we parted. I hope that Hai and Nakia have strong SAD powers too. These are powers you must call forth throughout your life, no matter your age or situation. But alone they are not enough.

I have recorded...

It appeared that Tata had grown weary or lost his way as the sentence wasn't finished and the last few words tilted down. There appeared to be a blank space and then a new paragraph began again.

I have recorded in English and K'iche' which only you will understand. My prayer is that you listen first in English and share it with whoever you trust to be a holder of this story. You were born here and are an American citizen.

Though I hope you will always speak K'iche' and Spanish and English, it is important that you embrace being an American. Never fear sharing your heritage. The flavors of our people can be a salve to sustain you and others in troubled times.

When you have the time to ponder the story, perhaps go back and listen in K'iche'. Then perhaps you will gain new meaning from the language of our ancestors. As you know, not all thoughts are easily translated.

I have one final request before you hear the story. That is that you ask a special person to listen to this story with you. Someone you love and trust. I ask this because the story is a difficult one, and it may help to talk about it after. This story is a heavy burden to bear; but it is also a story of perseverance. It is a story of the power of SAD and how it has run through our family —the ancestors before us and now through you and Hai and Nakia. It is up to you to pass those powers onto all those you love. SAD powers strengthen when supported by love and a community of believers. Without love, strength and determination are not enough.

Sharing a burden makes it easier to bear. No one person must take the full weight alone. In doing so, others will trust you and share theirs as well.

I always shared my burdens with Nana and she with me. Your Mama also shared her burdens with Nana and that meant I shared them too—three instead of one. IF one faltered, the other two could carry their load until they could carry it themselves. Do you understand?

Please find someone with good, strong SAD powers and an abundance of love to share this with you.

Love survives long after death, Akna. It survives in each person who remembers.

Forever yours,
Tata

Akna closed her eyes and pictured him in her mind. They were his words. As she read, she could hear his voice in her head. She could see the look in his eyes, the way he would lean forward and sometimes whisper to hold her attention. She knew exactly where he would have held her hand or pulled her onto his lap in an embrace.

She pulled the small rectangular thing from her pocket. It was coated in metallic sapphire and aquamarine. When she moved it back and forth under the light, it shimmered against a black background like a living thing swimming in the depths of the ocean. She knew it was a jump drive. It held files, just like the one she used to make her presentation in Language Arts. They could be video files or audio files for him to tell the story.

Akna closed her eyes. She knew who could share this burden. Mama Lois had very strong SAD powers. She'd also share it with Gianna. The one who understood Akna from the first day. The one who also had a mama with addictions.

She placed the drive back in the fold of the letter. Then she placed the letter back in the envelope and all of it back in the puzzle box.

Later in the evening, Mama Lois waved goodbye to Papa Virgil, Hai, Nakia, and Polly as they left in the minivan. She'd arranged for them to have a special night out at the movies and then a treat at the ice cream parlor. Sandra was gone as well, participating in a twenty-four-hour prayer vigil at her church and would not be home until tomorrow.

Gianna had hooked up her tablet computer to the TV so the video would be large enough for everyone to see. The lights were off, but she had brought her candles from the park and arranged them in a very large circle that encompassed the entire family room.

Then she queued the video. She stopped on Tata's face before he began to speak. He looked very large on the TV. Akna sat with Mama Lois on one side and Gianna on the other. Akna had control of the video. Mama Lois said she could pause at any time, or chose to stop completely and finish another day.

Akna stared at Tata's face, trying not to cry. She missed him so much. She bit her lip and squeezed a hand on either side of her as her eyes filled. "Go ahead," she whispered.

Tata smiled and his eyes twinkled. "I know you are afraid, Akna. I know your amazing mind is moving back and forth, at the speed of light, between watching or waiting.

I am sorry that your childhood has been difficult. But you are not alone in that. Millions of children around the world have difficult lives. You are fortunate to be in America where you have a chance. You are blessed by the gods to have such amazing SAD powers to shield you and propel you forward. You must do more than live from day to day, Akna. You must thrive."

Akna nodded her head and swallowed. She had. They all had, except Mama.

"This is your Mama's story to tell," he began. "But I am not sure she will ever be able to tell it. I don't know when, or if, her heart will heal in this life, in this earthly world."

He swallowed and is mouth turned down. He closed his eyes and said, "Oh yes. Your Mama's heart has been broken many times. It is only her SAD powers that have kept her alive at all."

Tata blew out a big breath and swallowed again. His eyes raised to the sky as if waiting for the gods to give a blessing in the telling of Mama's story.

Akna took in a deep breath. He looked exactly how she remembered him. It was as if she were right there in front of him now. "What is it?" she asked in a whisper. "Tell me now and I will remember it forever."

He swallowed and nodded as if he heard her. "This story begins before your Mama was born. It begins before Nana and Tata were born. It is important to know the beginning to understand the now. Our people, the K'iche', were a strong and proud people for thousands of years. We were strong because we shared our land with each other. We were strong because we shared our food and our stories. We were not perfect, but we learned to live in harmony because that was the only way we could live in a world of many dangers and evils.

"Nana and I grew up in the central highlands of Guatemala. Before Guatemala became a country, the land was known as the Tezulutlan, the land of war.

"Nana has told you stories from the Bible, the stories of the Jewish people. These are shared among many churches in America, including the Catholic Church. But the K'iche' have their own stories. The story of our people, and our kings, and our enslavement by the Spanish conquistadores. The early stories are in the *Popol Wuj*, the Book of Community. This is an important story to know, to understand how much the gods loved the K'iche'. I hope that you find a way to learn these stories if you haven't already."

There was a minute in the video when no one was there. Tata's chair was empty. Then suddenly he was back. He'd changed to his pajamas and he was slumped in his recliner a little more than usual. His eyes were closed and then they opened slowly.

"This is the hard part," Tata started. "When you learn about the history of our people, you will find that even three hundred years ago still feels like yesterday. From the time of the Spanish enslavement to today, K'iche' lived in poverty. We had no land, no homes, no freedom. In my own lifetime, Guatemala lurched from one dictatorship to another.

"Nana, Itza, tu madre, and I fled Guatemala in 1981 during the civil war. All Maya, including K'iche', were being killed for no reason than being different from those who were descended from the conquistadores. The soldiers believed we were sympathizers with their enemies but we were not. They just needed someone to blame. They burned villages, murdered people in horrific ways. Even if we ran into the hills, they would find us and kill us.

"I saw my parents killed and Itza saw both of her brothers killed who were seventeen and nineteen. They were your Mama's older brothers. Itza was only fifteen years old. Too young to see her brothers die. Some say we should have stayed and fought to the death. I say we chose to live.

"You should always choose life, Akna. Always choose life.

"We traveled with a group of twenty to thirty K'iche'. At night we hid in the fields. Some would stay awake to watch for soldiers who were looking for those who ran. When we got to the border with Mexico, we could not cross the Suchiate River because Mexican officials would not permit us to cross.

All of us had sold belongings and brought money for a coyote—a person who is hired to protect us in the journey. He took our group in a raft, ten or eleven at a time. Once we had all crossed the river, as we were walking to our next destination, the coyote and Itza disappeared. We thought perhaps she had been hurt or she'd wandered off and he went in search of her. Two days later, Itza reappeared. She said she had paid a debt to ensure our continued safety. We never saw the coyote again.

Your mother was never the same after that.

By the time we reached the border at Nogales, the United States had made laws that made it impossible to cross. They said we were economic refugees, not asylum seekers. They did not understand that the K'iche' were being slaughtered by the military junta. We spent many months in Nogales waiting.

In November of 1981 we were connected with the Sanctuary Movement. These were many churches—Jewish, Catholic, Protestant, Unitarians—who provided sanctuary for any immigrants coming from Guatemala or El Salvador. I will not share how we made it into the U.S. because this network is still in use today, decades later and there are those who would want to take it down forever.

We lived in a Sunday School classroom with four other families for a while. Itza turned sixteen while we were there. It was soon after that we learned she was pregnant. We were shuffled from church to church to stay ahead of any immigration searches. We lived like this for a year, doing cleanup work for the church or sometimes building and fixing things. When her baby was born, she did not want it because it was from the seed of the coyote. A family at the church agreed to adopt the child. I believe that was the beginning of the demons who haunted Itza. The same demons that kept her from having good relationships with her children.

Because I had good farming knowledge, I was able to find good work in California where I began working in the vineyards. After President Reagan signed the 1986 Amnesty Act, we no longer feared deportation and the vineyard owners no longer feared the scrutiny of the government. The owner of the vineyard purchased land in Oregon for a new vineyard; and I was able to go from being a seasonal worker to a full-time manager of seasonal workers. The vineyard owners transferred me and my family to Oregon where I was able to help with all the new plantings. Nana and I and Itza could also make plans for becoming American citizens.

Itza chose not to come with us. She stayed in California with a boyfriend she was planning to marry. Instead, like all the others, when she became pregnant he left. Her heart was broken once again. Over the next decade, she had four more children each with a different man. Every man left once she was pregnant. We tried to talk to her about dating, about not getting pregnant, about talking to a counselor. She believed she was not worthy of love. She believed she was cursed because of what happened with her and the coyote. She believed God was punishing her and she had no choice but to accept it.

I don't know when the drinking started or the drugs. I only know that she tried to kill herself two weeks after the ninth child was born and she ended up in the hospital.

"Stop," Akna said in a whisper. "Stop. I can't breathe."

Gianna stopped the video.

Her mother tried to kill herself? If she'd succeeded, Akna would never have been born. Her sisters would never have been born. Suicide was a sin in the Catholic church. Her soul would have never been allowed into heaven.

She bent over and tried to take deep breaths like Gianna had taught her so many times before. Mrs. Bohn lightly ran her hand on her back in circles.

Gianna sat in front of her. "Look at me, Akna. Follow my breaths." She slowly drew in a breath and slowly let it out again. "Match me. You can do this."

After several tries, Akna was able to match her. She concentrated only on her breathing until she didn't feel so lightheaded.

"Perhaps we should save the rest for tomorrow," Mama Lois suggested.

Akna shook her head. "No. I want to get through the whole thing. I want to understand. I can do this. I *must* do this."

"Tell me when you're ready," Gianna said.

Akna took a couple more breaths and then sat up straight and looked directly at the screen. "Go. I'm ready."

Tata appeared to wipe a tear from his eye. Had she missed that before she had her meltdown. Then he continued.

Child Protective Services in California took away all of her children and put them in foster care. This is why you only know their names. Most of them have made a decision not to have Itza in their life at all. Nana and I occasionally get a Christmas card from them, but that's about it. They've all made lives elsewhere.

Nana and I drove from Oregon to the hospital in California and insisted Itza come back and live with us. She was good for almost two years. She saw a counselor here. She had medication to help with her depression. She worked as a cleaner for several vineyard owners' homes.

Itza became pregnant with you when she lived with us. She said it was a man from one of the homes she cleaned. She would not tell us which one. She said they had been dating for two years, and he promised he would leave his wife and marry her. Instead, he bought her a mobile home in the park where you grew up and then never spoke to her again.

Once she was on her own, she again had difficulty with raising you and over the next few years was when Hai and Nakia were born. We did not know how difficult things had become until Itza was pregnant with Nakia and she admitted to Nana that she had returned to her old ways. I wish you had been old enough to tell us what was going on. We did not know. Perhaps we suspected but did not want to know.

I wish I had an answer to heal Itza's heart. But even a parent cannot force an adult child to seek help. She must want it. She must make the decision.

Please do not judge your mother too harshly. She was brave for so long. Itza believed she was not worthy of love. Even our love was not enough, because she did not love herself.

There are many stories in the Popol Wuj where the gods must descend to the underworld to fight a battle or to sacrifice themselves in order to be reborn again. Perhaps that is what Itza will have to do. When she has used all of her options for escape, she will be forced to face herself in the underworld. That will be her chance for rebirth.

Wherever you are, Akna, if your Mama is not with you, please reach out for help. Whatever age you are, even if you are an adult, please reach out for help. Your SAD powers are strong. I want your heart to be strong as well. I want your love for yourself and your sisters to be the strength that will keep your powers strong.

Our love is forever. Never forget that. I am always in your heart. Loq' alaj wixoqil.

Tata made the sign of eternal love on his chest.

The screen froze on the television.

No one spoke.

No one moved.

Akna didn't dare look away. If she could keep looking at Tata she would not lose him again. She stared hard until her eyes could no longer stare. She blinked to clear her vision.

When she looked up again, Tata was frozen with his hand to his heart, it was as if she had imprisoned him in this world because she couldn't say goodbye. It was wrong.

She wanted him to be free. She wanted him to fly with the Tzuultaq'a" as he believed. She wanted him to be reborn or have a chance to become a god, too. Perhaps he was helping protect K'iche' even now. Perhaps…

Her eyes filled making his still picture blurry again. The more she tried to hold onto his image, the more he disappeared into the sea of tears that silently snaked down her cheeks. One day she would listen to him tell this story in K'iche—perhaps when she is older. But not now. She couldn't hear it again today, or tomorrow, may be not for a long time.

"Let him go," she said, her words choking as she spoke it. "Let him return to the Tzuultaq'a".

Then he was gone.

Mama Lois leaned in and gathered her until she couldn't see anymore. Akna wept for Tata, for Nana, for Mama, for herself and Hai. She wept for Nakia who never had the chance to know Mama without a broken heart.

When she had cried herself out, she opened her eyes and Gianna was sitting cross-legged in front of her holding a single lit candle.

She glanced around the room. All the others had been extinguished.

Akna focused on the candle. "What is it?" she asked her voice still wobbly.

"It's the light of your mama's heart," Gianna said as a tear slid down her cheek as well.

"I don't understand," Akna said.

"I don't either." Gianna wiped a hand across her eyes. "But I think it's true. I think…" Then she shrugged and looked down as she let out a big breath.

"Your Nana and Tata sheltered a piece of the light of your mama's heart inside them, so they could share it with you when she could not," Mama Lois said. "Now that you know the story, you can shelter that piece inside you, and share it with your sisters when they are old enough to understand."

Akna waited a moment and then carefully took the candle from Gianna. "But what happens if I blow out the candle?"

"It is still there," Gianna offered. "When I light my candles to calm my mind and ask my questions, it is not because I believe they hold something magical that I only see when they are lit. It is because they remind me of the magic inside me."

"What if she never gets well?" Akna asked. "What if I can never give her back the light of her heart."

"It's not you who can heal her heart," Mama Lois said. "She has the light inside her, but she doesn't have the eyes to see it right now. When she does, she will find the light."

"But…"

"When you stand outside in the sun and enjoy its warmth on your face, are you stealing the sun from someone else who needs it?" Mama Lois asked.

"No…" Akna said, trying to understand.

She worked it in her mind over and over again, trying to understand the sun, the candle, the light, and Mama. No one said anything more. They gave her time. Patient and loving silence.

Then a smile started to form. A tiny thing. It felt like that day in early March when there had been a cold storm bringing a dusting of snow to the valley. She'd been confused and hurt after Mama's phone call. She'd needed to run, but it was too icy to be safe. She'd sat at the window coaxing the sun to quickly melt the snow. Each day a little more melted. By the time it had all melted she no longer needed to run to escape. Instead, she started running for joy.

Her heart may feel numb right now, but she knew she had many summers ahead of her. She and her sisters had a story to tell—an important story. The story of the Sales sisters and how they would now choose to live. To thrive. To love.

ACKNOWLEDGMENTS

As with all books, no author writes and publishes alone. I have many, many people to thank. I'm fortunate to have a good many authors in my life—people who punish with Windtree Press as I do, people who are part of an accountability group where we weekly report our word count and how we are progressing toward our individual goals. My large family is always there for me, and want to see me succeed. All of those above were important in being this loving group that forms the base of my daily life.

There are some very specific people I want to thank, because the helped me on this project. This is my first upper middle-grade book. I've written a chapter book for young readers and a YA fantasy series. And many adult books, but this was different and close to my heart. I was uncertain as to what age range it would fit, if the topics were too difficult, and if my protagonist (Akna) spoke and acted like an 11 and 12 year old today.

I am grateful for two professional editors, and authors of middle-grade and YA books themselves, who read this book in its early stages and provided great feedback. Lisa Rojany at Editorial Services of LA read an early edited draft, agreed it was at the MG level, and provided some good story feedback to make it better. Lisa is an author of more than 40 books and has edited hundreds. Most of them children's books. Sarah Zarr read a later finalized draft of this book, and provided excellent feedback particularly around structure, character traits, and my use of metaphors throughout the story. I wanted Sarah's feedback in particular because she has written several MG books about difficult topics. Sarah is an award-winning author of middle-grade and YA books, and a National Book Award finalist. She also is faculty in an MFA program, and occasionally provides story edits to authors when she has the time. I was lucky to get her between projects. She had good ideas, new feedback I hadn't received and was on target about the market and the pitfalls of difficult contemporary topics.

I have also been well-supported by my longtime editor and good friend, Jessa Slade/Elsa Jade of Red Circle Ink. She has supported me in good times and bad for more than a decade. She is always honest but kind, and is the best person to hide away with on a writing retreat because we actually write and don't talk much. Silent support is an art that she has mastered and it makes a world of difference when on retreat.

Two particular Middle Grade authors—Laura Stegman and Sherrill Joseph, have steadfastly met with me monthly over Zoom for the past two years. Those Zoom moments provide each of us both professional and personal support in our often circuitous and challenging journeys to bring a story to publication. I look forward to our Zoom time every month, knowing that I will leave it feeling better and with the energy and spirit to keep moving forward no matter the challenges life presents. They are both now friends and I can never thank them enough for their support throughout this book's progress.

Finally, without my husband I don't know if I would have made it through the past two years. He was by my side during the pandemic and our relationship got even better. Over the past two years of family and health challenges, as well as grief and death of family members, he kept me going. When I needed to get away to write on retreat, he kept the home fires burning, took care of the cats, and made sure I was only bothered in an emergency. He is steadfast in his love and support, which is what allows me to write and to see how my characters can triumph over tragedy every time.

A NOTE FROM MAGGIE

Dear Reader,

When I shared this book with some children before it was published, they always asked me: **"Is it true. Is this based on real people?"**

The answer is yes and no. That is a K'iche way of thinking. The ability to hold two opposite things in your mind and know both can be true.

What I mean is that the things that happen in this story have happened to some people I know. There are many children in foster care because of one or more people in their life having a drug addiction or alcohol addiction or both. There are many children in foster care of different backgrounds. It is not just one group that always ends up in foster care.

As of the Spring of 2023 there were over 355,000 children in formal foster in the United States. That does not include the estimated 150,000 children who are living with friends or relatives outside of the foster care system. It is likely that one or more people in your school are in foster care. But, just like Akna, they don't talk about it because they are still figuring out what they want to share or not share with others. They are still wondering if their classmates will change their behavior if they know about their past.

This story and future books about Mariposa Lane is inspired by the experiences of real foster children I grew up with during my childhood and early adulthood. My maternal grandparents took in over 100 foster girls over a period of 25 years. Just like the Bohn family in this story, they were licensed for six girls at a time.

My family lived only a few blocks away from my grandparents' home. These girls were like close cousins to us. We played together, cooked together, attended the same schools, and spent holidays together. They were, and still are, part of our extended family.

My grandparents weren't the only relatives who took in foster children. An aunt and uncle, who lived nearby, also took in foster children during that same time. They were licensed for only two children at a time. They helped over twenty foster children over the same period of time. Whereas my grandparents mostly had girls from age eight to seventeen, my aunt and uncle mostly cared for children from infants to five years old.

Though I never formally had foster children myself, my husband and I took in two teenage girls (about five years apart) who were 16 and 17 when they joined us. Each of them needed a home, but was not eligible to enter foster care because they were within two years of graduating from high school.

The stories in this series reflect a variety of real problems and transformations I witnessed in myself and in these girls lives. Though no characters in any of the stories are the true experience of any one foster child. The stories contain elements common to many.

The character of Akna and her sisters in this book was created from two distinctly different experiences I wanted to include in this story. First, though my grandparents usually had only one girl at a time brought to the home, when I was ten years old I remember three sisters being brought all at once. They were very young, I don't remember the exact ages, but I know I was a couple years older than the oldest (so maybe 8, 6, and 3). Just as in my story, the oldest was the one who felt responsible for the other two. She was also the one with the best memory of their home with their mother. All three lived with my grandparents until they reached 18, or graduated high school. That is when they must leave foster care and make way for another child to come into the home.

Though Akna, Hai, and Nakia's story is different from those three girls, their connection and many of their feelings are true to their experience. Even today, 40+ years later, those three girls are very close to each other and to our extended family and always will be.

I created the story of Tata and Nana's immigration to the United States based on my work with the Guatemalan refugees in my church. I wish I could speak K'iche but I never learned enough to make a conversation. I learned phrases and a few common words. In writing this book, I did a lot of research of the culture and contacted someone I knew to help me learn to speak and translate a few of the longer passages.

I would love to hear from you and if you liked the book. I'd also like to know which of the six girls you met in this book that you would like to learn more about in the next Mariposa Lane book. You can email me at maggielynchauthor@gmail.com and tell me whose story you most want to read next and what questions you'd like answered about that characters life.

Thank you for reading *The Power of S.A.D.*

Maggie Lynch

ABOUT THE AUTHOR

Maggie Lynch is the author of 30+ published titles, as well as numerous short stories in anthologies, literary journals, and magazines. Her fiction tells stories of ***people making heroic choices one messy moment at a time.***

Her love of lifelong-learning has garnered degrees in psychology, counseling, computer science, and education; and led to opportunities to consult in the U.S., Europe, Australia, Southeast Asia, and the Middle East. Since 2013, Maggie and her musician husband have settled in the beautiful Pacific Northwest where they have retired from the corporate and academic world to follow their dual creative pursuits of music and writing. Her fiction spans contemporary coming-of-age stories, as well as romance, suspense, fantasy/SF, and mystery titles. Her non-fiction titles are focused on helping other authors become successful in their careers.

Maggie is also a sought-after speaker and workshop presenter. She has presented workshops for authors at conferences, for readers from children to adults at libraries and at school assemblies. She's often spoken at chapters of national organizations, and teaches online through consulting and small classes via POV Author Services.

You can learn more about Maggie at her website: https://maggielynch.com

If you'd like to join Maggie's email list, you'll get a regular newsletter with information about upcoming books, including future titles in this Mariposa Lane series featuring other foster children.

The newsletters often have good bargains for past books—sometimes even free only to newsletter subscribers. Sign up for her list at https://bit.ly/maggielynch

If you use social media, please do contact her on Facebook, YouTube, Pinterest, and at BookBub.

ALSO BY MAGGIE LYNCH

THE MARIPOSA LANE SERIES

Upper Middle Grade / Younger YA

Ages 11 -15

- The Power of S.A.D - Akna's Story
- Black and Blue - Gianna's Story
- Mindplayer - Polly's Story
- A Question of Faith - Susan's Story

THE FOREST PEOPLE SERIES

Contemporary YA Fantasy Novels

- Chameleon: The Awakening
- Chameleon: The Choosing
- Chameleon: The Summoning
- Forest People Boxset (contains all three of the above novels)

SWEETWATER CANYON SERIES

Romantic Women's Fiction

Novels:

- Undertones
- Healing Notes
- Heart Strings
- Two Voices

- Thanks for Love (Novella)
- Christmas Courage (Novelette)
- The Hogmanay Stranger (Novelette)
- **A Sweetwater Canyon Trio (Boxset)** Contains: Thanks for Love, Christmas Courage, and The Hogmanay Stranger stories all in one book.

SCIENCE FICTION BOOKS

Obsidian Rim: Cryoborn Gifts Series

- Gravity
- Magnetism
- Singularity

Eternity (stand-alone novel)

Pax Reborn (novella)

The Vow (novelette)

The Payment (short story)

Rhythms: A collection of 7 stories

SUSPENSE / MYSTERY

Shadow Finders Series

- Expendable
- Vanished
- Silenced

Two Turtle Doves (mystery novelette)

NONFICTION

Career Author Secrets Series

- Secrets Every Author Should Know: Publishing Basics
- Secrets to Pricing & Distribution: Ebooks, Print Books, Direct Sales
- Secrets to Effective Author Marketing: It's more than "buy my book"
- **BOXSET** Secrets to Becoming a Successful Author: three-volume boxset of all three books above

Teaching & Learning

- Learning Online: How to succeed in the virtual classroom
- The Online Educator: A guide to creating the virtual classroom
- Project Managing E-learning: A handbook for successful design, delivery and management
- Best Practices in Teaching and Learning in Nursing Education (multiple authors).
- Design and Implementation of Web-Enabled Teaching Tools (multiple authors).

THANK YOU for purchasing this Windtree Press Novel. The author has planned many more novels featuring the foster children residing at Mariposa Lane.

For more books of the heart, from anthologies to memoirs, non-fiction, and novels, we have books for all ages: children's books, middle-grade, YA, and adult books. Please go to our **website at https://windtreepress.com**. There you can learn about all of our authors, their books, and where to contact them directly.

9 781962 065283